The Curse of Braeburn Castle

Karen Baugh
MENUHIN

For my parents,
Gordon and Jean Palin,
with love.

CHAPTER 1

Late October 1921

'Are you absolutely certain he said skeleton?' I asked, with a degree of scepticism.

'E did, sir. Really, 'e did. An' it was in a wall.'

Tommy Jenkins had answered the telephone in the hall while my time had been spent on a visit to the gunsmith in our local village, Ashton Steeple. I would have returned home a great deal earlier and a great deal drier if my temperamental Bentley tourer hadn't broken down on a quiet country lane in the pouring rain. It had taken forty-five minutes to fix the damn magneto and now I was sitting in front of a roaring log fire in my library with my dog, Mr Fogg, at my feet, trying to make sense of what Tommy, the boot boy, had heard from Braeburn Castle.

'Where was Greggs?'

"E said 'e wasn't allowed to answer the telephone on your orders, sir.' Tommy replied as he swept thick dark hair from his eyes.

'Hum. Well, that was true: Greggs, my aged butler, wouldn't admit to deafness and his messages made even less sense than Tommy's.

'I think there was summat about a crown, too, but it were a bad line, sir. Sounded like 'e were calling from the back o' beyond, 'e did.' Tommy nodded for emphasis.

I eyed him from my wing chair, my hands clasped around a hot toddy, sodden clothes steaming gently from the warmth of the fire. I had visited Braeburn Castle; it was indeed in the back of beyond having been built in the wild days of Scottish marauding, inter-Clan warfare and bloody revolution. It sat on top of black rocks surrounded by ancient trees ringed by a sandy shore in the middle of Loch Laich and hadn't progressed much since the Middle Ages.

'And it was Swift on the telephone?' I asked between sips of whisky, lemon, honey and hot water.

'Ay, that Chief Inspector as was. 'E said there'd be a telegram, sir, but I 'aven't seen one.'

'Better go and ask Greggs,' I told him.

'Yes, sir.' He grinned broadly, but didn't move. He was a freckle-faced thirteen-year-old wearing trousers too short for him, a jacket too large, a collarless grey shirt and a muddy green jumper which had been darned more than once.

'Who do you think the skeleton was, sir? I've read about castles. Sometimes they drop people down in dungeons and forget about them. Do you think it was one of them?'

'Tommy, I have not the slightest idea. Go and find Greggs, would you,' I told him again.

'Will do, sir,' he continued. 'But if 'e was in a wall, they didn't drop him in a hole, did they? Do you think Mr Swift was looking for him? He was in Scotland Yard, wasn't he? Maybe he missed detecting and wanted to find someone who's been murdered?'

I pointed toward the library door, which he'd left open, admitting a cold draught. 'Tommy, go – now!' I ordered.

He opened his mouth to say something more, noted my expression and finally crammed his cap back on his head and dashed out of the room.

I let loose a sigh and placed my feet up on the footstool. Tommy's father hadn't survived the War, the Spanish flu had taken his mother and the lad now lived with his auntie, who was my cook. A clothing allowance came with the job of boot boy, but I knew he was saving for a bicycle, so I'd turned a blind eye to the ragamuffin hand-me-downs he wore.

I regarded the flickering flames reflecting off the leather-bound books lining my small library as I mused the message from the distant highlands.

Chief Inspector Swift had been the cause of my visit to Braeburn Castle a few months ago in the height of summer when he'd married the Laird's only child, the lovely Lady Florence Braeburn. They'd met in the spring when we were all gathered at Bloxford Hall for the wedding of my childhood friend Lady Caroline Bloxford, and, as it turned out, to investigate a few unpleasant murders. Swift had subsequently exchanged Scotland Yard for the highlands of Scotland itself and was now an ex Chief Inspector. Not having much else to do, he'd taken to carpentry and masonry – and possibly, as Tommy had speculated – investigating ancient murders.

Greggs entered at a dignified pace. He wore his usual butlering togs: black tails, dicky, white tie, waistcoat and cotton gloves, with which he held a silver tray. He announced in a drone, 'A telegram has arrived, sir.'

'Read it out, would you, Greggs, old chap?' Not that I was incapable – but I was stiff with cold and had no desire to move or let go of my hot toddy.

Greggs straightened up, paunch to the fore, a slight frown between his eyes as he struggled to bring into focus the small imprinted type on the yellow telegraph card.

'Major Heathcliff Lennox. The Manor. Ashton Steeple. STOP. Uncovered skeleton. STOP. Now infested with Archaeologists. STOP Suspect they are actually Treasure Seekers. STOP Head gone missing. Am investigating. STOP Florence with child. Bit short-handed. Could do with some help. Jonathan Swift. STOP.'

Greggs looked at me as I raised my brows.

'*Head gone missing*,' I mused. 'I wonder if he means the Laird?'

'I couldn't possibly say, sir,' Greggs replied, in a dull monotone.

'And why "treasure seekers"? The Braeburns have barely two farthings to rub together.'

'Very unfortunate, sir.'

'Yes… We'd better send a reply,' I decided.

'Certainly, sir.' He remained impassive.

'You know. Felicitations and all that,' I explained.

'About the baby, sir?'

'Well, I'm hardly going to congratulate them on the skeleton, Greggs.'

He didn't bat an eyelid. 'Will you be going to the castle, sir?'

My gaze turned back to the flames in the hearth as I contemplated another sojourn at Braeburn. It wasn't that I didn't want to go, it was just that I didn't particularly want to exchange my cosy home for the discomforts of the ramshackle castle.

'I suppose I must, Greggs. Better pack some of my winter togs. Dig out the old trunk, would you.'

He sighed.

I took a longer look at my old retainer. He swayed somewhat – no doubt he'd helped himself to the whisky while he had prepared my toddy. He had a fondness for the stuff, although he preferred Irish whiskey to Scotch. But Greggs hadn't shown any curiosity in the peculiar contents of the telegram. And I'd noticed that his habitual hangdog expression was becoming decidedly basset hound, and a very glum basset hound at that.

As he turned to leave, I called out, 'Greggs.'

He made a slow volte-face. 'Sir?'

'What happened to the operetta? You know, Gilbert and Sullivan and all that?'

His ears turned pink – I'd hit a nerve.

'I have retired from the group, sir.'

'Really? Rather a shame, thought you were a leading light amongst the "players",' I said, blowing steam from my tumbler. 'Any particular reason?'

He stared at the ceiling for a moment and then coughed as though his collar was too tight. 'I have relinquished my role, sir, to make way for the younger generation.'

With that sparse explanation, he escaped the room before I could interrogate him further. My sleuthing skills may still have been in the early stages, but it didn't take Sherlock Holmes to deduce that Greggs was suffering from a bout of melancholy. And he wasn't telling the truth about the cause, either.

I turned my mind back to Swift's telegram and contemplated what to make of it. Marriage may have softened Jonathan Swift's temper, but he was still a determined and resourceful man and it was a rare circumstance that would lead him to ask for my help.

'Sir, sir, there's another one!' Tommy Jenkins came bouncing back into the room waving a yellow card.

'Hum?' I enquired as Mr Tubbs, my rotund black kitten, jumped up onto my lap — a sure sign I was drying out and warming up. I rubbed his ears as he purred.

'It's from Lady Caroline, sir. The one as married the cowboy.'

'Hiram Chisholm has a ranch in Texas, Jenkins, he is not a cowboy. Have you been to the moving picture show again?'

'Ay,' he nodded, grinning. '*The Bronco Kid* — it were smashing. Didn't have no skeletons in it, though.'

He handed the new telegram to me, and I read it out while he manoeuvred round to read it over my shoulder. 'Lennox. You must go to Braeburn. STOP. Florence terribly worried about Jonathan. STOP. He is trying to rebuild the castle single-handed. STOP. But has unearthed old bones and a curse to boot. STOP. It is utter chaos. And Florence is preggers. STOP. And so am I! Isn't it wonderful. STOP. All love, you old crum dudgeon C. and H. Bloxford Hall. Oxford. STOP.'

Well, I heartily object to the '*old*' — I'm not that much older than Caroline herself.

'A curse, sir!' Tommy said with relish. 'It must be the skeleton. Do you think 'e wrote a curse on the wall with his own blood as 'e was dying? Like in *King Solomon's Mines*? Can I come with you, sir? Please, sir?' He was practically hopping with excitement.

'No, you can't.' I was re-reading the telegram with a frown. Caroline was a no-nonsense country girl; if she thought the castle was in chaos, then it would indeed be chaotic. Although I'm not sure what anyone expected me to do about it.

Tommy continued to plague me with questions.

'But you've been there, sir. Someone must have said something about it.'

My memories of Braeburn Castle were somewhat hazy. I do remember that despite the rudimentary nature of the place, we'd all had a marvellous time — actually, it had been one long celebration. Florence's father, the Laird, was a master of hospitality, although you wouldn't think so to meet him. We guests were plied with champagne, wine, brandy and plentiful quantities of whisky from the moment we arrived. There were pipers to meet us at the castle gates and evenings were spent with music and Scottish dancing, including a ceilidh on the eve of the wedding itself. On the last night we were all pretty exhausted and had gathered around the massive fireplace in the upper drawing room clasping tumblers of whisky when someone had asked about the history of the old place.

'I think there was talk of a "Black Dougal",' I answered slowly.

'Who was he?' Tommy asked.

'An old foe — I vaguely recall the Laird telling us about the rival clans and chiefs.'

Tommy's eyes grew round. 'What did 'e do, sir? Did 'e massacre them in their beds? Or steal away with their treasure, or was it 'im who cursed them all in the castle.'

'Umm ...' I was trying to cudgel my fuddled memories of the few facts that had emerged amid the light-hearted chat and laughter. 'I think he may haunt the place.'

That delighted the young lad. 'A ghost! They've got a ghost, too! Please can I come, sir? I'll be ever so good.'

'No,' I told him firmly and withdrew my fob watch.

'Aw, sir.'

'Afternoon tea,' I remarked, finishing my drink. 'And I believe cook has been baking Dundee cake.'

The boy was torn between trying to extract more information from me and the thought of the warm kitchen below stairs where a copper kettle would even now be boiling on the stove and cook would be extracting said cake hot from the oven. The cake won and Tommy dashed off, no doubt to raise the hairs of our small household with grisly tales of blood and bones, terrifying ghosts and deathly curses.

Greggs arrived shortly afterwards with my tray of teapot and whatnot, and placed it on the table at my elbow. I was still staring into space as he clattered cup and saucer about.

'Another baby, Greggs. Two, I mean,' I told him.

'Very productive, sir.' He poured my tea.

'I suppose so. Natural sort of order, really.' The Dundee cake was very good, and still piping hot.

'Possibly, sir. Will that be all?'

I regarded the old fellow. 'Greggs, I think you need a change of scenery. It might buck you up a bit. Put a bit of zest back in your step. You can come with me.'

He turned pale, even paler than usual. His hands shook, making the milk jug he held spill a dribble.

'To Scotland, sir? To Braeburn Castle … in the *Highlands?*' he almost stuttered.

'Yes, why not?'

'But sir, when you last returned, you said it was primitive, without hot water, electricity … heating or … or … proper bathrooms…' His voice tailed off.

'Yes, but it wasn't too bad. What it needs is more staff, Greggs. More hands to the pump and all that, especially with Lady Florence in the family way. And there are historians running loose about the place, so there will be even more people to cater for.' I picked up another slice of cake.

'B-b-but ...' Greggs seemed to be having some problem finding the right words. 'My back, sir,' he finally managed. 'Bad, very bad. You remember, sir. That incident in your aeroplane when I was injured. I ... I don't think the cold will be of benefit, sir.' I glanced at him; the similarity to a basset hound was even more pronounced.

'Nonsense, Greggs. You fell out of the plane because you failed to fasten your straps properly. It was a very minor crash landing and it was only a short drop onto the grass, for heaven's sake!'

We had been through the War together, Greggs and I. He was my batman, usually confined to base as I flew sorties into battle against the Boche. On occasion we'd had to move headquarters with the squadron and Greggs had developed a fear of flying — with good cause, actually.

'But bathrooms, sir, without hot water. And no electricity, or gaslights ... it will be like ... like ...' His chin began to wobble.

'It will be like France. Yes, I know. But there's no war on now and no one will be tossing bombs or bullets in our direction. And no aeroplanes either.' I gave him a direct stare. 'Greggs, if I leave you here, you will merely mooch about the place. And eat and drink too much. In a word — you will *fester*. So pack yourself a bag. We're catching the morning train.'

CHAPTER 2

The hearse awaited us at the steps of the Manor early the next morning. Nobody had died, but there were no taxicabs in our rural corner of the world and the under-employed hearse doubled as a carriage for hire. And my trunk fitted very nicely in the back.

'Greggs, assuming it is you in there, will you please go and get in the car,' I told the figure standing in the hall. He was wearing a voluminous black cape, thick leather gloves, a knitted muffler about his neck, a dark-green balaclava, motorcycle goggles and a bowler hat. 'And if you don't take that ridiculous headgear off you won't be allowed on the train.'

He stared at me, or I think he did, and then offered some sort of muffled explanation.

'Greggs, we are going to the Scottish Highlands, not the damned South Pole.'

He went and sat in the hearse.

I shoved Foggy under my arm and followed. We were rather squashed along the way and I wished we could have taken my Bentley, but I couldn't leave her at the railway station as she leaked about the hood. It was a slow trip through countryside already melting into shades of autumn and shedding leaves upon the hedge-lined lanes.

The train was in the station. Steam billowed down the platform, washing the alighting passengers in wreathes of white mist. I hailed a porter and left Greggs to oversee the luggage as Fogg and I headed for the comforts of first class.

My little dog was generally a happy traveller, actually he was happy in most circumstances providing he was well supplied with his basket, blanket and choice titbits as were available. He was a golden spaniel, rather runtish in size and had been a parting gift from my late father when I returned from the Great War. On this occasion Fogg was, however, rather depressed and gazed at me with liquid brown eyes holding a hint of reproach. I'd made the decision to leave Mr Tubbs behind, and as the rotund black kitten was the object of Fogg's adoration, the decision had not been well received.

Whistles blew, doors slammed and there was much shouting of uniformed guards as the train rolled forward with a loud hiss. I ruffled Fogg's gold-tan fur as he sat on my lap watching the station platform vanish in a cloud of smoke.

'Major Lennox, sir. Your sleeping cabin is being prepared. You will find it in the adjacent carriage, room 7a.' A very smartly turned-out train attendant came into my compartment and addressed me. 'Could I bring you any refreshments, sir? Lunch will not be served in the dining car until we reach York.'

'Erm … coffee,' I said, and then thought that as it was a new adventure I might as well start it off on a sound footing. 'And brandy, please. Something decent, aged and all that.'

'Certainly, sir.' He went off with a nod of the head and not a crease to his uniform. Must say, the service had improved magnificently since I'd travelled the trains during wartime. And the attendant didn't raise so much as a sniff about my partaking so early in the day.

It was a marvellous journey. I watched the orange and autumn gold of the English countryside pass by; russet-brown cows ambled in fields, pale sheep nibbled green grass, dray horses drew carts of late-harvest beets and earthy potatoes along winding lanes. We huffed and puffed alongside villages, towns and the occasional sprawl of a hurly-burly city.

The rhythmic clicker-clack of the wheels sent me dozing over my book and brandy, and I didn't wake up until the attendant returned to announce that we'd reached York and lunch was ready.

It was a jolly good meal served in quite the smartest dining room I'd been in for ages. Deep polished mahogany-lined walls with gleaming gilt liberally inlaid, and electric light from silk-shaded lamps reflected gloss and gold in shimmering glory. I was served fresh-caught salmon with a light white wine and Foggy sat next to me on the cushioned seat.

'Ay, and a good afternoon to yerself and yon wee doggie, sir.' A different attendant came by my table, a

Scot by the sound of his accent. He sported a beard and kilt and very smart he looked too.

'And a good afternoon to you, old chap,' I replied.

'I'm yer man for the Highland line,' he told me. 'You'll be going home, then?'

'Um, no, I'm going to Scotland.'

'Ay, the Lennox,' he said with a nod.

'What?'

'The Lennox. You're a Lennox, are ye not?'

'Yes,' I agreed. 'I'm Major Lennox.'

'Well, there ye go, then. And don't ye be worrying, we Scots are always looking out for one another.' He went off with a wink and a nod.

Fogg and I wandered back to my compartment somewhat bemused.

I had brought with me a book on Scottish history and read it in the comfort of my carriage as the train followed snaking lines in a northerly direction. My book told much about revolution and clan warfare, but nothing of Black Dougal and whatever misdeeds he may have enacted.

After a sumptuous supper in the dining car I went to find Greggs.

'Come and join me, old chap,' I told him.

He'd removed the cloak and headgear and was quietly reading a book in his seat by the window, a snifter at his elbow. He looked at me with an expression such as Foggy adopted when the word 'bath' is mentioned.

'Greggs, it is not that bad!'

'As you say, sir.'

It appeared that I remained unforgiven.

'Look, we can play cards. I know how you used to enjoy it. You were rather good at it, as I recall.'

He sniffed.

'Well, I'll be in my compartment if you change your mind.'

I went off. Twenty minutes later he turned in from the long corridor, swaying slightly with the movement of the train.

He won seven shillings and fourpence ha'penny before ambling back to his quarters. I have now forsworn cards, particularly in the company of Greggs.

Next morning, I woke to crisp sunshine reflecting off the shores of a Scottish loch and some of the most stunning countryside I can ever recall witnessing. A forest of foliage in flaming red, bright yellow, warm orange and brittle tan flamed across gnarled tree branches. Berry-bearing rowan and juniper spread between moss-encrusted trunks and ran down to the shore to trail filigree fingers in the loch. The water lay like silver mercury and I watched an osprey languidly circle above, searching the depths for rainbow trout or a fat Atlantic salmon returning home from the far seas to spawn.

'Will ye be taking breakfast before ye leave, sir?' the kilted attendant asked when I arrived for my favourite meal. He was holding a tray of the most sumptuous breakfast I'd ever seen. It had everything from kippers to black pudding and all things in between.

'Um, yes, I'm not getting off for a while,' I replied.

'Not at the Lennox, then?'

'Um, no. Where is this Lennox?' I asked.

'Here!' he said with brows raised at my ignorance. 'Loch Lomond and thereabouts, that's the local name: the Lennox.' He leaned back and eyed me carefully. 'Are ye saying you're not Scots, then?' He withdrew the tray as he spoke.

I watched his movements, as did Fogg.

'Well, probably a bit.' I saw him hover in indecision. 'Quite a bit, really. Actually, I'm almost entirely Scots,' I said as the tray moved back in my direction.

Fogg and I enjoyed the meal as the train chugged across a viaduct and through spartan valleys where only sheep and deer roamed. With a sigh of contentment, the little dog and I returned to our carriage and settled in.

I was reading an out-of-date newspaper when a lady entered from the corridor laden with luggage, an umbrella and a beaming smile.

'Greetings,' I called out, and stood to help her unload.

'Oh, dear boy. Thank you so much,' she replied rather breathlessly.

'Porter not helped you?' I asked as I tossed her carpet-bag and whatnot up onto the overhead rack.

'I have moved seats,' she replied, unwinding various scarves from around her neck. 'There is a strange man in the carriage. He is wearing a balaclava and goggles with a bowler hat. Most disconcerting.'

'Erm, he's with me actually,' I admitted.

'Oh dear,' she smiled and leaned down to stroke Foggy's fur. 'What a beautiful doggie.'

'Yes, he's called Mr Fogg. Do please take a seat, Mrs, erm …?'

'Miss,' she smiled. 'Miss Lavinia Fairchild.' She held out a hand and shook mine firmly. It was customary for older ladies to tender a gloved offering for a formal peck, but Miss Fairchild had obviously adopted modern ways. It was quite refreshing.

I introduced myself.

'Major Heathcliff Lennox, and I'd rather you didn't call me Heathcliff. Please,' I added and waited for her to sit before doing the same.

'Your mother was …'

'Of a romantic nature. Yes, and I'm not.' I explained.

Fogg took an instant liking to her and I must say she seemed a good sport. Wavy grey hair in a loose bun falling adrift from hurriedly placed pins, a kindly face with rose-coloured cheeks, brown eyes full of life and lips creased with laughter. Her figure was enveloped in a heavy pale-blue cloak over a cream blouse with a frilled neck and blue and red tartan below in the form of waistcoat and skirt. I'd say she was built on the pillowy side — very pillowy, actually.

'Phileas Fogg?' she asked as she smoothed the fur on the top of the dog's head.

'From *Around the World in Eighty Days*,' I said. 'Yes, excellent book. Always liked it.'

'He's not very adventurous, though, is he,' she smiled, causing a crinkled dimple to appear in one cheek.

'Erm, no. But "Fogg" suits him; he's a bit of a duffer, really. Hopeless gun dog — lovely nature, though.'

'Hold out your hand,' Miss Fairchild said.

'What?'

'Your right hand. I will read your future.' Her eyes shone bright as she looked at me. 'Come along.'

Just as I had taken a liking to her, she proved to be verging on the batty. I held out my paw with a silent sigh. She didn't say a word, just stared at the lines on my palm. The train continued to rock gently as it chugged and chuffed between crags of bare rock.

'You are at a crossroads,' she said at last.

I stared at her. 'Is that it?'

She laughed. 'Would you like to know more? I thought I had detected a hint of scepticism.'

'Well, I suppose now that you've started … I mean, you did ask me, so …'

'Major Lennox, you have an interesting future ahead of you,' she told me, still clutching my hand. 'If you should choose to take it. But you have a tendency to withdraw from the world. This is because you have lost so much — your family, many of your friends … and you are not proficient with money, so you don't have much of that either, do you?'

That made my eyes open, but then it occurred to me that since the War, the same could be said of many people. 'Thought you said you were telling my future,' I retorted.

'The future is forged in the past,' she replied calmly, and again fixed her gaze upon my palm. 'Love has evaded you, but now it is near.' She paused, her voice taking on a wavering note. 'There is something more awaiting you, something of the dark. It is a cruel force, a threat to you and to others. You must overcome all. This will lead you to your destined path. Should you fail or take another route, you will drift and flounder.' She let go of my hand suddenly and smiled, almost as though she'd woken from a daze.

I gazed at her as she plumped back against the cushioned seat, her feet barely touching the carpet. 'Not sure if that was terribly enlightening, actually, Miss Fairchild.'

'The fates don't give much away, dear boy. But do take heed, won't you. I'm rarely wrong.'

Fortunately, the stop for Braeburn Castle was coming up so I wouldn't have to suppress my incredulity for much longer.

'Erm, well, thank you anyway.'

The attendant appeared in the doorway. He must have met Miss Fairchild, as he smiled brightly at her.

'Good morning, madam,' he addressed her, and raised his cap then turned to me. 'Would you be taking lunch, then, sir?' he asked.

'Erm, I'd like to but I understood we were almost at the stop,' I remarked.

He pulled out his large fob watch and peered at it. 'Ay, you're right. Well, you'll be going hungry.' And he went off with another smile in the lady's direction.

I stooped to pick Foggy up. 'Do excuse me, madam. Getting off now.'

'Yes, of course you are. You're going to Braeburn, aren't you!'

'Um, yes …' I replied warily.

'I'm a clairvoyant and a medium, you know. I've been called by the spirits.'

'Really. Spirits, eh. Called where?' I asked.

'Braeburn, of course, I'm coming with you!'

CHAPTER 3

Two hearty young chaps unloaded my trunk from the guard van and carried it along the platform. Actually it wasn't a proper platform, it was a row of wooden planks running beside the track. They carried on down to the shore of the loch a few yards away and onto a jetty where a rowing boat was waiting. They hoisted the trunk deftly aboard and returned smiling and wiping their hands on their kilts. I was terribly impressed and gave them a shilling each for their trouble.

I'd been fully occupied in helping Miss Fairchild descend the carriage whilst holding Fogg firmly under my arm. Greggs came to join us at a dignified pace and together we faced the crisp wind blowing in from the sea and stared at the castle standing proud on a small island in the distance. It had a romantic air, with a saltire fluttering above a high tower, the dark stones stark against a horizon formed by the mountains rising above the remote Isle of Mull.

Donald MacDonald broke into our collective gazing.

'Ye'll be getting aboard now, I cannae be standin' aboot all day.'

'Greetings, old chap,' I hailed him, having encountered him on my earlier visit.

'Ay, Major Lennox,' he nodded.

Greggs was again attired in his ridiculous get-up and the Scot gave him a hard stare.

'He's with me,' I assured him.

MacDonald was the Laird's personal Ghillie-mor, a term meaning a carrier of armour and weapons for his master. He had been to war with the Laird but he'd carried rifles and revolvers into battle rather than claymores and shields. He looked as though he'd fought hard, too, his skin riven with deep lines, a cold expression glinting from eyes almost hidden beneath a thicket of wiry brows, thin lips behind a clipped white beard. He waited for us at rigid attention, clad in a kilt of blue and green threaded with red, and a bonnet to match. He wore a dark cape across his broad shoulders and it blew in the breeze.

'Major Lennox, sir. I dinnae have notice of a lady in yer party.'

'Erm, I believe Miss Fairchild has been summoned,' I replied. 'See that she's seated safely, would you.'

He aimed a severe frown at the poor lady and I could see he was ready to argue the point. I was burdened by Fogg and Miss Fairchild's carpetbag, but she stepped forward and put her hand on his arm and smiled up at him. The effect was almost immediate: the man melted.

'Ay, well, 'tis a fair lady an' she must be carried safe across,' he said half to himself, and then more loudly to Miss Fairchild: 'Now, ye take a care, bonnie lass, hold on to my arm, now.' He helped her gently into the lurching rowing boat tied tightly with a sturdy rope to the dock and settled her at the prow. Then he turned to watch as Greggs clambered ponderously aboard. I passed down the bag and my dog and followed suit. Miss Fairchild turned and smiled at Greggs. He mumbled something in reply and raised his hat.

'You see, Greggs, it's not that bad, is it?'

There was no reply. I eyed him more closely; he didn't say a word, just stared at Miss Fairchild until his goggles misted up.

It was a fairly short trip across the water. Blue green waves washed against our bows as MacDonald made good time with the oars. The air was scented with salt, pine and seaweed; screeching gulls wheeled about our heads. Greggs relinquished the headgear – I think he was trying to impress Miss Fairchild. MacDonald refused all help so I enjoyed the view as Fogg leaned into the breeze, his long ears flying behind him.

A group had gathered on the sandy shore. Lady Florence stood foremost to the landing jetty, her blonde hair caught in a coiled plait, and her peach and cream complexion warmed by the wind. She wore a lavender shawl wrapped about her shoulders above a dress in dark-blue wool. Swift was at her side, while the Laird, white-haired and handsome in full highland rig, stood aloof and staunchly upright on a rock behind them. As we closed on the beach a piper blew into his bagpipes, and after the usual terrible drone he cudgelled a tune from the tartan-clad sac and filled the air with a merry Scots medley.

'Oh, Lennox!' Florence's face lit up. 'I'm so pleased you're here!'

I jumped the boat rail and strode up to kiss her on both cheeks, being utterly delighted to see her again. 'Greetings, dear girl,' I declared with my best grin.

Swift didn't say a word; he stared at both the other passengers, obviously unaware that I was bringing my butler with me. Greggs had probably omitted the fact of his attendance from the telegram in the hope that I would weaken at the last moment.

I gave Swift a good long stare back because he was wearing a black jacket, kilt and all the usual getup, including a sporran. His dark, hawkish looks were weather-blown, and he was rather red in the face – which was hardly a surprise given the unaccustomed draught he must be suffering about the nether regions.

'Greetings, to you Swift,' I called. 'Brought Greggs with me.' I waved an arm in his direction then turned to the lady now being helped from the boat by both my butler and MacDonald. 'And this is Miss Fairchild, whom I assume you know.'

They obviously didn't know, judging by the blank looks on their faces, but Florence welcomed her kindly as Fogg leapt ashore and chased about, ecstatic to see everyone. Greetings complete, we ambled slowly beneath the huge stone archway between the twin towers forming the Gatehouse-Keep. The Laird hadn't said a word, he'd merely nodded stiffly in our direction. He and the gaily playing piper brought up the rear.

Once within the inner courtyard surrounded by its high wall, Greggs was marshalled by MacDonald somewhere or other while Florence took Miss Fairchild in hand and they went off chatting together. The Laird took his own direction with the piper at his heel, so that left me alone with Swift.

'Lennox, you can have the East Tower,' Swift announced, and went to march across the grass-fringed cobbles. Excited barking broke out as I made to follow: Fogg had discovered chickens and chased them with great glee. They scattered with loud cackles and squawks and he ran in happy circles as a couple of them launched themselves into the air. They finally escaped behind a barred gate where a group of fat sheep were housed in an old byre. I shouted at him and he returned, entirely unabashed. Swift was frowning at me as I caught up with him, and we went up the steps into the squat tower.

'It's quite comfortable, once the fire stops smoking,' Swift told me as we entered the upper floor. I couldn't see much on account of the haze, and coughed as the woodsmoke caught in my throat. As the room cleared I took a look around. It was as spartan as everywhere else to my recollection. An old tester bed with a thick quilt and tartan coverlet took up much of the space, the bare boards were covered in threadbare rugs, and heavy curtains hung across a draughty window cut into the dense stone walls. There was a pokey dressing room resembling a cave just off the bedchamber. The fireplace was huge and dominated the room, as did most fireplaces in the castle. It was almost tall enough to walk into and had a bread oven, various iron brackets, chains, and a lead-weighted spit-jack hanging from bars driven into the stonework. A black kettle on a swing arm was suspended above flames licking around pale logs. Two wing chairs stood either side, and there were also a couple of stools, a desk and chair, an antique wooden chest and a washstand. My trunk hadn't arrived yet; I assumed it would be brought up by someone or other.

'Swift,' I started.

He turned to look at me.

'Just tell me what the devil's going on, would you.'

He let out a sigh and sat down by the fire, then shifted a cushion behind him. I took the chair opposite and waited.

'Someone tried to kill Florence,' he said at last, 'or hurt her, anyway.'

'*What?*' Well, that came as a nasty shock.

'I couldn't put it in the telegram …' He ran his fingers through his hair. 'Too many people would see it …' He stopped again.

'But why call me, why didn't you call the police?' I asked.

'Because I can't prove anything. Look, Lennox, she doesn't realise. No one does.'

'If it was deliberate, then somebody does.'

26

'Yes, yes, you're right,' he mumbled.

'Tell me what happened.'

He shifted in his chair. Swift has always looked hawk-ish but his appearance had become sharper and leaner in the months since I'd seen him. Married life certainly suited him, but the responsibilities of living in such a singular environment must have been testing his mettle — and now he feared a hidden threat of some sort to his adored wife.

He sighed and began his tale. 'Every morning Florence goes down the outside stone steps from our bedroom in the Keep and washes her face in the waters of the loch. It's a habit she's had since a child,' he explained as I raised my brows. 'Superstitious — they all are. Anyway, the stone steps were loose and had been for years, so I repaired them. I hammered slate and pebbles into the gaps and tested every one of them until the whole structure was completely solid. Then last week, Florence went down at dawn as usual and one of the steps rolled away under her feet – and she fell.' A haunted look slid across his face. 'Someone must have sabotaged them, they must have, I *know* they were safe.' He slapped a fist down hard on the arm of the chair.

'But she seemed in good health today,' I put in.

'Yes, but she was badly bruised. She was fortunate, her legs went from under her and she slipped down. If she'd fallen sideways she could have been badly injured, or worse. I've locked the door and hidden the key, I'm not risking a repeat.'

It was my turn to sigh. 'Is this connected with the skel-eton? I couldn't make any sense of your telegram.'

'Ha! That would be amusing if it hadn't been for those damned archaeologists invading us.' Swift smiled wryly. 'I found it a couple of weeks ago — I've been trying to make our quarters more comfortable. We're in the Keep, which is one of the oldest sections in the place and has the thickest walls, so it hasn't fallen apart quite as much as the rest. I've been constructing a library from a disused room and realised that there must have been an interior passageway between that and the Lady's Parlour, so I decided to open it up.'

A knock sounded at the door, interrupting us. Greggs entered carrying a tray of tea and a slab of something on a plate.

'Ah,' I clapped my hands 'lunch at last, Greggs! And it's already past the hour.'

'No, sir, I'm afraid the trunk has not yet been delivered. I enquired in the kitchens for provisions, but Cook was not minded to be co-operative,' he intoned, and looked about for a place to put the tray. 'I am informed that this is all that is available until dinner. I trust it will prove edible, sir.' He deposited it carefully on the desk in front of the window and commenced to pour two cups of tea.

'Erm ... what is it?' I asked as he placed a slab of something on a chipped saucer and handed it to me.

'I have no idea, sir.'

'Clootie dumpling,' Swift informed us. 'Made with dried fruit, suet and a drop of Scotch. You'll get used to it. Very sustaining. Try it.'

I did, and there was more than a drop of whisky in it.

It was rather good, actually. The fire picked up and lapped around the pine logs, yellow flames flickered brightly and the logs crackled and spat in the momentary silence as we chewed on the cake.

'Skeleton,' I reminded Swift through mouthfuls.

'Yes, I was coming to it,' he retorted, sounding more like his old self. 'I took a large pick and hacked at the wall. Once I'd forced a decent sized hole, the rest started to crumble away. I could see there was a hollow space behind, and when the hole was big enough I shone a torch into the void.' A grin suddenly lightened his expression. 'A skull stared back at me! Black sockets in white bone — I almost dropped the flashlight. I must have let out a shout because the maid came to see what I was up to. I told her to take a look and shone the torch through the gap and she screeched blue murder. Ran off shouting "Black Dougal, Black Dougal!" He laughed, then tried to be serious. 'I shouldn't have done it.'

We heard a splutter behind us; it was Greggs. We turned around and he immediately resumed his usual po-faced demeanour.

'Greggs,' I said.

'Sir?'

'For heaven's sake man, sit down, will you. Come on, we're not at home now. No need for formalities.'

'I couldn't possibly, sir.'

'Yes, you can. And it will save me having to tell you about it later. Find a cup, pour yourself some tea and pull up a seat.'

He hovered for a while, unhappy about crossing the old demarcation lines. But the castle was like many of the ramshackle buildings in France we'd had to share and there was no point in standing on ceremony in a bare-bones billet.

He refused to take tea, but his curiosity finally got the better of him and he deigned to sit stiffly on a wooden chest as Swift turned back to his tale.

'I continued to hack the wall down as the household came and gathered about. Then MacDonald joined in and between us we pulled the remaining stones down and stood back to let the dust settle.' He took another wedge of clootie and chewed slowly.

'Yes … and?' I encouraged him.

'There he was. Full-sized skeleton, half buried in the back wall, wearing a golden crown. Had pretty good teeth actually, only a couple missing. Bones, too. I examined him with my magnifying glass — all intact. Must have been walled-up in one piece.'

'Swift,' I said abruptly as he carried on eating cake.

'Uhum?'

'Golden crown? Black Dougal?'

'Yes … We can go and have a look. Then you can see for yourself.' He stood up. 'Except the head's been stolen.'

'What?'

'I wrote to you, Lennox, it was in the telegram,' he replied snappishly.

'And the crown?' I asked.

'Yes, of course,' he said. 'Come on.'

'Right.' I brushed crumbs from my tweeds. 'Coming, Greggs?'

'I have duties to attend to, sir,' he began fidgeting about the room. I know he was a touch squeamish – well, very squeamish, actually – so we left him to it.

We stepped from the wide stone doorway of my squat tower into the courtyard and then froze in our tracks. An ear-splitting scream echoed up from the ruins at the farthest point of the castle. Swift's face turned ashen and we both broke into a run.

CHAPTER 4

A maid came racing towards us.

'It's him, Black Dougal, it's him!' she yelled, her apron flying, red hair streaming under the mob cap falling askew from her head.

'What? Wait. Stop,' Swift held his hand out to wave her down. 'Ellie, stop right this minute,' he shouted, which did the trick.

'Oh, sir,' she stumbled to a halt in front of us 'I saw the head, over yon. 'T'were the skull, starin' at me. Pitch dark it was, except for the head, which was all white, like a ghost.' She was almost sobbing as she caught her breath. 'He had black holes fer eyes, like the devil himself. He's come back alive!'

'Where?' Swift demanded.

'Away back there, in the gin-gang.' She pointed toward the far end of the castle.

We looked over to where a large wicker basket of washing was overturned and a line with a few shirts had been pegged to flap in the breeze. Beyond that was the sprawl of buildings that made up the other half of Braeburn Castle, the half that lay in ruins.

'Why did you go in there?' Swift demanded.

'I …' The maid tried to catch her breath. 'I heard a noise, sir.'

Florence had come running from the Keep along with other servants and met us in the middle of the courtyard. One was a young footman and I noticed he and Ellie exchange looks. Florence took the poor maid back toward the kitchens as Swift and I strode toward the jumble of ruins.

'Careful going in,' Swift warned me. 'It's dangerous. The roof is tumbling in and there's rubble on the floors. Even the walls are giving way to the weather.'

The castle had been built within a huge curtain wall following the contours of the island's highest point. At one end were the twin towers of the Keep, which were occupied by Swift and Florence. Then came the Kirk and Great Hall which had been inhabited almost continuously for hundreds of years. But the jumble of buildings in the farthest quarter had been designed to house a sea-going militia and only been used in times of extreme need — which in the past had occurred fairly frequently given the many enemies the Braeburn clan had fostered. But peace had eventually prevailed and over more recent centuries they had fallen into disuse and decay.

'What's a "gin-gang", Swift?' I asked as we trod carefully over the threshold of the ruins.

'Horse-driven mill; well, it was a donkey actually — can't keep a horse here. The donkey was tethered in a pit and walked in circles to power the blacksmith's bellows. There was a huge forge here at one time making weapons.' He dropped his voice as we stepped further inside, and held his finger to his lips. 'Quiet now.'

We trod carefully. It was dark. Loose stones shifted under my feet, I felt in my pocket for my torch but Swift beat me to it and switched his on. He ran the beam into dark corners where cobwebs hung in skeins draped with dust and small silk-bound corpses. A few shafts of daylight filtered from missing slates, but somehow that made the dark seem darker. There was no sign of ghostly skulls or anything akin. I stood on a twisted branch and it broke with a loud crack.

'Quiet,' Swift hissed.

Nothing seemed amiss in the first building so we went through a broken doorway, deeper into the labyrinth of interconnecting buildings. Detritus tripped us up more than once, causing us to curse: should anything, ghost or man, be hiding in the darkness, they would have had no problem hearing us coming. As we bent below a fallen roof joist, a pale form skimmed over our heads and we both ducked instinctively. It was an owl, and it escaped on silent wings.

'Perhaps that's what she saw?' I said.

'Hum.' Swift was rubbing a grazed knee. 'We'll assume it was. Come on.' He turned and we both made our way back to the courtyard, brushing cobwebs and dirt from our clothes.

Florence had returned and was standing with Greggs, who must have heard the commotion and come outside to see the cause; he looked chilled and probably wished he was still wearing his ridiculous balaclava. Fogg wriggled out of his hands and came to run around my feet.

'Sweetheart, you look quite dreadful,' Florence said to Swift.

'Owl,' he replied. 'Nothing to worry about.'

'Should I put the kettle on, sir?' Greggs asked. It wasn't quite the heroes' return you'd expect.

'Later,' I replied. 'I haven't seen this skeleton yet. As you're here, Greggs, you can come along.'

'But sir ...' He tried to prevaricate, then gave it up and followed at a reluctant pace.

Swift was limping.

'Hurt my knee,' he told his wife.

'You don't have to wear the kilt.' She spoke quietly to him. 'Trews are fine, really, my darling. Nobody would mind.'

'No,' he said with determination, and limped on, blood dripping down his knee to soak into the top of his long cream woollen socks. The couple leaned in toward each other, chatting quietly as they went.

I followed them back toward the twin towers of the Keep, but Florence halted and let go of Swift's hand.

'I must go and see Cook in the kitchens, my love, we were in the middle of baking. I will join you later.' She kissed him tenderly and waved to me, then we watched her go.

'Right, come on.' He turned into the huge arched gateway forming the entrance to the castle, and then through a narrow doorway set in the wall. It was an old guardroom, now hung with coats of many sizes, and boots and shoes serried in a line below.

'Lennox, I want you to take notice of the lay-out of the rooms,' Swift ordered.

'Right-o … Why?'

'Because you need to understand how I discovered the skeleton,' he snapped. Swift may have been late of Scotland Yard, but he was still a detective at heart, and just as short-tempered.

'Hello, my dears. May I join you?' Miss Fairchild came in, still enveloped in her pale-blue cape and no doubt snug and warm beneath it.

'Um, of course. Delighted, Miss Fairchild,' Swift said.

Greggs's ears turned pink.

I offered a quick greeting as Swift strode off toward a narrow door in the corner of the boot room and started to climb the winding stone steps. 'These are Florence and my quarters now,' he said. 'Each room in both towers is the same size, about eighteen feet square, with arrow slits opening seawards and a single window facing the courtyard.' He sounded like a tour guide, his voice echoing up the stairs. 'There's a fireplace in each room; almost all of them are equipped with cooking facilities. The walls are around six feet thick — more in some places. Now …' He arrived at the top of the worn stone steps and waited for us to follow.

Fogg beat us all to it and raced into a cosy music room where a pretty harpsichord stood in a corner, with music sheets and whatnots spread about. 'If we go through the music room…' he waved his arm about then walked through a doorway, 'we enter our drawing room. This occupies the area that forms a bridge between the towers. When the place was a fighting fortress there were gullies in the floor for pouring burning pitch down onto invading enemies below.'

We all went to have a look at the floor, which was covered in pale flagstones with patched mortar roughly spread over filled-in holes.

'Was there a portcullis?' I asked, being familiar with such arrangements.

'No,' Swift replied. 'There's a yett below us. It's similar to a portcullis but it's hinged to the walls rather than being raised and lowered. It's a common feature in Scottish castles.'

I would have to give him a tip if he carried on with the history tour; or hand him a furled umbrella.

'It's a lovely drawing room.' Miss Fairchild was looking about with obvious pleasure, her bun adrift and wispy strands curled about her face. 'Dear Lady Florence has made it very comfortable. I simply adore chintz, you know. I make a lot of my own cushions and curtains, too,' she remarked as she raised a hand to feel the flower-patterned fabric hanging at the windows.

'Yes, yes, my wife is very good at that sort of thing.' Swift moved quickly on. 'That door there…' he pointed to a heavy oak door on the far side of the room 'leads into the twin tower on the other side of the Keep and is the same size as the music room in this tower.'

'What's it used for?' I asked, wishing he'd get on with it and show us the bones.

'Our bedroom, actually.' He reddened lightly and turned back the way we'd come. 'Right, come on, we're going upstairs.' He turned around and shooed us back through the music room and then to the winding stairs up to the next floor. 'This is known as the Lady's Parlour.'

'Oh, how delightful,' Miss Fairchild exclaimed. She was right: it was very pretty. The stone walls were entirely covered in tapestries, the chairs were deep cushioned, the ceiling was plastered and painted with cherubs and winged horses and half-dressed ladies in the classic style. Even the tiled fireplace was delicately embellished, and it was warm in the room from the brightly blazing fire. I imagined it was where Florence spent much of her spare time.

'Yes, well, never mind that. If you'll come this way.' Swift crossed to the far wall and opened a black oak door heavily studded with nails and iron hinges and pulled it open to admit a very cold draught. 'This leads onto an open walkway overlooking the inner courtyard.'

We duly walked out to a narrow passage that I calculated was above the drawing room, and stared over the crenellated wall. It was a marvellous vantage point actually; I could see the whole courtyard, enclosed by the curtain wall. Slate roofs, square towers and stone buildings met my gaze in a confusing jumble, but I began to construct the layout in my mind. In the centre lay a huge round well. To my right lay squat, whitewashed buildings – they were the kitchens and stores, from my recollection. Chickens were pecking about in front of the neighbouring byre. To my left was the little Kirk with its steeply pitched roof; beyond that, the tall rectangular building housing the Great Hall, containing reception rooms, guest bedrooms and the Laird's quarters. Then there was my tower, which butted onto a steep set of steps rising to the battlements, and next to them was another tower, which was known as the Armoury. At the very opposite end to where we stood between the twin towers, were the ruined militia buildings. I squinted my eyes to observe them carefully, half expecting to see something flitting about in the shadows.

'Come on, come on.' Swift hurried us on to a door at the other end of the passageway. 'In here is my library.'

'Which is above your and Florence's bedroom,' Miss Fairchild observed with a dimpled smile.

'Yes, yes,' Swift muttered as he led us into a book-lined room that smelled of oiled leather and sawn wood and the whiff of something strange and slightly unnerving. 'And here…' he went over to a heavy tartan rug hanging on a wall 'is where I found the skeleton.'

'About time too,' I remarked.

Swift scowled at me. He reached up and pulled the rug aside to reveal a large dark opening.

'Why is it behind a curtain?' Miss Fairchild asked, peering into the cavity.

39

'Because my wife isn't very keen on it,' Swift said. He pulled out his flashlight while I fumbled for mine.

We both shone a beam into the darkness and everyone said, 'ohhh ...' at the same moment – except Swift, of course, who'd already seen it.

It was a tall skeleton, very white, the bones, I mean. It was entirely upright, straight-backed, feet together, and arms by his sides. He was half buried in the mortar on the wall behind him. It was too narrow for us all to enter, so we gathered in the entrance.

'Rather a shame about the skull and crown,' I mused aloud.

'Yes, I could kill the ba – um, apologies, Miss Fairchild – the blighter who stole it,' Swift swore.

We stared at the smooth concave hollow in the mortar where the head should have been.

'And what did the crown look like?' I asked.

'Gold,' Swift replied. 'Thick and heavy. It was virtually cemented to the skull by its weight.'

'Was it elaborate?' Miss Fairchild asked.

'Not really,' Swift replied. 'It was a simple circlet with spikes – you know, like triangles, the sort of thing you'd expect on a crown. The Laird said it could be the old Norse crown belonging to the King of the Isles. If it was, then it would be almost a thousand years old.'

That made us all stop and wonder, and we stared at the headless skeleton for quite some time. It was rather spooky the way it was pinned into the wall, with rough-hewn stones forming the dark hollow where the man had been sealed up.

40

I asked, 'Could you explain again the series of events, Swift?'

Swift had been staring intently at the skeleton, but he now turned to face us. 'Yes ... very well. After the discovery, I spent a few days scraping the mortar away from the bones; it was damp and crumbled away easily. He was hollow inside, so he must have been flesh and blood when the mortar was poured over his head. There's a hole up there – look.' He aimed a beam of light a couple of feet above the skeleton to show a gap in the ceiling and the rafters beyond. He carried on: 'Then the archaeologists arrived and demanded to see it. The Laird, MacDonald and myself brought them up here and the first thing the ringleader did was snatch the skull and crown away from the body. The Laird was livid and grabbed it back. MacDonald was reaching for his dirk and we were all shouting at once. The Laird replaced the skull and crown, then ordered them out and gave them a dressing down,' Swift recalled angrily. 'Then the skull and crown vanished the same night, and we banned the blasted archaeologists from setting foot in this room again.'

We all paused to digest the details, then I asked, 'Why did they stay on the island, then?'

Swift replied, 'Because they had come a long way and we couldn't actually prove it was one of them. The Laird held a discussion with them and finally allowed them to research the castle's history if they agreed to behave, which they did, and so we agreed to put them up until the month's end.'

'May I ask a question, sir?' Greggs piped up.

'Yes,' Swift said.

'Do you think the thief has smuggled the crown off the island, sir?'

'No,' Swift answered. 'We have only one boat and MacDonald checks the archaeologists and all their kit before taking them to the mainland. It's still here somewhere, I'm sure of that. I haven't found it yet, but I will.'

'But who *was* he, sir, and why was he interred in the wall?' Greggs continued.

'Black Dougal,' I replied.

'Suspected to be Black Dougal,' Swift cut in. 'We can't be certain.'

'But *why* is it thought to be "Black Dougal", sir?' Greggs persisted.

'Yes, and who was Black Dougal?' I rejoined. 'He must have done something to warrant all this effort. They could have just tossed him in the loch if they'd wanted to be rid of him.'

'I can't tell you the story.' Swift looked embarrassed. 'Hector, the Laird, he must tell you — if he wants to.'

'It's a secret, is it?' I remarked.

'Skeletons in the closet,' Miss Fairchild giggled.

'In the *wall*,' I added. 'Better class of skeletons in castles, you know.'

Greggs stifled a laugh and Swift frowned. 'Very amusing,' he retorted, and started to pull the rug back over the opening.

'Just a moment, Swift,' I said. 'Few questions, old chap. How long since this room has been used?'

'No idea.' He paused and waved an arm toward the smart new library he'd constructed. 'It was just a store-room when I decided to turn it into my study. It was full of old weapons, shields, rusted chain mail, that sort of thing; I cleared it all out and put it in the basement. The roof had been leaking for decades, so I repaired it, then started to strip out the old panelling lining the walls.'

'And what made you think there was an opening here?' Miss Fairchild asked.

'Once I'd removed the rotten panelling, the outline of this doorway became apparent. There was a pattern of the cracks around it, you see. And I realised it was prob-ably an old interior passage that had once connected this room and the Lady's Parlour.'

'It would not have always been the Lady's Parlour, would it, sir?' Greggs observed.

'No, it wasn't,' Swift agreed. 'This is the Keep; it would have been the guards' quarters when it was first built and for hundreds of years afterwards.'

'Was there nothing at all left to indicate what may have been done?' Miss Fairchild had returned to the mystery. 'A name, or a warning, scratched into the plaster?'

'No, not a thing; but I found an iron crucifix hanging around the skeleton's neck. It fell off when I was uncover-ing him, so I fixed it above the opening, see?'

Swift shone the lamp onto the stone wall above the jagged edges of the opening.

'Damn and blast it!' he swore.' Some bloody swine has stolen that as well!'

CHAPTER 5

'Chief Inspector!' Greggs exclaimed in horror.

'Erm, sorry – sorry, Miss Fairchild.' Swift looked round to see her smiling at him, not in the least bit shocked. He ran his fingers through his dark hair and stared at the place where the crucifix had been.

Greggs took the opportunity to take Miss Fairchild by the arm and steer her from the room and, no doubt, escort her for a little tête-à-tête somewhere quieter. Fogg had stayed resolutely away from the cavern-like space holding the skeleton, but now came to wag his tail at me so I picked him up.

'Swift,' I began, then went and sat down on a leather-backed chair in front of the fire and placed my little dog at my feet. 'Swift, you'll have to come clean about Black Dougal and whatever this curse is about.'

He came and dropped heavily into the chair opposite me, stretching his legs in front of the fire. His knees were grazed and grubby.

'I can't, Lennox, because the Laird won't tell me about it and Florence says she doesn't know anything either.'

'The maid knows something, I heard her shout Black Dougal.'

'Yes, but it's a sort of bogeyman name around here,' he said wearily. 'Any supposed ghost or ghoul is called Black Dougal, but no one knows why, or if they do, they won't say. As far as I know he's part of their local superstitions. And now it seems they think the curse has been let loose to haunt them, or some such nonsense.' He breathed a long sigh. 'Lennox, I'm a foreigner here. It's a different world and I try my best to fit in, but ... it's in their *blood*, this clan thing. Hundreds, probably thousands of years of fighting and feuding, making pacts, breaking them, forging alliances, committing acts of treachery ... nothing is forgotten and they inhale their history with every breath they take. And here I am, blundering around trying to learn, and I haven't a clue.'

'Are they being kind to you? The family, I mean.'

'Yes, couldn't be nicer,' he replied. 'Actually, there's only Florence and her father, Laird Hector; there's no other family here. And the servants are friendly and willing. Even MacDonald is amiable — well, his version of amiable. But the castle is just the tip of the iceberg: back on the mainland, the Laird owns thousands of acres of land. There are farmers, tradesmen, shepherds and blacksmiths, gillies, woodsmen – hundreds of people ... and they're all part of the clan. The Laird is the chieftain. And I'm an Englishman from London, coming in as father to the future Laird.' He sighed. 'I can feel them watching me, gauging everything I do. It's unnerving.'

'And the first thing you do is uncover some sort of ancient murder.' I laughed. 'And now it's stalking the halls.'

'Yes, exactly!' He grinned wryly. 'I make my best efforts to renovate the castle and manage to uncover a skeleton in the process. And it probably really is some dreadful deed they buried centuries ago, and now it's been dragged out into the open –by me, a damn Sassenach!' He laughed, then frowned as his mood changed. 'And my poor wife tumbled down the steps. She could have been killed and the baby with her …' His voice broke across the words.

I regarded him quietly. His confidence must have been badly knocked by the circumstances and recent events. I reached into my pocket and drew out my hip flask.

'Brandy,' I said, unscrewing the lid.

'I've got something better.' He reached into his sporran and withdrew a battered old silver flask.

'I always wondered what the Scots kept in those things,' I grinned.

'The essentials,' he replied with a smile. 'Florence gave it to me. Belonged to one of the ancestors; still got the dent where it stopped a bullet.' He held it up. 'And it holds the best whisky you'll ever encounter.' He poured a pale capful and passed it to me.

He was right: it was marvellously smooth – dangerously smooth.

'They've got their own distillery on the mainland,' he said. 'Can you imagine owning your own whisky distillery? And they don't export any, it's all distributed locally.'

'Good Lord, there can't be a sober man in the district!' I remarked.

'I doubt there is. How do you think they survive the highland winters wearing kilts!'

I laughed as he topped up my cap. We savoured the fine spirits for a moment in silence, then turned to more serious matters.

I asked: 'These archaeologists you talked about. Where are they now and how did they come to be here?'

'They're going to the mainland today; MacDonald is taking them to catch the local train. They said they want to study the archives at the records office in the town. We have a lot of documents here in the muniment room, but they wanted to research something or other. They came to the castle because I stupidly reported the skeleton to the coroner's office in London and happened to mention it to a friend at Scotland Yard. Within days I received a telegram announcing that this team of experts had been appointed to investigate, and they arrived the next day. Six of them.' He ended on a flat note.

'Are they staying here?' I asked. 'At night, I mean.'

'Yes, I've put them as far away from the Keep as possible. They're in the old Armoury building next to your tower. It's mostly habitable.'

'And you think one of them stole the skull and crown?' I asked.

'Yes, who else?' he retorted. 'And probably that crucifix, too.' He glanced up at the vacant stone wall where it should have been. 'And no, I don't know when it disappeared, before you ask.'

'Right.' I thought about it. 'Was there anything special about the crucifix?'

'I've no idea. There was an outline of a crucified man etched onto one side, and some writing inscribed on the back. Runic, I think, same as the crown.'

'You handled the crown, then?' I asked, rather surprised.

'I only cleaned the mortar off it. I told you, the day I discovered it, MacDonald came and helped dig it out and everyone else was there too. Once we'd exposed most of the skeleton, we all just stood back and stared. The Laird was adamant we must not move any part of it, we could look at it, but that was all.'

'Whereabouts was the lettering on the crown?' I asked.

'It had been incised on the band running around the rim of the crown,' he replied. 'But as it was still partly in the wall we couldn't read it all and no one understood runic form anyway.'

I ruminated on this while Swift poured another capful of whisky for me and took a swig for himself. 'And were there any strange reactions when it was discovered?' I asked.

He raised his brows with a wry smile.

'Yes, yes, stupid question,' I admitted. 'But I meant, any stranger than you'd expect?'

He shifted in his seat. 'MacDonald. He was shaken, I think. He's a hard man and doesn't give much away, but he couldn't take his eyes off the crown. Seemed alarmed and mesmerised in the same measure.'

'Hum.' There was much here to think about and I was trying to shuffle my thoughts into order. 'Did they examine the skeleton, or the crown?' I asked.

'Who?' Swift asked back.

'The archaeologists, of course.'

He frowned at me. 'They asked a lot of questions, and after the argument caused by the leader grabbing the skull they were told to leave the room. Then the skull vanished overnight. They denied any knowledge, of course. I questioned them thoroughly and searched their rooms but didn't discover a thing. Since then, they've kept their distance and so have I, although I've continued to search for the skull. I'll be glad when they leave, actually.' He took another swig from the flask and passed it to me for my own tot. I handed it back and he slipped it away in his sporran.

'Why did you bring that woman?' Swift asked suddenly. 'Miss Fairchild. I don't mind, you can bring whomever you like, but…'

'I didn't bring her,' I protested. 'She was on the train and I came to her aid. I had no idea she was coming here.'

'Fine.' He looked sceptical. 'Anyway, Florence has taken a liking to her. We put her in the rooms you were supposed to have.'

'So that's why I'm stuck out in the tower,' I remarked.

'Yes.' He grinned. 'And you can come to the seance they're holding tonight after dinner.'

'Oh, for heaven's sake! No, I'm not going,' I told him firmly.

'If I must go, so must you,' he replied equally firmly.

Florence appeared on the doorstep and interrupted before I could argue the point. She looked flustered.

'Darling, the water pump has broken and one of the maids has had to collect buckets of water from the well. You couldn't take a look at it, could you? The kitchen staff are becoming quite upset and it's set Cook on the warpath, and you know what she's like.'

'Oh hell, yes, of course, my dear.' He got up, kissed his wife and left me with a cursory goodbye.

'Heathcliff.' Florence turned to me as I stood to greet her. 'I'm terribly grateful you are here. Poor Jonathan needs someone to bolster him up. There's so much for him to do and he takes it all so very seriously.' She slipped into Swift's chair. 'It's really rather tiring,' she said with a smile.

'Um … Not Heathcliff. Lennox, old thing,' I reminded her. 'Swift's a capable man, Florence, don't worry about him, he'll settle down. Although – this is all a bit out of the ordinary,' I remarked while admiring her large blue-grey eyes. 'The skeleton, I mean; and the archaeologists. And you took a tumble, I believe?'

Her smile faded. 'It was nothing. I was clumsy. But it has been rather a strain, and now we have all these people. They're terribly nice, but … Anyway, at least you brought Miss Fairchild with you, she's really quite delightful.' She brightened up, her pretty features suddenly sparkling.

'I'm so pleased to have such an interesting lady here. She is quite remarkable and we are holding a seance later. Isn't it fun?'

I didn't have time to answer as she glanced at her watch.

'Oh dear, I must be going.' She jumped up and I followed suit.

'Actually, I didn't bring Miss Fair…' I began to protest, but too late: she reached up to kiss my cheek and swept off.

I shoved my hands in my pockets, took one more glance around, and made my way back down to the courtyard. Fogg aimed straight for the chickens and scattered them once again. I called him to heel and lectured him quietly, which he ignored, of course.

The wind had died down. I walked out below the arched gateway and down the stone causeway, then turned off, away from the castle and onto a worn path between the trees. The last time I was here had been for the wedding ceremony, and although there had been very little time for solitary exploration, I had managed to identify a good spot for fishing. I'd brought my new travelling rod with me, a lovely seven-piece Hardy, and tomorrow at dawn I intended to try it out.

Fogg started barking and I turned around to identify the cause. MacDonald was just shipping oars and bringing the wooden boat up to the jetty near the causeway. There were a number of men on board and they jumped out to help secure it. I assumed them to be the archaeologists, and returned to my contemplations.

I wandered slowly beneath the boughs while Fogg foraged ahead, nose to the ground. The ancient trunks were black with mould and a thick shroud of green moss clung along the snaking roots weaving in and out of the dark earth. Pale lichen hung from twigs and branches, trailing lacy tendrils to catch the unwary in a clammy caress. Stone cracks and crevices held long-fingered bracken spun with silver-stranded spiders' webs that sparkled in rays of golden light from the setting sun. A clump of gorse, deep green and bristling with thorns, formed a dense thicket amid a jumble of grey rocks in the centre of the copse. I followed the path around it going downhill as I went.

The shore was a beach of sand and pebbles. I padded down to a comfortable rock at the edge of the water. Ahead of me, across the loch, lay the mountains of Mull; behind me, about the same distance, was the broad expanse of the tree-lined mainland.

A fish rose for a fly, then a few more, leaving rings rippling across the still water. Mist that had clung to the mountaintops all day now crept down the valleys and gullies to touch the sea. Haunting and silent, the loch held an ethereal beauty and I took a deep breath of crisp salt air — if ever there was a taste of heaven, it was here.

Fogg came to join me on the rock. Time ticked by as I waited for the sun to sink into the sea, and slowly turned the sky and gathering clouds shades of orange and pink, before finally letting loose a bright flash of white and melting below the horizon.

I remained in the peaceful silence, listening to the sea-birds returning home with quiet calls across the water; then, as the chill set in and a thin drizzle began to fall, I rose to make my way back to the castle in search of a snifter and dinner. I had no sooner stepped onto the beach when an awful sound, like a bone-crunching thump, rang out. I looked up ahead, trying to peer into the dusk. Fogg and I raced up through the trees toward the castle walls set high upon the crags, then stopped. Sprawled across jagged black rocks lay a body, spreadeagled and bloody, and very, very dead.

CHAPTER 6

Rather breathless, I peered up at the looming castle walls. A piece of paper fluttered in the faint breeze and drifted slowly to the ground. I glanced at the body: he was obviously beyond help, so I strode over to retrieve the paper before it was blown into the loch. I shoved it into my waistcoat pocket, then went quickly to the corpse. The dead man stared glassily up at me, well, one eye did; the other was rather damaged by the fall. I had no idea who he was. He was badly broken from the long drop: his arms and legs were contorted at odd angles, which was rather disconcerting.

Dusk had gathered quickly and I pulled out my torch and shone it over him for a better look. He had a pleasant face, unlined, relatively young, my age anyway, around thirty, pale-blue eyes, sandy-coloured hair, dirt under his fingernails and he was marginally overweight. He wore the clothes of an outdoorsman, being mostly shades of green apart from the thick, cream-coloured flannel shirt he wore under a tweed waistcoat. I assumed he must be one of the archaeologists, given the English appearance of his attire. I could detect a hint of whisky and leaned in — in fact he stank of the stuff, and now that I was close to him I could see the puffiness under the eyes and broken veins over his nose that indicated a heavy drinker. I straightened up, frowning, then had the sense to pull out my fob watch and noted the time at just after half past five in the evening.

I stared up at the walls, but nothing showed other than a light in one of the arrow-slit windows. Fogg held a deep dislike of anything dead, so he had raced off to the sanctuary of the castle. I decided I'd better follow suit and inform Swift that his problems had just become a great deal more serious.

'*What?*' Swift stared aghast.

'Dead and rather mangled, I'm afraid,' I told him. I'd found him in the outhouse next to the kitchens, where he was just putting the water pump back together; a small diesel generator was humming beside it, the only piece of modern technology I had seen in the place. He rolled his sleeves down and pulled his black jacket over his shirt.

'Come on.' He grabbed the storm lamp under whose light he'd been working. 'Show me.'

It didn't take long, as nothing was far away on this small island. We stood over the victim for a moment as Swift cast a cool, professional eye over him, then remarked: 'Soused.'

He knelt down for a closer inspection while I held up the lantern. '*Why?*' he muttered half to himself, then stood up to follow the line of the dead man's fall to the top of the wall thirty feet or more above us. 'The Armoury,' he said.

'Is he one of the archaeologists?' I asked.

Swift nodded. 'Yes: Maxwell. Frederick Maxwell I think his full name is.'

'What do you know of him?'

'Virtually nothing,' he said firmly. He was searching the pockets of the corpse as he was talking, rain was falling more steadily and there were more and more drops on the face and clothes of the dead Maxwell. Swift stopped to look dispassionately again at the body. 'I need to have a look behind him; give me a hand, will you.'

I put the lantern aside and we rolled the poor chap over. There was a lot more blood beneath him, but no knife in the back or any such drama. I retrieved the lamp and watched Swift finish his task.

'Was he the leader?' I asked.

'No, that's an American called Jackson, from New York City. He's a brash loudmouth; this chap was very quiet, barely said a word.' Swift stood up. 'Nothing in his pockets except a grubby handkerchief and a few coins.' He tugged the body back again by the lapels of the jacket, then leaned in to study the dead man's face. 'Very strange,' he muttered.

He straightened up, wiping his hands on his kilt. 'Come on, we'd better go and break the news.'

I hesitated for a moment, hovering by the corpse. I stopped to bow my head and send a silent prayer to the man upstairs, wishing Frederic Maxwell a peaceful passing — should such a journey exist — and then followed in Swift's footsteps.

In the brief time it took us to return to the castle, Swift had metamorphosed back into his role as a chief inspector of Scotland Yard. His face had set hard, his lips firm in a thin line; he looked more hawkish than ever as we passed under the elaborate lantern hanging from an iron bracket under the archway into the Gateway-Keep.

'Swift,' I called. He stopped as I pulled the stray piece of paper from my pocket. 'Found this near the body.'

He took it from me, unfolded it, then turned it over in his hands under the lantern light. It looked like an etching of a crucifix, or rather a rubbing, such as somebody would make of a brass engraving.

'It's from the crucifix — the stolen one. Looks like someone made a copy,' he remarked.

'And that's the inscription?' I frowned at it.

'Yes,' Swift said, then folded it back up and stuffed it in his own pocket. 'Come on, we'd better inform the Laird.'

We crossed the wet cobbles and entered the main living quarters of the castle, which lay between the Kirk and my tower. The Great Hall was the best room of all, to my mind: high stone walls with suits of heavy armour standing around gathering dust, the walls awash with pikes, halberds, swords, dirks, shields and the rest of the paraphernalia designed to wage medieval war. There were a couple of stuffed stags heads, too, with magnificent antlers. The place was alight with wall sconces and a roaring fire in a monumental fireplace. Our footsteps echoed as we trotted up the broad oak stairs and along the balustraded corridor. The Laird and Donald MacDonald were seated before the fire in the upper drawing room, smoking pipes with a dram of pale-gold whisky at their elbows. The room was cluttered and cosy, with more weapons on the walls, and some very nice paintings — I particularly liked the highland cows. There were tartan rugs for comfort, with high-backed chairs and deep sofas with plump cushions, and a battered suit of armour in the corner. A large desk stood next to it with the usual pens, blotters and whatnots, this room was used by the Laird as his study too.

The Laird raised his leonine head to look at us, I suddenly felt like a crass schoolboy and thought we should have knocked.

'Body, sir,' Swift said, a touch breathless. 'Out on the rocks.'

The Laird frowned in question.

'Fallen from the wall, above the Armoury. He was almost certainly pushed,' Swift added. 'I'm pretty sure he was, anyway.'

'He had been drinking,' I added. 'But we found a piece of paper nearby. It was a likeness of the stolen crucifix.'

Swift dug it out and handed it to the Laird and he and MacDonald stared at it, and then each other.

'Ay,' MacDonald's voice rumbled. I noticed his boots gleamed wet in the firelight.

'We are going to keep it to ourselves until we've made further investigations,' Swift said.

As one, they placed smoking pipes on the stone-flagged hearth and rose to their feet.

'Ay, we'll take a look,' MacDonald growled. They were men of few words, but he reached up to the high mantle above the fire and took down a lighted lantern. They all seemed to keep lanterns about the rooms, which on an island without mains electricity was a good precaution, in my view.

'Right, Lennox.' Swift turned to nod at me.

I followed him and we strode quickly in the rain to the three-storey Armoury building set between my tower and the jumbled ruins at the far end of the castle courtyard.

'Jackson?' Swift called out as we entered a narrow passageway.

A call came down the circular stone stairway. 'Hello?' the voice shouted down.

We raced up the winding stairs and into a corridor.

'Come on in,' a fair-haired chap said, holding the door open. He was dressed in similar garb to the dead man and was grasping a boot in one hand whilst hopping on the other.

'Campbell! Where's Jackson?' Swift paused on the threshold.

'Haven't the foggiest, old boy,' Campbell replied, slipping his stockinged foot into his boot whilst speaking. The sock had a hole in the toe, I noticed.

'We need to take a look at the battlements. Campbell, you can come with us.' Swift turned and strode to another door, which he dashed out of. From the cold draught I realised it opened onto the steep steps rising to the battlements.

'Greetings, old chap.' I said hastily. 'I'm Major Lennox.' I waved a hand at the startled Campbell, who was frowning after Swift, then raced up to the top of the castle wall. The rain had almost stopped; it was very dark with a sprinkling of stars and a waxing moon. A crenellated parapet ran all around the curtain wall and we leaned over it to see lamplight moving below, presumably that of the Laird and Donald MacDonald.

'Search along there,' Swift told me, pointing to the right. He strode off to the left, holding the storm lantern low in front of him. Campbell arrived, a little breathless.

'Best follow Swift,' I told him.

He went, looking decidedly puzzled.

I switched on my torch, gave it a shake as it flashed on and off, and then shone the beam at the stone floor of the parapet walk, searching for clues.

The rooftops of most of the buildings rose to this level, their lead-lined gutters butting up to the inner edge of the battlements. Despite the buffeting wind, I felt perfectly comfortable ambling slowly along with my eyes fixed firmly on the uneven stones, searching for whatever might be found. I'd gone a few more feet, lost in concentration, when I realised there was no roof to my right. I swung my torch to have a look, then stepped back swiftly as my heart skipped a beat. It was a black void beyond a crumbling brink — nothing but pitch darkness lay at my side. I'd always been scared of heights —which is a bit of a disadvantage for a pilot, actually — and sweat suddenly pricked cold on my brow. I was above the ruined militia buildings. I moved sharply to the battlement wall and stayed there.

'Over here,' Swift shouted.

I turned and went back quickly with some relief to join him and the confused Campbell.

Swift was holding an empty silver hip flask. 'Found this.' He held it out. 'It has Maxwell's initials engraved on it. This must be where he went over.'

I leaned over the battlements, saw MacDonald's lamplight directly below and nodded agreement.

'Could you please tell me what you are talking about?' Campbell asked.

'Maxwell,' Swift replied. 'He fell from here.'

'Good Lord, no!' Campbell looked convincingly astonished.

'When did you last see him?' Swift began an interrogation.

'After we got off the boat. About an hour or so ago,' Campbell replied. 'Why on earth did he fall off this wall? And what was he doing up here?'

'That's what I'd like to know,' Swift growled.

Campbell took an involuntary step backwards. 'Well, I have no idea.' He turned to look at the awful drop again as he realised the import of what Swift was saying. 'You mean he's *dead*?'

'Of course he's dead,' Swift snapped.

'Good Lord,' Campbell said again. 'Poor fellow. I was rather fond of him. We all were.'

'Well, somebody wasn't,' Swift said.

'I suppose he'd been drinking,' Campbell remarked, leaning over the wall again and staring down into the darkness. 'And he toppled over.'

'Nonsense; how could he?' Swift dismissed the idea. 'Nobody would fall over these walls, however drunk they might be.'

He was right: the crenellations came to waist height at the lowest points and up to my shoulders at the highest.

'He wasn't exactly happy, you know,' Campbell said. 'He had debts and drank a great deal. He was quite miserable, actually. Nice enough, of course, but laden with problems.'

'So you think he may have jumped?' I said.

'Possibly,' Campbell suggested. 'Wouldn't be surprised, anyway.'

'No, he didn't,' Swift argued. 'Look.' He pointed at fresh scratch marks on the old stones. 'He must have had a scuffle with his attacker.'

'Could have been made by his boots as he clambered up,' Campbell suggested.

We peered at the fresh marks scraped into the moss and lichen on the dark stone walls.

A flash of light in the far distance caught my eye. 'What's that?' I said, aiming my torch toward the horizon.

We all stared at a light like a blazing flame floating on the dark waters of the loch. Puzzled, we watched silently as the burning light flickered and then sank into the moonlit night.

'I think it was a boat,' I said.

We all looked at each other.

'Damn and blast it!' Swift shouted suddenly. 'It must be our skiff!'

CHAPTER 7

Swift turned to run down the steps shouting as he went.

'Campbell, show Major Lennox to Maxwell's room, then gather your people together in the mess. I'll be back to interview you all shortly.' I heard his boots clatter downwards in the darkness, then he called back up. 'Lennox, make sure you do a thorough search.'

I opened my mouth to protest at being ordered about like some lowly police constable, but he was out of earshot.

Campbell's blond brows were raised above brown eyes.

'Used to be a detective,' I explained. 'Scotland Yard.'

'Ah,' he nodded. 'Well, better go and muster the troops. It'll come as a bit of a shock, you know. Maxwell I mean.'

'Yes.' We were trotting down the steps following the beam of my torch until we came to a low door set in the wall of the Armoury building.

'In here,' Campbell said.

We entered a rectangular room where stood a long wooden table with benches either side and a couple of oil lamps illuminating the whole. I don't know what it had been in the past but it appeared to have been adopted as a temporary mess by the archaeologists. A man with thick black hair, wearing a dull-green outfit over a cream shirt, was stirring a cauldron suspended by a chain over a crackling fire. It smelled rather good.

'Buggins,' Campbell called out. 'Maxwell's had a bit of a reverse. Took a dive over the top, apparently.'

'Napoo?' The dark haired man at the cooking pot asked, having turned to regard us with a dripping ladle in hand. 'Napoo' was old army slang for dead and gone, a mangled Anglicisation of the French 'il n'y a plus'.

'According to accounts, yes: entirely done in,' Campbell replied. 'Lennox, this is Barclay Huggins. Better known as "Buggins".'

'Greetings,' I extended a hand and was given a hearty shake in return. 'I assume you went through the war together?'

'We did, and came out the other side.' Buggins raised a brief smile.

'What was your line?' I asked

'Intelligence,' he replied, his eyes darkening.

He turned to Campbell. 'Maxwell had a few too many?'

Campbell had opened his mouth to respond when he was interrupted by the entrance of another chap. A tubby little fellow came in; he bore thick round spectacles over red chubby cheeks and looked like a ham actor done up to be everyone's idea of the archetypal archaeologist. He even wore a khaki neckerchief and a hat with a broad brim. I was surprised it wasn't a pith helmet.

'When is dinner?' he asked in a voice more contralto than tenor, which I suppose was to be expected of someone who still sported shorts at thirty. 'I'm hungry,' he complained.

'Could be a bit of a delay, I'm afraid,' I told him.

His brows furrowed, 'But it is time for dinner.' He sounded peeved. 'We always have dinner at six o'clock.'

Campbell sighed. 'Dennis Dennis, our archivist. This is Major Lennox.'

Dennis Dennis? His parents must have been entirely lacking in imagination. He stared at me through those thick lenses, then gave me a sort of wave, or possibly a boy-scout's salute, I wasn't sure which. As he hadn't come round the table to shake my hand I stayed where I was and gave him a cursory nod.

'Greetings, Dennis. You do know that Maxwell is dead, do you?' I watched for his reaction.

He jumped as if someone had given him a poke with a sharp stick. 'Why?' he shouted.

'I say, old boy, that was a bit brutal,' Campbell tried to cut in, but I ignored him.

'What do you mean, *why?*' I walked around the table to stare down at him.

He stared up, eyes magnified by the thick lenses. 'Why is he dead?' he shouted in his squeaky voice.

'Because someone pushed him off the battlements,' I replied.

'Well, it's not allowed,' he replied, blinking rapidly. 'He drank a lot, you know. That's not allowed either.'

He backed away, then went over to Buggins by the fire and stared into the bubbling pot of stew until his glasses steamed over.

Campbell arrived at my shoulder and explained: 'He's better with dusty old tomes than people.'

'Damn strange chap,' I remarked, not at all sure what to make of him.

'Why did you say Maxwell was pushed?' Campbell was looking perturbed. 'You don't *know* that, do you?'

I stared at him; he had a point. 'Well, erm … Look, let me go and see Maxwell's room, maybe it will help. Perhaps there will be a note, or something like that.'

Campbell nodded and led the way across bare wooden floorboards, through the far doorway and down the interior stairs. He opened a door to let me in the dead man's room then set off to call the rest of the archaeologists together.

The room was even more spartan than the usual castle accommodation. A camp bed was placed near the hearth, and grey woollen blankets lay rumpled and untidy, as though the occupant had recently climbed out of it. The fire had been lit but was dying for want of wood and a pan full of water had been left in front of it. A tin mug and a packet of black tea told its own story.

Maxwell had appeared to be camping out in the room, which I assumed was standard practice for the archaeologists given their usual activities out in the field. There was a large canvas rucksack in a corner and I went to have a rifle through it. Nothing but grimy working togs smelling of must and mould – as did the blankets, which I yanked off the camp bed and shook out, sneezing as the dust flew. I found nothing of interest and moved to the centre of the room to scan the place. There was a folding stool made of canvas and wood beside the fire. On the mantelpiece itself was a larger tin with a red cross painted on the top. I opened it. It contained a simple medical kit, the sort carried by soldiers during the war. I suppose the archaeologists would all have one if they were working in remote spots. It was fitted with standard medical stuff and I closed it firmly against the ever present dust.

A heavy green rug had been hung across the arrow-slit window, so I pulled it aside and found a row of empty whisky bottles in the deep embrasure. In another corner were propped a workman-like shovel and a large hand-pick – for digging, presumably.

I stood up, deflated. I'd formed the idea in my mind that Maxwell had been murdered for filching the iron crucifix. He may have stolen the skull and crown too, and if I had found them I could have returned to Swift in triumph. But then, I mused, the killer would have taken them, so it was rather an irrational hope. And it suddenly occurred to me that I should have worn gloves — fingerprints and all that. I stifled a sigh and returned to inspect the hearth. Along with the kettle and brackets, hooks, chains and whatnots, there was a spit-jack. It was similar to the one we had in the kitchen at home.

I gave the handle a couple of brief turns to wind up the counterweight and set it off. It worked like a simple clockwork mechanism, using two heavy lead weights. I watched as it clicked away, turning the empty rotisserie before finally slowing to a stop as the counterweight reached the floor. It didn't seem to be hiding anything, so I took a closer look at the embers of the fire.

The crisp remains of burnt pages lay under charred logs. I prised the lumps of wood away with a poker and knelt to peer at the blackened paper. I could see the impress of scrawled writing but couldn't make out any actual words. I tried blowing on the rectangles of carbonised sheets but they broke into fine fragments and floated off up the chimney. Only one solitary piece at the very bottom remained legible; I could just make out a couple of words: '*Heaven's doom*', it looked like, before that too disintegrated.

I gave up and left.

Silence met me as I entered the archaeologists' mess. Swift was scowling at the room in general as a group of chaps were each quietly engaged in writing with ink pens on creamy sheets of thick paper.

'Statements,' Swift informed me. 'They're giving an account of their movements between arriving from the mainland earlier this evening and now.' He eyed me more closely. 'You did wear gloves, didn't you?'

'Umm,' I replied noncommittally. 'You do have fingerprint powder with you then?'

'Yes, of course. I've already taken everybody's prints.'

Campbell had been listening and held up inky black fingers to waggle at me with a wry grin.

'Come outside,' Swift ordered, and walked out of the room and onto the steps that led up to the battlements. It was very cold and dark. He stopped when we were out of earshot of the archaeologists.

I told him what I'd found in Maxwell's room, and he frowned at me. "*Heaven's doom?*" he repeated, then shrugged. 'Look, Lennox, MacDonald and I are going to move the body, put it in the Kirk until we can contact the mainland. Don't let anyone leave until you've got a written and signed statement from all of them,' he ordered. 'I've taken Jackson's already. He's in a fury and demanding that the police be called. I haven't told him that the boat has gone – and don't mention it to the others, will you.'

'Campbell knows,' I reminded him.

'Yes, but I've told him to keep it under his hat,' Swift said. "The culprit may give himself away.'

I thought that highly unlikely but didn't say so.

'Right, get to it,' he ordered me.

'Swift,' I said rather tersely, 'I'm not one of your damn bobbies, and it's almost dinnertime. I need to clean up.' And find my dog, I thought, because he'd be hungry too, although Greggs had probably done the necessary.

'Yes, yes. Erm, Lennox ...' Swift paused, then ran fingers through his hair. 'It's all a bit ...'

'Close to home.' I finished the sentence for him. 'Yes, I understand. Have you told Florence?'

'No, not yet.'

'Why don't we leave the death a bit vague? Just tell everyone he may have jumped,' I suggested. 'Because for all we know he may have done.'

'The staff are already spooked,' Swift replied. 'Even if it were true, they wouldn't believe it. And that paper; and now the boat …'

He had a point there. 'Well. Fine. I'll go and collect the statements.' I sighed.

'Yes …' He hesitated. 'We should interview them tonight, while it's all fresh …'

I cut in. 'They're not going anywhere, Swift, we're all stuck here now.'

He gave me a perturbed frown, and then left abruptly with a swirl of his kilt.

The quiet hum of chatter broke off as I entered the mess room. Most of them had finished writing and there was a stack of papers in a neat pile beside the oil lamp in the centre of the table.

'Is it true that there's only one boat?' Campbell asked. He was trying to light a pipe as he spoke and sucked on it without much result.

I gave him a hard stare but he remained oblivious while prodding his pipe.

'Thought you were supposed to keep that to yourself?' I retorted, rather annoyed.

He stopped and looked at me. 'Oh yes! Damn. Apologies, old man. Took a bit of a battering on the bonce, you know.' He pointed to his head. 'Forgetful, aren't I,

Buggins. Since that bomb went off in '17. Nearly blew my top off.' He laughed.

Buggins nodded in support.

I let out an exasperated sigh and picked up the statements. I was folding them when I realised one of the archaeologists was still writing. 'Get a move on would you, man?' I snapped.

'It's Carruthers,' Campbell said. 'Not ...' He started to splutter as his pipe caught hold with a puff of smoke.

Carruthers stopped writing, put the pen down slowly, and then pushed the paper towards me. He wore the usual archaeologist's get-up: cream shirt, dull-green waistcoat and trousers and a tattered fedora low over the eyes. He glanced up from under its shadow, then slowly reached a hand to the rim and pulled it off. Glowing blonde hair fell to the shoulders and, with a twist of disdain upon sculpted lips, Carruthers turned to look me squarely in the eyes. It was a girl – a woman. And she was quite, quite ... exquisite.

CHAPTER 8

I opened my mouth, then closed it firmly. I was hopeless with women and didn't want her to think I was a complete idiot by babbling. She was regarding me coolly, so I stared back, which didn't help.

'Ummm …' I said. 'Greetings, ermm … Carruthers. I mean *Miss* Carruthers. I'm Lennox. Major Lennox. Well, Major Heathcliff Lennox, actually, but I don't like my name. My mother, you know, had strange ideas about romance. Romantic names, I mean, not, not …'

She stood up and came over, and held out her hand.

I shook it, mesmerised by her cool blue eyes and lovely face with its delicate high cheekbones and small nose … 'What?'

'I said *hello*, Major Lennox.' She was still looking up at me, a faint smile on her lips. 'I don't like my name either.'

'Really?' I stammered. 'Well, I suppose Carruthers isn't very interesting but it's perfectly reasonable. It could be worse, you know …'

'I mean my Christian name,' she interrupted before my babbling became entirely incoherent. 'Heathcliff's not too dreadful, I think rather apt actually, although you're too fair to be Heathcliff proper.'

'Oh.' I wondered what she meant by that.

'Persephone,' she said.

'Really?'

'They call me Persi.'

'Ah, rather unfortunate. Why don't you use your middle name?'

'Nefertiti,' she said without inflexion, then raised her brows — as did I.

'Carruthers it is, then,' I said, still gazing into her eyes and quite oblivious to my surroundings.

She nodded. 'Mother specialised in ancient Greece and father was a professor of Egyptology. They're both archaeologists.'

'Ah,' I uttered, then stopped, wondering what else I should say.

A cough came from behind me, and was repeated.

'Sir?'

I spun around. It was Greggs.

'Dinner, sir,' he said, looking rather anxious.

'Oh, hell. Right, um, goodbye, Miss … Carruthers.'

She raised a hand.

I went a bit pink, then turned to push off, but realised I'd forgotten the statements and had to go back to the table for them. I noticed that all the other chaps were watching me. I blinked a bit, then dashed out after Greggs.

He went with me to the steps of the tower, then left with barely a word, I assume he was heading to the kitchens to take a meal with the castle staff. I called thanks but he was deaf as usual and didn't hear me.

Foggy was delighted to see me and bounded in my direction for a fuss, then returned to his basket by the fire with a happy sigh and wag of the tail. A rotund black kitten was comfortably ensconced in said basket.

'Tubbs?'

I went and picked him up, looked him over and concluded he was indeed our little cat. But how on earth had he got here? There was a note propped up on the mantle piece:

'*Sir, the trunk has arrived and with it Mr Tubbs, who had stowed away. He made himself comfortable in your socks, but had to perform his toilette in your hat. It is drying by the fire. He has subsequently been supplied with a suitable box of ash and soil. They have both dined. Yours, etc., Greggs.*'

I really don't know why he couldn't just have told me himself. But I was very pleased to see our little chap, and Foggy was, of course, ecstatic. I noted the kitty tray in the far corner and my trunk at the toe end of the bed. The good butler had boiled the water on the fire and left it in the ceramic washbasin on the marble-topped washstand, and he'd dusted down my evening wear and laid it out on the bed. Once I'd spruced up and donned fresh togs, I called Fogg and we set off for dinner.

I arrived late and earned a frown from the Laird as I strode into the grand dining room. It was a spacious room with a high ceiling, but had been set for only a small gathering, with a linen-draped circular table placed in the middle. Candles glowed amid sparkling glasses and gleaming silverware. The fire was blazing in the huge hearth and everyone was already seated and waiting for me. The castle factotum, Natty Brown, was presiding, and greeted me with a grunt, so I pulled out my own chair and sat down. Fogg settled at my feet where I could drop titbits in his direction.

'A murder!' Miss Fairchild said to me as I made myself comfortable between her and Swift.

I frowned at Swift but he ignored me.

'We are trying to keep it quiet, Miss Fairchild,' I said.

'Silence,' the Laird announced suddenly, in the deep, booming voice I recalled from my last visit. 'Prayers.'

We lowered our heads and eyes as he intoned a blessing in Gaelic, which I didn't understand although I enjoyed the lilting cadence. He had a richly resonant voice with barely a hint of accent, Scottish or otherwise. It was often the case that the Scots aristocracy spoke more precisely correct English than the English themselves.

I was just about to reach for my glass of red wine when the piper came swirling in. He played a couple of rounds of hearty highland tunes before exiting. We were finally allowed to start.

'Lennox,' the Laird addressed me loudly as I raised my glass to my lips. I put it down again.

'Sir?'

'You and Swift will put an end to the skulduggery being perpetrated in this house.' He informed me.

'Right, erm, yes …'

'Report to me in my quarters tomorrow at o six hundred hours.' He turned to glare at me with dark brown eyes under thick white brows. 'I want an explanation. This has gone far enough,' he growled, and then added in a furious undertone: 'My *boat*. They burned my bloody boat, the heathen …' He stopped and glanced at Miss Fairchild, who was seated between us and watching avidly. Then he picked up his glass and downed the wine in one and shouted, 'Brown!' who appeared instantly and poured him a refill.

The soup was cold, but it was more stew than soup and very tasty. The bread rolls were like rocks — should we ever suffer invaders we could pelt them to death with Cook's buns. I wrested them into pieces and soaked them in my soup while I turned to Miss Fairchild.

'I hope you are enjoying your stay, Miss Fairchild.'

'Oh, dear boy, it is most delightful. Lady Florence and I made ourselves comfortable in the Lady's Parlour and had a cosy afternoon by the fireside. And before that I took a bite with your dear man Greggs. He was quite attentive. We had cakes and tea and a lovely long chat.'

'Hum.' I almost let loose a sigh because I *knew* Greggs would form an attachment. Indeed, his bout of doldrums back home in Ashton Steeple had almost certainly been caused by a misplaced *coup de coeur*. Miss Fairchild may seem eccentric, but, I mused, she was essentially a level-headed sort of lady and perhaps would prove a good match for my old butler.

She drained her wineglass and looked around for more, as Natty Brown came over and wielded the decanter for a top-up. She downed that in one, too.

'Is there anythin' more I can be gettin' fer ye, dear lady?' Natty Brown asked in a heavy highland accent. He had thick red hair and was togged up in the usual highland kilt, bonnet and whatnots, as were all the Scotsmen on the island.

'Well, just one more.' Miss Fairchild looked up at him with bright eyes and an empty glass. She had the most remarkable effect on the older men — one smile from her and they became mush.

She turned to gaze at the brightly burning fire in the hearth on the far side of the room, and suddenly whispered: 'There are lost spirits here.'

Yes, because she and the Laird have just drunk them all, I thought but didn't say.

I finished my soup and stared around. The room had once been part of the original Great Hall where the Lairds of old would have caroused with their clansmen in full medieval style. But as medieval carousing had fallen from fashion the room had been reworked and a new wall constructed to split it in half. The outer part was now the front hall, with the stairway leading to the upper rooms. The remodelling hadn't detracted from the grandeur of the place, though. The room was broad and long, the high ceiling dark and distant; it was easy to imagine ghosts from the turbulent past in the shadows above us.

Natty Brown came back and topped up Miss Fairchild's

glass and then the Laird's, so I drained my own, too. I had a feeling this was going to be a long night.

The soup dishes were cleared away and a mound of mashed meat on a plate was placed before me.

'Haggis,' the Laird boomed. The piper appeared, played another merry medley, and then went off again. I had another drink.

'Did you discover why they interred the skeleton in the wall?' Miss Fairchild asked me.

'Only the Laird knows,' I said. We both looked at him; he was draining his glass and his eyes were beginning to take on a glazed look.

'I don't think we'll hear the story this evening,' she giggled.

Florence called over to her father. 'Daddy, please don't fret over the skiff. Fundit will be over with the stores on Monday. It's only three days away and the larder is well stocked for the winter.'

'Thank you, Florence,' he answered in a soft tone. 'But we have a duty to that dead man and his family. We must tell them, wee lass — and the police.'

'Yes, I suppose we must,' she answered solemnly.

'Fundit?' I asked, my brows raised.

'Our man ashore,' Swift answered. 'Absent minded, but when he finds whatever we've asked for he tells us he's "fundit".'

'Will he remember to come?' I asked.

Swift didn't crack a smile. 'Yes, he's perfectly reliable.'

'We won't be isolated for long,' Florence told me. 'And

it isn't unusual for us to be cut off. Sometimes we have dreadful storms and we can't reach the far shore for a week or more. We have plenty of food in the stores and it's really quite cosy. You'll see.'

MacDonald cut in with a growl. 'Ay, but if yon laddie hadn't taken the old boat ashore for mending, we'd' have had another.' He nodded towards Swift.

'I wanted it to be ready for the winter,' Swift said in his defence. 'The planking was lifting. And if the spare skiff had still been here, the arsonist would probably have burned that one too.'

'Humph,' was the only reply he received as MacDonald fell back to brooding.

'My dear Donald…' Miss Fairchild leaned forward to beam at him across the white clothed table 'I would like to pray for the poor dead man. May I ask where you have placed his remains?'

'Crypt,' MacDonald rumbled in reply. I could see him softening as she gazed at him. 'The auld crypt below the Kirk. I'll take ye t'morrow, bonnie lass. Ye must nae go alone, ye hear me?'

'Indeed, dear Donald,' she replied.

I listened with surprise: I hadn't realised there was a crypt. I knew the little Kirk from my last visit when I had attended Swift and Florence's wedding; it was a spartan place squeezed between the towers of the Keep and this building.

Miss Fairchild turned back to me. 'Poor Maxwell, he was pushed, you know. I heard an echo of his distress.' She finished another glassful of wine.

'You heard him fall?' I asked.

'Oh no. Just the call from his spirit.' She looked up at me. 'It's a terrible shock when the soul is made to leave before its allotted time. It causes quite a tremor in the ether.'

'Um, yes,' I muttered.

Dessert was another slice of clootie with a lump of custard. I waited for the piper but he must have gone off so we were allowed to chew our way through pudding in peace.

I glanced at Florence on the other side of Swift. Her pregnancy wasn't apparent, although the pretty pink shift dress she was wearing was loose fitting. Her skin was almost glowing and so was she. She was a picture of happiness and contentment despite the horrible death that had just happened. Perhaps she didn't quite believe it was murder; I knew her for a dreamer and she was probably quite proficient at denying unpleasant circumstances. I saw her glance at Swift, her eyes soft with love. He returned her gaze and put out a hand to place over hers.

'She's quite safe.' Miss Fairchild had followed my regard. 'I heard about the tumble she took. And although a villain stalks, she is not the target.'

I frowned at her, my spoon poised over pudding. 'What, or rather, who, is this villain?' I asked pointedly.

'There is evil within these walls.' She spoke softly so only I could hear. 'They are searching, they are stealing and now they are killing. We must be wary.'

'Who is it, Miss Fairchild? If you know anything at all, please tell me,' I almost snapped, being annoyed at the half-revelations.

'I cannot,' she whispered. 'Their mind is devious and I cannot discern such things, Major Lennox. Only that which wishes to be known can be known.'

I finished my pudding in silence.

'Ladies, withdraw,' the Laird suddenly bellowed.

Florence turned toward her father. 'No, Daddy, we're not going to. There's only Lavinia and myself and we'd much rather go to the drawing room all together. Isn't that so, Lavinia?' She looked at Miss Fairchild.

'Indeed,' Miss Fairchild answered. 'But we cannot leave this room yet.'

'Why?' The Laird asked, turning his dark eyes upon the lady.

'Because the spirits are gathered about us, I can feel them,' she told us. 'They grow restive. Everyone join hands now. We must hold a seance and communicate with the departed. They have much to impart.'

CHAPTER 9

'I'll not be holdin' hands with a man, Laird or no,' Mac-
Donald objected.

'Nor I,' the Laird rejoined.

'You must.' Miss Fairchild focused her bright eyes
upon them each in turn and I watched as they both
slowly held out a hand in compliance.

We all joined hands to complete the circle. I considered it all nonsense, but there was no point in arguing,
and I admit I had a quiet curiosity about the proceedings.

'Natty Brown,' Miss Fairchild called out. 'The candles.'

The factotum armed himself with a brass snuffer and
put out the flames one by one until just one candle in the
centre of the table was left burning.

'You may leave us now,' Miss Fairchild called out again.

Brown exited with a sharp nod of the head and
opened and closed the door with a soft thud as he went.
A draught blew through the room and extinguished the
remaining candle. Only the flames from the dying fire
remained to wash flickering lights into the shadows that
massed about.

'Come forth,' Miss Fairchild called out, her voice wavering. 'We await you. We welcome you.'

I expected some sort of ghostly whisper in reply, but she was met by silence apart from the crackling of the logs.

'I sense your presence, dear lady, please come closer.' Miss Fairchild now spoke in a softer tone.

We all held our breath while nothing happened. I heard Fogg let out a snore beneath the table, then he suddenly shifted and sat up with eyes and ears alert.

A faint wreath of smoke swirled slowly in the far corner. I blinked, assuming it to be my imagination. The smoke drifted upwards in a haze of fine mist and spun very gradually in an upward curl until the shape of a pale, hooded face above a slim body could be made out. It drifted closer.

Miss Fairchild spoke kindly. 'You wish to contact your child?'

The vision didn't move, but I could see the face more clearly; it looked awfully like my mother.

'What message do you have?' Miss Fairchild called out.

The room was now frozen and hushed, and the hairs on the back of my neck stood rigid as I stared at the translucent wraith.

Miss Fairchild's voice took on a lighter resonance, not like her own voice at all. 'My beloved child be at peace. I am with you. I am watching over you. I walk where you walk, I am ever at your side. I am your loving mother.'

Miss Fairchild's voice faded away almost to a distant echo. As she fell silent, the pale wraith dissolved before my eyes. I stared at the void where she had appeared, wanting her to come back, wanting the chance to speak to her, but she was gone. I breathed a faint scent of her perfume and felt tears prick my eyes; then I closed them and prayed.

'Here comes an unquiet soul.' Miss Fairchild broke into my reverie.

I opened my eyes expecting to see another apparition but there was nothing, or perhaps there was darkness within the darkness, I wasn't sure.

'Is that you, Frederick Maxwell?' she called out. 'I believe it is you. I feel your anger, your rage.' She took a deep breath and let it out gradually. 'Put aside your fury, Frederick Maxwell, you cannot pass with hate in your heart.'

None of us moved, but I felt a tremor run through Swift's hand, which was sinewy and cold. Miss Fairchild's hand felt soft and warm holding mine with a light touch.

'Who did this to you?' Miss Fairchild asked abruptly. She seemed to be staring somewhere just above the fireplace.

I scanned the spot but couldn't make out anything other than the carved crest set in the stone wall, cast about with shadows.

'Ah,' she gasped. 'It was an evil-doer. One who was known to you. One who aspires to greater things. One whose grasping for vainglory and ambition has killed you.' She tensed and clutched my hand tightly. 'The name, tell me the name.'

Silence fell again. Miss Fairchild's deep breathing broke into it.

'You cannot? Yes, I understand. It is so, and you must repent, you are not free of sin.' She stopped and paused as though waiting. 'Go in peace, Frederick Maxwell. Do not linger, you have no cause to remain. Do not be trapped by the weight of impotent anger.'

Silence fell again. I glanced around the table from under lowered brows. It felt rude to break into Miss Fairchild's performance but there were a couple of questions I wanted to ask.

'The dark one comes,' she whispered suddenly.

That spooked me.

'From a distant time, a terrible place, you have dwelt in darkness and you have earned it.' She paused, then shouted: 'Spirit, you are damned.' Then she sighed. 'Why should we help you? By your actions you have been justly punished. Who are we to release you from righteous retribution?' Her eyes suddenly flew open. 'This house has suffered from your malignancy. Have you learned repentance?' she shouted.

A howl of wind gusted down the chimney and blew ashes and fiery splinters into the room.

Miss Fairchild continued, her voice harsh. 'I cannot answer you, spirit. Your story may be brought into the light, but forgiveness? Can you be forgiven? I know not. Should such a day come, the dark will claim you as you deserve.' She shouted all this, and then fell quiet. A moment passed and then she took a deep breath as smoke drifted about us. 'Enough of your black devices – leave us, we will hear no more from you.'

She sighed, let go of my hand and turned to look around as though waking from a daze. We all unclasped hands and blinked.

She turned to me. 'It's terribly dark in here. Would you light some candles, dear boy?'

'Yes, of course.' I got up and took a taper from the mantelpiece, lit it from the embers of the fire and blew life into the candles on the table.

'What did you mean?' Florence had risen from her chair to go to Miss Fairchild's side.

'I don't know, my dear, you will have to tell me what I said.' She looked up with a sweet smile. 'You see, when they come, they take me to the edge of their world. It takes me a little time to return to ours.'

'I'll get ye a wee dram,' Donald MacDonald told her, and went to the refectory table where a decanter and glasses had been set on a pewter tray. She drank it quickly then stood up.

'Very reviving, dear boy,' she told him. 'Now, may we retire to the drawing room? I feel rather cold.'

The Laird answered. 'We can, madam. Come along with me.' He held out his arm and she took it and they led the way with MacDonald following behind. Swift took Florence's hand, I glanced at him with raised brows, he shook his head slightly and we all trooped upstairs.

Natty Brown was waiting for us and had made the drawing room cosy. It cheered us all to enter the homely warmth where the fire crackled merrily and oil lamps and candelabra spread wide pools of light into the corners and up to the ornate plaster ceiling. The cushions were plumped and rich tartan blankets draped about and we settled around the fire on broad-backed sofas, the Laird and MacDonald on the same carved chairs they'd occupied earlier when Swift and I had crashed in on them.

Brown placed a large tray on the low table. There was a choice of whisky or brandy, and a platter of cheese with salt biscuits. Apart from Florence, we all took a dram and I shared some of the snack with Fogg.

'Lavinia,' Florence started, then broke off in hesitation. 'Please could you tell us what it meant.'

Miss Fairchild sipped from her glass and smiled at us, the dimple showing on her cheek, her hair curling about her face. 'You will need to refresh my memory, my dear.'

I answered: 'Mother, Maxwell and Black Dougal, in that order.'

'Ah, yes …' She nodded and remained quiet for a few moments as we watched her closely. 'I am so pleased your mother was able to find you.' She smiled around at us all, which I thought rather odd. She continued. 'Poor Frederick Maxwell was terribly upset, and rightly so.'

'So he didn't throw himself off the wall?' I asked.

'He did not,' Miss Fairchild replied with conviction.

I hesitated in my turn. She couldn't possibly know that, or could she?

'Who pushed him?' I asked.

'I do not know,' she replied. 'They cannot interfere,

you see. The spirits must not cross into this realm or they risk changing the path of fate. Fate is set and it must pass in its own time. None can interrupt its flow.'

Well, that's as clear as mud, I thought, but held my tongue.

'Ye spoke of a dark presence?' MacDonald asked quietly. 'What did ye ken of that?'

'It was very disturbing. I sense restlessness. After so many long centuries he has been uncovered. He veers between a desire to escape this earthly confinement and excitement about the evil he detects taking root here. Forgiveness will free him, but evil will feed him. He is in turmoil. He has yearned for release for centuries and yet he knows he might now have a way to take the revenge he desires.'

I listened to her and glanced again at Swift. His brows were lowered and I could see he had no patience with this. But I did think we might be able to use Miss Fairchild's strange account to lever the secret of the curse out of the superstitious Laird.

I asked, 'What did you mean about "bringing his story to light"?'

She looked directly at the Laird. 'You cannot hide him any longer. His history may be evil but he wants to be heard.'

'No,' the Laird growled in a deep bass voice. He sat straight backed in his chair, every inch the clan chieftain in tartan kilt and sash, dark jacket, white sporran, cream hose and dirk. He glared at us all. 'You delve into things you do not understand. The past should have been left in peace.' He slammed his hand down on the arm of the throne-like chair, then spoke softly, as though to himself. 'And yet … he is found …'

'Hector.' MacDonald spoke. 'Ye cannae reveal it — ye know ye can't. The curse is the secret of the clan, and it is yer sworn duty to uphold it.'

'Enough, Ghillie-mor. It is not your place to order *me*, man,' the Laird snapped. 'We should not be bridled by superstition.'

'Dinnae tell, Hector, I'm asking ye, have a care now.' MacDonald was almost pleading.

An uncomfortable silence fell across the room, and then Florence rose to her feet and went to her father.

'Daddy, I'm going to my bed,' she said quietly.

'Wee lass.' His voice softened. 'Sleep well, my girl.'

Swift came to take her arm and they wished us good night. This gave us all the cue to leave and I bowed out whilst offering to escort Miss Fairchild to her comfortable guest quarters in the rooms upstairs.

'Did you not find Donald MacDonald's reactions rather odd?' Miss Fairchild asked me as I walked with her along a carpeted corridor on the upper floor.

I'd found the whole damn evening odd, but thought it better not to say so.

'Um …' was the best response I could come up with.

'He's involved, you know,' she said.

'MacDonald?' I was incredulous. 'Surely not. I mean, he's a good chap. I'd never have thought…'

'The curse is playing on his fears. There is danger! *He* is dangerous,' she murmured enigmatically, and then went into her room, leaving me entirely nonplussed.

CHAPTER 10

Greggs was fidgeting about my room folding socks.

'Greggs, what are you doing?' I was tired and cold and wet, as it had started to rain again.

I dried Fogg with his blanket, then he went and jumped up onto the bed, turned three times and fell almost instantly asleep. It had been a long day.

'I am attending to duties, sir,' Greggs intoned as he slipped the last pair of socks into a drawer and slid it closed.

'Well, there's no need, it's late and you're not usually up at this hour.'

He looked rather embarrassed and tried to hide it in a cough. 'Very well. I will retire now, sir.'

'You're not nervous about crossing the courtyard in the dark, are you?'

'No, sir,' he replied. 'I am not residing in the servants quarters.'

'Why?' I asked.

'The facilities, sir …' He dropped his gaze. 'They are … they are basic, sir. *Wooden.*'

I will never understand why he was always so damn fastidious about toilets. We'd been through a war, for heaven's sake! There had been far worse matters to deal with.

'Greggs, we were lucky to get a hole in the ground in France. Why on earth are you concerned about a wooden toilet seat? They're all made of wood! And they will be well used, so there's no risk of splinters.'

'It is not the wooden seat or splinters.' He paused. 'There were two, sir.'

'Two?'

'Holes, sir, in a bench. One is expected to *share*.'

'Ah.' I looked at him for a moment, then sighed in defeat. 'Where are you billeted, then?'

'In the room downstairs, sir. I have made it quite comfortable and will be on call at all times.'

'Really?' I raised my brows. 'And you're not going to keep me awake at night with your snoring?'

'Certainly not, because I do not snore. May I wish you goodnight, sir?'

'Oh, very well. Goodnight, Greggs.'

That must have caused his earlier agitation; no doubt he had gone to inform the other servants that he was decamping to more comfortable quarters. I hope he was diplomatic about it because this was a very small island and we were now all marooned on it together.

He did snore, very loudly. He had already started when I delved into the trunk and pulled out my brand new notebook. It was rather handsome, actually, bound in red leather with thick creamy pages. I'd brought it along for the very purpose — assuming any sleuthing be required, that is.

Tubbs came to join me at my desk where I'd settled to write. It felt homely to have the little cat with me. He had developed a fascination for the moving pen and sat to watch as I jotted down the times of events, the names of the archaeologists, pausing at Persi Carruthers, and then the few facts I'd accumulated. I was writing the details of the seance when he jabbed a soft black paw at the tip of my fountain pen, causing me to flick a few spots of ink across the page. I scolded him to his face and he stared at me with wide blue eyes in a sooty face with long black whiskers — the very picture of innocence. I carried him to join Fogg on the bed, gave him a swift ruffle behind the ears until he purred, and returned to finish my notes.

What on earth was all the hocus-pocus about? Did Miss Fairchild know something and didn't want to disclose it openly for fear of her life? But if so, what? Or was she given to the dramatic and it was merely a show? And what had she actually revealed? Anything, or nothing? I was inclined to dismiss it as smoke and mirrors, although the vision of my mother drifted into my mind, and the memory of her scent. I shook my head, put down my pen, blotted the ink dry, and joined my little duo under the covers. Weariness propelled me through Greggs's snores reverberating from the floor below and I slept deeply and soundly.

Swift was banging on my door before dawn the next day. I cursed as I fumbled for my dressing gown and let him in.

'Where are the statements?' he demanded.

'On my desk.' I pointed him in that direction while tying my belt. 'Haven't seen my butler, have you?'

'No,' Swift replied tersely while scanning through the papers. 'They all say much the same thing.'

'Yes, I know, I've already read them.' I replied, picking up the handbell on my bedside table and giving it a good ring.

Swift summarised the archaeologists' statements. "Went to my room, cleaned up, waited for the call to dinner" – or variations of the same.'

'Well, what did you expect them to say? "Met Maxwell on the roof and tossed him over the wall"?' I retorted. 'He should have brought a cup of tea by now.'

'Who?' Swift snapped.

'Greggs,' I replied. I ran fingers through my rumpled hair. 'What time is it, Swift?'

He was carrying a flickering lantern; it was the only light in the room. The fire had died in the night and Greggs hadn't got it going yet.

'Five forty-five, and it's threatening a storm outside. Better get a move on.'

I'd forgotten how annoying Swift could be when he was on a murder case. I sighed and lit the oil lamp on my desk, then chivvied the remains of the fire, adding twigs and logs until bright yellow flames rose from the embers and licked around the kindling.

Greggs knocked and came in dressed in his usual butlering togs and looking quite perky, given the hour.

'Tea, sir?'

'Yes, and one for the Inspector. I'll spruce up while you make it.' I left them to it. Greggs swung the hook holding the blackened iron kettle over the flames while Swift ensconced himself in one of the chairs in front of the fire. I almost froze to death in the tiny stone-walled dressing room with only a candle for warmth.

'Jackson stated that he went to fetch water for tea from the well around dusk,' Swift told me when I returned. He was waving a sheet of paper, so I assumed it was one of the statements.

'Greggs, I need breakfast,' I told him. 'So does Fogg, and Tubbs.'

'I fed them while you performed your ablutions,' he replied. 'Your tea, sir.' He held out a chipped mug.

'Lennox, are you listening to me?' Swift broke in as he took his own cup with both hands.

'Yes, yes. I read it. William Jackson.' I drew out my fob watch and glanced at the time. 'Greggs, have breakfast ready for when I come back. Half an hour or so.'

'Certainly, sir.' He was suspiciously compliant this morning. 'May I presume to take some time off today, sir?'

'Only if you supply said breakfast, Greggs. Where are you going, anyway?' I tried to comb my unruly hair into some semblance of order. I hadn't forgotten the exquisite Miss Carruthers and I thought there should be an opportunity for furthering our acquaintance today.

'Lennox, will you stop prattling about breakfast and listen!' Swift broke in.

'Yes. What?'

'Jackson. We need to interview him properly. And the others.'

'Yes, after we've talked to the Laird.' I made for the door.

He followed, then went back to grab the lantern and we walked outside into the face of a breaking storm.

The blustery wind shrieked down over the high castle walls to buffet us about before escaping through the arched gateway between the towers of the Keep. A cockerel crowed half-heartedly from the byre on the other side of the courtyard, but otherwise the place seemed deserted. Our hair and clothes were blown awry by the time we reached the Great Hall. I decided that fishing was probably off for the day.

'You're late,' the Laird barked at us as Natty Brown admitted us into the upper drawing room. He was seated behind the large desk near the suit of armour, the fire blazing up the chimney. Swift and I crossed the rug to join him as he pocketed his fob watch into his tweed waistcoat. They wore kilts as usual, despite the weather. Considering the continual cold and damp around the criticals, it was a mystery to me how the Scots managed to propagate the population at all.

Swift and I sat down in front of the desk trying to brush wind-blown hair from our faces.

'Status report,' the Laird snapped, and then realised we

were no longer in the War and we weren't his soldiers. 'I mean, what have you *learned*, Jonathan?'

'Maxwell was a drinker and had financial problems,' Swift answered. 'But I don't believe he threw himself off the battlements. Someone pushed him.'

'It would have to be a very powerful man,' the Laird replied. 'The fellow would have put up a fight for his life.'

'Someone may have hit him over the head first,' I speculated. 'It wouldn't be difficult in the dusk, and any evidence would be destroyed by his fall.'

'I think he was drugged, sir,' Swift said, and withdrew the silver hip flask wrapped in a white handkerchief from his sporran. 'We found this up on the walls. I tested it last night, look.' He held the flask under the lamplight. 'See the red crystals? They are formed by the reaction of the chemicals I used in the test. I suspect morphine was added to his flask. They all carry medicines.'

We stared at the tiny flecks around the rim of the flask; they looked like sugar granules to me, but tinged with carmine.

'You brought all your detective's testing kits with you, Swift?' I eyed him.

He reddened slightly. 'Yes. Why not?' He bristled.

I was about to state that he was supposed to have retired from the Force and given up detecting, but was interrupted.

The Laird said, 'What action have you taken so far?'

'We've taken statements from the archaeologists and will question them in more detail today, sir.' Swift answered. 'One of them is responsible for the murder, and the boat, and all the rest of it.'

I was beginning to wonder why I'd come, not having much to add to the proceedings. And I was missing my breakfast.

'But ...' I began, thinking about what Miss Fairchild had said to me about MacDonald last evening. They both turned to stare at me and I hesitated, decided it was nonsense, and changed tack. 'Erm ... Given that we are investigating a murder, sir, don't you think this curse should be exposed? Without knowing the content, we can't be sure if it is relevant or not.'

The Laird was dismissive. 'It's an old superstition, man. It has no pertinence whatsoever to anything.'

'I disagree,' I said. 'You've left us hamstrung, sir. The archaeologists are here because the skeleton was found. Everybody talks about Black Dougal but nobody will tell us what it's all about. I think we need to know.' I was a bit short-tempered because it was early and I was hungry and I didn't like being hampered by damned secrets.

Swift had been looking at his feet, or his sporran, or whatever, and was no doubt unwilling to upset his father-in-law, but he spoke up.

'Actually, I do think we should hear the story, sir.'

The Laird looked from one to the other of us, then sighed.

'I'll be breaking a centuries-old oath ... but ...' He paused, and I could see he was battling with his conscience.

The door banged open and Donald MacDonald entered, very wet and wind blown. He straightened his bonnet and wiped a hand over his trim white beard. 'There are slates come loose on the kitchen roof, laddie,' he said to Swift. 'Water's comin' in and Cook's fair crabbit. I'll be needin' ye tae give me a hand now.'

'Look, MacDonald, we haven't finished here,' Swift started to argue.

'There's nae breakfast until the leak is stopped.' MacDonald cut him off.

I saw his shoulders slump and he nodded in defeat. He turned to us.

'We can meet back here later. Do you agree, sir?' he said, addressing the Laird.

'I'll make no promises,' the Laird replied.

MacDonald looked with narrowed eyes at each of us, then turned sharply about.

'Swift,' I called to him as he was about to leave.

'What?'

'I'll start the interviews with the archaeologists. Let me have the statements, will you?'

He handed them over and we departed in different directions. It was frustrating not to be told the history of Black Dougal and about the curse, but at least I had a good excuse to see Miss Carruthers again.

The storm had picked up and brought hail and rain with it. I could feel ice in the sharp droplets that stung my face, I took the courtyard at a run but was still dripping wet on arrival.

The squat tower smelled of frying bacon and eggs, tea and toast. The castle inhabitants might be suffering domestic strife, but I knew Greggs would have unpacked our supplies from the trunk and be cooking my favourite meal of the day.

Fogg greeted me. He was as wet as I, having been let out by Greggs to perform the necessities, poor little dog. I rubbed him with his blanket as Greggs steered the contents of the frying pan onto a plate, and I ate the bacon-and-egg feast at my desk with Tubbs on my lap and Fogg at my feet. Hot buttered toast followed, complete with marmalade — I quietly congratulated myself for bringing Greggs along.

'Excuse me, sir. I am going out now and may be gone for some time.' He made the announcement as he poured my third cup of tea.

'Really?' I quizzed him. 'Where on earth are you going at this hour?'

'Miss Fairchild has expressed a desire to further her acquaintance with members of the staff, sir. I have offered to accompany her to the servants' hall for breakfast.'

'Have you been outside, Greggs? It's turning into a raging storm out there. Your best togs will be wet and wilted by the time you get halfway across the courtyard.'

'I am quite aware of that, sir. I was about to prepare for the crossing.'

He returned some short time later wearing the voluminous black cape, his balaclava, goggles and bowler hat tied in place with a scarf. He looked like a crow in an Easter bonnet.

'Good luck with impressing Miss Fairchild in that get-up, Greggs.'

His nose turned pink but he didn't answer.

'And you have a rival, old chap. You'll have to put your best foot forward, you know, if you want to make any progress with the lady.'

He didn't seem to appreciate my advice and went off muttering something about kettles calling the pot black. I thought I'd better peruse the statements again before tackling the archaeologists, and I put my feet up on the stone hearth while rereading them.

I didn't learn anything new, but took quite some time over the pencil rubbing of the iron crucifix. The peculiar lettering was a scratched set of short lines set at sharp angles. I recognised it as the runic form the Vikings used. It meant nothing to me and no amount of staring at them helped. I took the page over to my desk and very carefully copied the whole thing into my notebook. Tubbs joined me — I ordered him back to the basket with a warning. He ignored me.

And now for the interviews, I thought, and Miss Persi Carruthers. I was wet and decided to change, so I went off to inspect my wardrobe – well, my trunk, anyway. I dug out a very smart cream Aran sweater which was bound to give the right impression. I even changed into my newer, less worn, pair of tweed trousers. I crammed a hat on my head, shrugged on my shooting jacket and then my waxed greatcoat for protection against the worst of the elements, and shoved my notebook into my pocket. I set off without Fogg, who had already suffered the weather and didn't intend to repeat the experience.

The storm had grown even more ferocious and I was thrust aside by the gale as I left the tower steps. Despite the hour, it remained near dark, with heavy clouds massed overhead in a broiling tumult of black, purple and grey. I could barely see for the icy slivers of sleet hitting my face and eyes. It was driven by a wind that had raised itself to howling point and screamed about my ears. I kept one hand on my hat and tried to fend off the whip-lashing with the other. I was close to the sturdy oak door of the Armoury when something caught my eye. I turned for a better look and was almost blinded by a volley of hail that blew my hat into the racing wind and over the castle walls. There was someone lying face down on the ground, their clothes soaking wet and muddy, a puddle of hail-spattered water already growing around them. I leaned into the blast and struggled to his side. I knew who it was, and as I knelt over his body my heart was pounding. I felt for a pulse and prayed I was not too late.

CHAPTER 11

I turned him over, and heard his breath come in ragged spurts. Water ran down his brows and into his white hair, into which blood had seeped and stained it with red streaks. I shouted at him, without response, then tried to yell for help but my words were thrown back in my face as another blast of icy hail hit me. I forced my arm beneath his shoulders to lift him out of the pooling water when another hand grabbed the unconscious Laird from the other side. I could barely make out Donald MacDonald in the roiling sleet that had become a near-blinding veil.

'What's this? What have ye done?' he shouted at me.

'I found him like this,' I yelled across the gale. 'Help lift him, will you.'

'*Dear God, tis the unborn ...*' I heard him mutter, barely discernible beneath his breath in the howling wind and hail.

Between us we heaved the Laird upright, and with his booted feet dragging through water and mud we carried him into the Great Hall.

'Brown,' I yelled up into the echoing room. 'Natty Brown.'

'He may be gone to the kitchens,' MacDonald shouted back, although we were indoors now, and, despite being drenched, could hear each other perfectly well. We carried the Laird upstairs and then up the next flight to his bedroom, trailing water and mud as we went. Despite our careful manhandling, the Laird groaned as we laid him on the huge and very ornate four-poster bed.

'What happened to him?' MacDonald asked as he pulled off the Laird's sodden boots and dropped them on the rug.

'I have no idea,' I told him, and went to toss a few logs onto the smouldering fire to try to get some heat into the room and dry the man out. 'I thought you were with Swift?'

'I had to leave him.' MacDonald had poured a shot glass of whisky and held it to the Laird's lips, trying to bring him round. 'The shutters on the storeroom worked loose and were tryin' to tear themselves away from yon wall.'

Natty Brown came in and stopped at the door in shock. 'What's all this? I saw the mud and mess coming up the stairs. God in Heaven, man, what happened to the Laird?

He went over and took the glass from MacDonald's grasp.

'And that's no way to warm him up. Away with ye both now. I'll see to him; he'll be catching his death if ye leave him in those wet clothes.' Brown was dragging the Laird's jacket off.

I hovered for a few moments before being firmly shooed away, and as there didn't seem much for me to do, I left Brown to it.

MacDonald followed me down the stairs.

'I'm assuming it wasn't *yerself who* knocked him about the head?' he asked sharply.

'Don't be ridiculous,' I snapped.

'Did ye see what occurred?' he asked with an undercurrent of fear in his voice.

'No, and what the devil was he doing outside?' I demanded.

I had stalked down to the drawing room and pushed open the door. Smoke met me on the threshold. I ran in, MacDonald at my heels, both of us alarmed and looking swiftly about. There was no sign of a fire outside the hearth, and the smoke seemed to be dispersing. What the devil was going on?

'Is the chimney blocked?' MacDonald asked as he looked about, then strode to peer up the flue.

'How?' I went to join him and we stared into the wide, sooty shaft. We saw swirling smoke but nothing more. 'If it was, it's clear now. Have there been problems? Crows' nests or some such?' I demanded.

'No, laddie, the fires rarely burn out and we have seabirds here, nae crows.' MacDonald was still staring up into the chimney while I prowled the room looking for anything peculiar.

'I think the chimney was blocked by something,' I began.

He turned to look at me, a deep frown furrowing his brow, lips drawn tight behind the white beard and moustache.

'Or some*one*,' I finished, and eyed him closely. He stared back, as suspicious of me as I was of him. It didn't help, so I gave it up and turned to make a better search of the room. If the chimney had been blocked deliberately, perhaps it was for reasons of theft rather than attempted murder.

I crossed to the Laird's desk, which was fairly tidy, or as tidy as you'd expect. Actually, I'm rather unobservant and wouldn't have a clue if anything was missing from the spot where it had been only an hour ago.

'What are ye lookin' fer?' MacDonald growled.

I'd yanked open a desk drawer and was peering inside. 'Checking if anything was stolen,' I retorted.

'And how would ye know?' he asked.

'Erm ...' He had a point. 'Well, I was just looking for anything obvious. Actually, it's probably better if *you* check – and, erm, tell Swift about it, would you. I'd better go and interview the archaeologists.'

I made a rapid exit and trotted down the stairs, confused and concerned about events. As I placed my hand on the front doorknob I paused and turned to stare back up toward the balustraded corridor and rooms beyond. There was nothing to see. I shook my head, then opened the door to battle the elements again.

Would it be heroic or just plain stupid to go up onto the battlements and take a closer look at the chimneys of the Great Hall? I asked myself as I was pounded by the wind and hail raging across the courtyard. The better part of valour won. I decided to leave such investigations for a later hour, and ran up the steps to the Armoury.

All eyes turned to face me when I walked into the archaeologists' mess room. I was dripping wet, with my hair plastered to my head, water running down my neck, and mud spattered over my coat and boots. I squelched with every step. It wasn't quite the entrance I'd hoped for.

'Where have you all been?' I demanded, rather too loudly.

'What do you mean?' Buggins asked. He was standing next to the long table, one booted foot up on the bench, and dressed as they all were in the usual tweeds and cream shirt.

'I mean ...' Oh hell, I thought, what *did* I mean? 'Well, has anyone been outside in the last hour, or half hour? Or at all?'

They looked at each other, bemused.

'Not me,' one said.

'Nor me,' came other replies.

'No, it's filthy out there,' one chap snapped. I assumed this to be William Jackson as I didn't recognise him and he looked out of place, dressed as he was in a city suit.

Campbell said, 'I put my nose outside, but it was raining cats and dogs, so I gave it up.' He was seated on the bench, next to where Buggins was standing. Carruthers sat opposite with the funny little archivist, Dennis, hunched next to her. He hadn't bothered to look up as I walked in.

Jackson was leaning back in a folding canvas chair at the far end of the table. None of them was in the least bit wet.

'There was an accident. The Laird was knocked over, or out, or something. Did anyone see anything?'

'No,' they all said almost as one.

'Right.' I restrained a sigh — this wasn't going well. I squelched to a vacant space on the bench and sat down dripping water.

'Statements,' I said, and fumbled in various damp pockets for the papers Swift had given me. I drew them out and placed them on the table, then peeled off my waxed coat. My notebook was soggy and curling around the edges. I found my pen, unscrewed the top and poised myself to hold a proper interview as water dripped from my hair.

'Is he all right?' Carruthers asked.

'What? Sorry, excuse me, dear lady … um, ma'am … Miss Carruthers,' I stuttered.

'The Laird …?'

'Oh … yes – probably. Pretty sure he will be, anyway. Now …' I pushed my hair back from my face and tried again. 'Jackson?'

He was a lean man in a black wool coat over a sharp grey suit, with dark brows and hair over a pale complexion. He looked straight down his long nose at me and answered with a New York accent. 'Yeah?'

'Did you see anything suspicious yesterday evening when you went to fetch water from the well?' I asked him whilst peering at his statement.

'No.'

'Are you sure?' I added. 'Round about half past five, or thereabouts?'

'Yeah, I'm sure,' he replied with studied arrogance. 'The guy was a drunk and a deadbeat. He probably threw himself off.'

'Right, well ...' I was beginning to wish Swift was here.

Jackson continued. 'I was going to kick him off the expedition. I don't pay for monkeys.' He jabbed a finger at me. 'He was useless.'

'Now, just a...' I was about to shout him down when Carruthers beat me to it.

'Absolute rot,' she interrupted fiercely, her eyes flashing. 'Poor Maxwell had dreadful problems and you made it worse. And you're not even here to study the site, you're here for what you can get out of it.'

I forgot all about taking notes and watched her: she was magnificent.

'Now, now.' Campbell tried ineffectually to intervene. 'Come along, old girl, you know this doesn't help.'

'He bought his way in. He's nothing but a treasure seeker.' She turned her blazing eyes at poor Campbell, who wilted. 'He should never have been allowed to come here.'

'You just shut your...' Jackson started to yell back but was shouted down as the whole room erupted.

'Enough!' A bellow came from behind me. A very wet and wind-blown Swift was standing in the doorway. He was wearing his trench coat over his kilt and Scottish whatnots; tightening his belt, he slammed the door behind him with a bang and stalked across the floor. He yanked a canvas chair from next to the fire, placed it firmly at the head of the table and sat down. Then he leaned forward and stared out from under hawkish brows.

I hid a smile — the Inspector was back!

'Lennox, take notes,' he snapped.

'What?'

He looked at me, then hesitated. 'Please.'

'Hum. Very well.' I tried again to flatten out the pages of my damp book.

Everyone else had stopped talking and waited to see what happened next.

'Jackson, what did you see?' Swift rapped out.

'I already told that guy there.' Jackson pointed at me.

'And now you can tell *me*,' Swift ordered.

'Nothing.' Jackson sat back and folded his arms with a smirk.

Swift growled. 'Did anyone see you?'

Jackson almost jumped, then retorted, 'What do you mean by that?'

'You were outside. Maxwell was outside. Everyone else states that they were inside,' Swift responded.

'You can't pin anything on me,' Jackson growled. 'I was seen by that man MacDonald. He was by the big building when I was at the well.'

'You snake, you should have told me that!' I growled at him. I liked Americans and I'd had some close friends from the States during the War and since, but I was beginning to take a serious dislike to this bounder.

'Lennox,' Swift snapped, then looked at me. 'Just write it down will you.'

I frowned, then returned to my task. My pen leaked a blot onto the damp page.

'Do you mean the Great Hall?' Swift snapped.

'Yeah – and why haven't I been invited by that Lord in there? You gotta learn to treat people right. Don't you know who I am?' He leaned forward and sneered at Swift. 'I got so much money, I could buy this miserable dump and everyone in it.'

'Don't think you can buy whatever you want …' Carruthers' eyes flashed with fury.

Jackson instantly turned on her and jabbed a long finger. 'And you can…' he started, but was cut off as everyone jumped to their feet and started shouting again, including me.

Swift stood up and yelled: 'Quiet! Sit down, all of you.' He slammed a hand down on the table, making it shudder, which shut everybody up. He waited a moment for the room to calm down. 'Now …' He leaned in Jackson's direction. 'Tell me *exactly* what time you were outside.'

Jackson leaned back, folding his arms. 'I dunno the exact time, do I. I wasn't keeping a diary. It was around five thirty. Just about sundown.'

Swift made no effort to hide his anger or his disdain. 'Right. Did you see anyone other than MacDonald?'

Jackson scowled. 'No,' he snapped back.

'Or hear anyone?' Swift continued.

'Only that racket the little guy makes with his type-writer as I was leaving.' He flicked a thumb in the direction of Dennis.

'Did you see him, or did he see you?' Swift demanded.

'No, his door was closed … What the hell do you think I'm going to do? Drop in on the little jerk for a cup of tea?' Jackson mocked.

'I was typing,' Dennis suddenly piped up. He was wearing the same get-up as yesterday, complete with hat. 'It's my job, I keep the records and I type reports. And I am not a jerk.' He jumped to his feet and went very red in the face; his little eyes shone with ire behind the thick lenses of his spectacles. 'You are very rude. You shouldn't talk to people like that.'

'Shut your mouth.' Jackson stabbed a finger in his direction. 'I wasn't talking *to* you, I was talking *about* you.'

Dennis opened his mouth to argue, but Swift cut him off.

'Sit down,' Swift barked. He didn't even look at the little chap, just continued to stare at Jackson. 'What did you do before going to the well?'

'Nothing. Why are you giving me the third degree? What about *these* loafers?' Jackson indicated the others.

'Because I haven't finished with you yet,' Swift snapped.

'Yeah, well, I've finished with you.' Jackson rose to

his feet, knocking his chair over. 'You're nothing but a jumped-up plug. Who do you think you are to talk to me like that?' the American shouted so loudly his voice echoed off the walls. 'I'm financing every dime of this dig and I call the shots. And don't any of you ever forget it. And what I say goes,' he finished on a bellow, then turned and marched from the room, slamming the door behind him.

We all watched him leave.

'He is insufferable,' Persi Carruthers said. 'Heathcliff, you are right. He is a snake.'

'Er, yes. Um, not Heathcliff, old stick. *Lennox*,' I reminded her.

'What the hell is he doing here?' Swift asked loudly, still smarting from the encounter.

Campbell shifted in his seat. 'I'm afraid it's as he said: he's the money, old bean.'

'Well, you must be desperate if you're letting him provide it,' I remarked.

'We are,' Campbell replied, sitting down and taking out his pipe.

Swift looked about. 'Right. I need to know how all this works.' He pointed a finger at Campbell. 'You tell me.'

Campbell frowned and brushed his fringe back from his brow. 'Well, you see, old chap, there's nothing left in the kitty. The government is on its uppers after the ballyhoo in France. War, I mean. And it doesn't provide funding, never has actually, but it should.' He fiddled with his pipe, his pale face creased with worry. 'So we rely on outside help. Philanthropists. And people who have money, like Jackson.'

'Jackson is an amateur excavator,' Buggins added. 'He heard about the crown and offered to finance an expedition, recover any historic artefacts, that sort of thing.'

'Buggins, he's not an excavator, he's a dealer,' Carruthers cut in. 'He sells to whichever museum is the highest bidder.'

'Well,' Campbell stammered, 'there wasn't anyone else, old girl. Without him, we wouldn't have been able to come at all.'

The tension was almost tangible, which was hardly a surprise given Maxwell's death, although I sensed there was more to it than that.

'How did you all come to be here in the first place?' I asked. I had stopped writing notes because they weren't making sense.

'We're the Highlands and Islands team,' Buggins replied. 'We're affiliated to the British Museum and they told us about it.'

Campbell broke in, 'But then we discovered the funding was being put up by Jackson. It was a bit of a dilemma, actually, and we dithered. But we were very keen to come because the crown might have belonged to the King of the Isles. So we came, and here we are.' He gave a grin as he finished talking.

Dennis spoke up in a squeaky voice. 'Our quest is of the utmost importance. History will remember us. We will be thanked and feted.'

Swift and I exchanged glances.

'He's very keen,' Buggins explained dryly. 'Always wanted to be an explorer of ancient ruins.'

Dennis jumped to his feet, red in the face. 'We will do our all to complete the task. We will uncover the truth and restore order and enlightenment upon the history of this island.'

We all fell silent and looked at him. He sat down again and placed his hands upon the table and stared at them. He really was an odd little oik.

Swift tried again. 'Did anything happen yesterday? Any arguments, or anything out of the ordinary?'

They looked at each other.

'No,' they replied in near unison.

Given this morning's episode, I didn't believe them, and I doubt Swift did either.

He asked, 'What did you do at the records office?'

'Examine the Chronicles,' Dennis chirped up. 'There are copies of the Chronicle of Man held in their archives, I have seen the originals and they are the same. I checked every word as it was inscribed.'

'Chronicle of which man?' I asked.

'The Isle of Man,' Campbell answered as Dennis sniggered. 'They date from the year 1000 AD; very interesting actually, it was when the Isle of Man was part of the Kingdom of the Isles. Highland history and all that.'

'Ah,' I said, and decided to shut up.

'Why?' Swift asked.

'Because it is one of the most comprehensive contemporary accounts of this region,' Buggins explained.

'Right. Fine. And the rest of you?' Swift looked about.

'I spent my time in the library next door,' Carruthers said. 'I don't have very much to do with the records, you see.' She smiled at me, and I smiled back with my best grin.

'We were rummaging, old chap,' Buggins replied for them.

'Yes,' Campbell agreed. 'Always worth a good rummage through old documents when the chance presents.'

'And there isn't much we are allowed to do here now,' Buggins added.

I picked up my pen again and noted 'library' down and 'Chronicles', and then 'rummaging'.

'What was Maxwell's position in the team?' Swift questioned.

'He was our excavator,' Campbell explained. 'We called him "Maxwell Mole". He was awfully good, although there wasn't much for him to do. You'd already found the bones, old chap,' he addressed Swift. 'If we'd been allowed to do some excavating he'd have been much happier, but we weren't, so he moped.'

'What?' I asked.

'Bad habit he had. Moping,' Campbell continued.' Needed to keep busy or he would start drinking. Depression. He had a tendency to it. Bit like Van Gogh.'

'Didn't cut his ear off, did he?' I quizzed.

'Lennox, just take notes, will you.' Swift frowned at me, then pointed at Buggins. 'What's your role here?'

'Artefacts, pots, beads, that sort of thing,' he said. He

had a rugged face, just the sort of chap you'd come across on the rugby pitch, or at cricket. Solid, unassuming, clever in a quiet sort of way.

'Old Buggins is awfully good,' Campbell said. 'Best there is in his field. Can date anything just from a shard of broken jug.'

'Humph.' Swift wasn't terribly impressed. 'And you, Campbell, what's your speciality?'

'History of Scotland, the clans, battles and buildings. All sorts really. Family's one of them. Clan, I mean. I'm a Campbell, but on the English side.'

'Dennis, you're the archivist, I assume you deal with papers,' I said.

'I do. It's very important. I study vital historical records,' Dennis said in his high voice. 'Important manuscripts, royal charters, land grants …' he droned on.

My mind drifted in the direction of Carruthers, noting the cut of her glossy blonde hair caught up in a couple of simple clips. It came to just below her shoulders and gleamed in the glow of the oil lamp … 'What?'

'I said, 'are you taking this down', Lennox?' Swift asked me.

'Yes.' I dragged my eyes away from her lovely face and back to my notebook.

Swift stared at me narrowly, then turned toward Carruthers. 'And you, madam?'

'Bones,' she replied. 'I am a forensic archaeologist. I specialise in human remains.' She spoke in a clear voice with an unaffected accent.

I stared at her, caught Swift's eye and leaned studiously over my notes.

Swift grunted, then glared round at them and demanded, 'And which one of you burned our damn boat?'

CHAPTER 12

'That is an unjust accusation. You are not allowed...'

'Shut up, Dennis,' the others shouted at him.

He shut up and turned red. There was something of the droll about him, but he was still an irritating little tick.

'Why do you think anyone here burned your boat?' Campbell asked as he banged his pipe on the table to force out the ash, then fumbled for his tobacco pouch.

'It was one of you, it had to be.' Swift threw the accusation at them.

The room fell silent. It seemed to me highly unlikely that the culprit would admit to it, even if they were present.

'Swift,' I said, 'I'm off.' I shrugged on my wet coat, gathered my damp notebook, handed him the soggy statements, gazed once more upon the lovely face of Persi Carruthers, and made an exit.

Swift wasn't too pleased about my abrupt departure, but I was cold and wet and we needed a different strategy. The wind was still howling; the rain and hail had abated. I extended my stride across the courtyard, crunched through a blanket of tiny white hailstones and trotted up the worn steps of my tower.

Fogg and Tubbs greeted me. There was no sign of Greggs, so I swung the iron bracket holding the black kettle over the flames of the fire to make my own tea between shedding wet clothing. I towelled down, rooted through the trunk for more clean clothes, combed my hair again, and by the time Swift arrived I'd made myself fairly decent.

'You heard what happened to the Laird?' I asked him as he peeled off his damp trench coat and hung it near the fire to steam. I had placed my notebook next to it and the pages curled as they dried.

'I did,' he said. 'I just went to enquire how he was before coming here. Florence is with him; he's asleep, but he should recover. But …' He hesitated. 'It will create fury in the clan. When we find out who did this, they'll be strung up by the…'

'Does anyone know what happened?' I cut in.

'They assume he fell.' He regarded me with troubled eyes as he took a seat.

I finished brewing the tea and poured us a cup each whilst we were talking, and now searched for Greggs's box of goodies. He had hidden it in the old bread oven. I extracted the gaudily painted tin box and opened it to share the contents.

'The archaeologists,' Swift turned to the subject. 'They're all lying and they hate Jackson,' he said, biting into a piece of shortbread.

'Yes,' I agreed.

'So why did they burn the boat?' he asked, a deep furrow on his brow. 'They're all trapped here now.'

'To prevent something being taken off the island?' I suggested.

'Yes, obviously,' he snapped, sounding more like his usual self. 'Who do you think killed Maxwell?'

'I don't know,' I replied. 'But you can't confine your suspicions solely to the archaeologists.'

Fogg came to stare at my biscuit until I shared a piece with him. Tubbs went to sit on Swift's lap and fell asleep. Cats really just don't care.

Swift eyed me narrowly, 'Who else is there?'

Miss Fairchild's words of warning had lodged themselves in my mind.

'MacDonald,' I said.

'Absolute nonsense!' Swift was adamant. 'He has an alibi: Jackson saw him.'

'He only saw him near the Great Hall around half past five; what was he doing before then?'

'Actually,' Swift admitted, 'I just talked to him about it in the Laird's room.'

'Hum.' I sipped my tea and watched him over the rim. 'And what did he say?'

'He said he was locking the chickens up – he always locks them up around five o'clock. And I wish you wouldn't try to implicate him. I told you, he's…'

'I'm not trying to implicate him, Swift,' I cut across his anger. 'And that doesn't answer what he was doing between five and half past.'

'He had to find the chickens first. He said your dog had scattered them all over the place and it took him almost half an hour to gather them together again.'

'Ah, right.' I eyed my little dog, who was only interested in biscuits. 'But it doesn't clear him, does it?'

'Will you forget it, Lennox,' Swift retaliated. 'MacDonald would never have burned the skiff, or attacked the Laird, he's dedicated his entire life to him.'

'Fine,' I said. 'What about Natty Brown?'

'He had helped me fix the pump before you arrived, so you can count him out too,' Swift retorted.

'Right,' I carried on. 'Jackson? Would he have had time to push Maxwell off the wall?'

'I doubt it,' he replied. 'He'd have had to run like a madman across the courtyard to be at the well at that time and MacDonald would have certainly noticed that.'

I poured another cup of tea each from the chipped white pot and dug into the biscuit tin. 'The attack on the Laird must have been to enable a search of the drawing room,' I remarked. 'But none of the archaeologists was even remotely damp.'

'They're used to being outside in all weathers, they'll have plenty of wet-weather gear.' Swift helped himself to another biscuit.

'We should have searched their cloakroom,' I said.

'I did. A few coats and boots were damp but that could have been from last night,' Swift replied. 'And some of them would have been outside today, for logs or water or whatever.'

'Hum,' I thought about it for a moment then changed tack. 'So why was the Laird smoked out?'

'I suspect it was to search the room, it's usually kept locked.' Swift gave Tubbs's ears a rub; I could hear him purring away like a little engine. 'The Clan Rolls are kept in the Laird's desk. They hold the real history of the place and nobody can read them without the Laird's permission.'

'Is anything missing?' I asked.

'Not according to MacDonald, he said he checked and everything is still there,' he replied. 'The thing is, Lennox, Jackson's a nasty piece of work, I'd put him at the top of my list for Maxwell's murder. But he and the little chap are the only ones with alibis.'

'Have you fingerprinted Maxwell's room?' I asked.

'Yes,' he retorted sharply. 'They were mostly yours. Learn to wear gloves, will you.'

'Yes, yes. Can't see how it would help anyway,' I said. 'Anyone and everyone could have been in there.'

He frowned at me, but I carried on before he started another lecture. 'Tell me the layout of the Armoury, would you.'

He sipped his tea. 'Well, there's an old vault below the ground floor used for storage; it's locked and bolted and has been for years,' he replied. 'Buggins, Campbell and Miss Carruthers have rooms on the first floor. Maxwell, Dennis and Jackson are housed on the second, and the mess is at the top. Each level has a washroom and a door opening onto the steps up to the battlements. There's also an interior staircase – and the cloakroom of course.'

'Right.' I nodded, making a mental map in my mind. 'Look, I suggest we interview the archaeologists on their own, it's hopeless when they're in a group,' I proposed. 'Campbell seems like a good candidate to start with.'

'I wouldn't put him at the top of my list,' Swift said.

'Not as a suspect, no.' I paused to put my thoughts in order. 'But we need to understand more about what they're actually investigating; what relevance they think the crown has,' I explained. 'And the lettering on the crucifix, what does it mean? It must have some significance or it wouldn't have been stolen.'

He sighed. 'Yes, agreed.' He lifted Tubbs off his lap and handed him to me. 'I'm going to see how the Laird is, then take a look at the chimney up on the battlements.'

'Right,' I told him, 'I'll join you shortly.'

I wanted to have some time to myself and as he closed the door I picked up my near-dry notebook from the hearth and went to my desk to jot down what little we'd discovered. I had to smooth the pages down first, then paused part-way through the first sentence. The puzzle that played through my mind wasn't so much the reactions of the archaeologists, it was the occupants of the castle.

They had reacted in fear and alarm when the skeleton had been uncovered. But the theft of the skull and crown, and now the murder of Maxwell — had that truly raised a hullaballoo? And MacDonald was an enigma, he was in the courtyard when the Laird was injured *and* when Maxwell died, and I wasn't sure if I believed the tale about the chickens. I sighed.

Tubbs came to sit on my book as I gazed at the misted window overlooking the courtyard. The single pane was ancient, with tiny bubbles in the rippled glass. It gave a distorted view of the ancient castle within the walls, dissolving them into mere suggestions of light and dark. Small droplets gathered on the uneven surface of the pane and ran down to collect under the base of a cream and blue water-jug set on the stone window sill.

Sunlight suddenly broke from the clouds and sent bright rays through the glass to catch drifting motes of dust floating above the ink-scrawled pages of my note-book. Tubbs closed his eyes and settled to sleep in the sun, as cats do, on the most inconvenient spot they can find.

I picked him up, put him with Fogg in the basket before the fire and donned my damp overcoat. I'd rather have stayed with the duo by the hearth, but as I opened the door and trotted down the steps my heart lifted as I stepped outside and felt the sun on my face. The wind had dropped to a brisk breeze and I strode with a lighter tread across the sodden cobbles, up the steep, narrow steps and onto the battlements. Swift was just clambering down the slates covering the roof of the Great Hall. The roof met the battlements' edge and he stepped from one to the other without any danger.

'It's covered in soot, look.' He showed it to me.

There was a distinct black ring on one side of the slate.

'Easy to do,' I said, 'though madness, given the strength of the wind up here this morning.'

'I think it was placed on the pot before dawn and it just took a long time for the smoke to build up. The chimney's flues are huge,' Swift replied as he tucked the slate under his arm. 'Then, once the wind really got up it was blown off. I found it on the leeward side of the stack.'

'Was the Laird able to tell you anything?' I asked.

'Yes, he's come round now. It's as we thought: he went outside to see what had caused the chimney to smoke. He didn't see or hear anyone and maintains he slipped and hit his head.' He shrugged. 'He has a gash, but it's not too bad actually.'

'I found him face down, Swift,' I reminded him.

'Hum.' He looked at me. 'Well, I didn't believe he'd fallen, either.'

We were being buffeted by the brisk breeze. I glanced out to the churning sea at the remnants of the storm, heavy and black on the far horizon.

'It came in like a runaway train and left just as quickly,' I remarked.

'Maritime climate,' Swift said. 'The only constant is change. They say that if you don't like the weather just wait half an hour and it'll be different again.'

The steps were slippery and we went down with care.

'Lunch in ten minutes, Lennox. We eat at midday here.'

'Fine.' I was rather hungry actually.

He went off and I peeled away in another direction; there was something I wanted to look at. Down by the beach and jetty there was a stone building that I knew to be used by MacDonald. It was he who rowed the skiff and took care of it, and I knew that all the paraphernalia of boating was stored in there.

I strolled with an air of casual insouciance beneath the great arched entrance with hands in pockets and whistling tunelessly. It was a squat little hut with a low roof and a single window, the blue painted door peeling and cracked. A speckled hen sat on the roof staring down at me with beady eyes. I decided to ignore it.

I looked carefully at the sand and mud around the building; there were washed-out hollows about the size of footprints that came from the direction of the gateway and went back again. They had paused on the threshold, so I pushed the door open. There was grit on the floor. I walked further inside, then stopped and looked about. Coiled rope, a small rusted anchor, iron buckets, a couple of old lobster pots, some mouldy fishing rods and the usual boating whatnots lay about. They showed every sign of someone having made a rapid search. I thrust my hands back in my pockets, disappointed. If MacDonald had been the culprit seeking the vanished crown, he would not have searched the shed, it being his territory. But as it had been searched, it obviously wouldn't have been him. Did that exonerate him or not? I wondered. The chicken was still on the roof. I meandered in thoughtful mood back to my tower.

Greggs had returned. He was wearing his usual butlering togs and entirely dry. He was staring into the empty biscuit tin.

'Swift came over for tea. Had to make it myself, actually,' I told him.

'Indeed, sir,' he sniffed.

'How did your breakfast go with Miss Fairchild?'

He mellowed, as I knew he would. 'Rather well, thank you, sir.'

'And did the lady enjoy the company of the servants?' I asked.

'I believe she did, sir.'

He poured water from the water jug into the kettle and placed it back onto the iron hook over the fire. 'Will you be staying for lunch or joining the family, sir?'

'Um, family …' I hesitated. 'Greggs, when you and Miss Fairchild were hobnobbing in the servants' hall, you didn't happen to hear about the skeleton, or the curse, or anything else, did you?'

He placed a couple of logs onto the fire from the pile by the hearth, then tossed the used tea leaves from the teapot onto the flames, where they burned with a hiss of steam and smelled rather pleasant.

'There was talk of a ghost, sir.'

'Really?' I asked. 'Was it thought to be Black Dougal?'

'It was, sir. And a number of members of the staff claim to have seen or heard him.' Greggs spooned fresh black leaves into the teapot as he spoke, then turned again to pick up the empty tin box of purloined biscuits, and looked at me.

'I will replace them, Greggs.' I may have sounded exasperated.

'Hum.' He sniffed again. 'Footsteps have been heard, and door handles rattled, sir. One of the maids claimed to have seen him twice, once by the wash-house and again in the log store. Always at dusk or just after dark.'

'And in the gin-gang,' I reminded him.

'That was a different maid, sir.'

'Yes, right. Did they say these sightings had only occurred since the skeleton was uncovered?'

'They did, sir.' He took on the po-faced look he adopted when speaking out of turn. 'They blame the Inspector, sir.'

'Hum, thought they might.' I nodded. 'And what of the curse?'

'They would not speak of it. They insisted they did not know the details. Miss Fairchild can be quite persuasive, but she could not elicit any information about the curse or the legend of Black Dougal.'

'That's rather a disappointment. I've noticed she is terribly good at persuading people.'

'Indeed, sir. But they believe that with the exposure of the skeleton, the curse is now unleashed and will bring about the total destruction of the castle, and death to all who dwell within.'

CHAPTER 13

'How can anyone believe a curse if nobody knows what it is?' I asked. 'It doesn't make sense.'

'It is superstition, sir. It is not required to make sense,' Greggs replied.

I suppose he had a point there. 'Right. I'm off to lunch, old chap,' I announced. 'And I left some damp clothes for drying.'

'So I observed, sir.'

Fogg decided lunch was worth confronting the weather for and we trotted downstairs with a light step. It had improved to the point of being almost pleasant; indeed, if the wind dropped a couple of notches, fishing might even be possible. I wondered if Carruthers liked proper outdoor pursuits, or just wanted to dig up old bones all the time.

My stroll in the direction of lunch was interrupted by the sight of Miss Fairchild leaning over the wall of the well and gazing down into the water.

'Greetings, Miss Fairchild,' I addressed her in familiar tones.

'Ah, there you are, dear boy.' She smiled up at me, then returned to her study of the well.

'May I offer you my arm to the dining room?' I asked.

'Not just yet,' she replied. She was wearing her voluminous light-blue cloak with a hand-knitted pink scarf. Her pale-grey hair had curled into a halo around her face. 'I am communing.'

I wasn't too sure what to make of that. 'Um ... who with?'

'*With whom*, Heathcliff. *With whom* ...' she corrected me just as my mother had done so long ago. 'The spirits, of course. They are disturbed.'

I went over and stared down into the dark water below. The well was as ancient as everything else in the castle and was formed from stones slick with moss and algae. I could smell the tang of cold and damp rising from its depths.

'I'm not surprised they're disturbed if they're lurking about down there,' I replied.

She raised her eyes and smiled, the dimple in her cheek suddenly forming. 'They are not down in the well, young man, as you are quite aware. I was looking into the waters because I feel a powerful force. It has significance.'

Clear as mud as usual, I thought to myself.

'Miss Fairchild,' I began in some exasperation, then softened my tone as I caught the twinkle in her eye, and changed tack. 'Is it at all possible you could explain to me what you mean in terms I could understand?'

She stared up at me. 'Dear Heathcliff, you are a handsome, intelligent and perceptive young man, and you are at last putting your hunting skills to good use, but the mysteries of the other world will forever remain an enigma to you.'

'I think you mean "no". Don't you?'

'Indeed I do,' she replied sweetly.

'It's Lennox, actually,' I reminded her. 'Not keen on Heathcliff.'

'Your mother and I are agreed on Heathcliff, and so you shall remain,' she replied, and then wandered off in the direction of the dining room, her cloak billowing in the breeze.

I remained peering down the well because it occurred to me that Jackson may have been searching for something yesterday. I didn't believe he was fetching water, or drank tea. So what was he doing here? Nothing sprang to view, and then I remembered I was supposed to be escorting Miss Fairchild to lunch. I was about to break into a trot to catch her when I was hailed from behind.

'Lennox,' a voice called out. 'I say, old chap. Do you have a moment?' It was Campbell.

'Off for lunch, actually,' I replied.

'Fine. Erm …' His face fell.

'But it doesn't matter. I wasn't terribly hungry,' I lied. 'Shall we?'

'Righty-o, yes, excellent.' He grinned and followed me back to my tower, where I could smell the meal Greggs was preparing for himself in his room. It was baked potato and ham, probably with lashings of butter and a layer of

Wensleydale cheese on top. My shoulders slumped a tad, but I stiffened my backbone and kept going.

'So?' I sat next to the fire as Campbell settled opposite.

He withdrew his unlit pipe and stuck it in his mouth. 'Thing is, Lennox,' he began, 'all is not well. It hasn't been since we started this expedition. In fact it's all rather a mess.' He stared at me glumly, a pleasant chap with even features and the weight of a heavy burden on his slim shoulders. 'You see, we've been struggling – the Highlands and Islands team, I mean. There is huge competition for funding and we're supposed to discover marvellous finds and promote them in the press, that kind of thing. Then everyone can see how useful we are and it will encourage proper philanthropists to come along and hand out the dibs. But we're not terribly good at puffing ourselves up and parading our finds. This little jaunt is our last chance; if we don't come up with the goodies, we're going to lose it all.' He sighed.

I regarded him quietly. 'We'll have some tea,' I decided, and pushed the kettle back over the fire without calling Greggs, who would refuse to come anyway. 'But I thought Jackson was the leader, isn't he supposed to do all this?' I asked.

'No,' Campbell almost laughed. 'He's not a leader, he's only here to see that we investigate the crown, then he'll clear off as fast as he can. Usually it's just me and Buggins and Maxwell.' He smiled, although he looked rather doleful. 'And there's Dennis of course, but he's a scribbler, you know, paperwork and all that.'

'He's a bit of an odd-bod,' I remarked.

'Oh, I suppose so.' Campbell fiddled about with the pipe, but made no attempt to light it. 'He's not used to being in the field; this is his first trip, actually. He's been with us about ten months now. He was terribly keen to see the skeleton and visit the records office, so we brought him along. He's not so bad, actually, just a bit of a fish out of water.'

'Hum. And Persi Carruthers? I assume she's not part of your regular team.'

'No, no, we called her in specially,' he explained. 'Bones! She's awfully good with them. Rather an odd obsession for such a pretty girl. I hope we haven't wasted her time. We're not making much progress. Well, none, actually ... and poor Maxwell ...' His words petered out.

'Jackson,' I said, and was about to expand on the theme when Campbell cut in.

'Yes, that's the problem.' He suddenly sat up. 'It's Jackson. Carruthers is right, he doesn't care about history, he's just a money-grubbing dealer.' His shoulders slumped again and he sighed. 'And this is what we've come down to, Lennox, accepting anybody with money just to enable a dig. It's a bally disaster.'

'Campbell...' I was beginning to get a touch exasperated with his convoluted meanderings 'will you tell me if you know anything? I mean about the crown, or the murder?'

'I don't, really I don't.' He fiddled with his pipe, then put it away when I handed him a mug of steaming tea.

'Poor Maxwell. He detested Jackson, said he'd grab the lot. And then look what happened.'

'But surely the British government wouldn't allow Jackson to walk away with the crown. I mean, it's a national treasure, isn't it?' I argued.

'It doesn't work like that, old chap.' Campbell sipped his tea. 'Rich chaps sponsor expeditions all the time, it's a hobby with some of them. They usually donate the goodies to their museum of choice and get a jolly good slap on the back. Some of them get gongs. But then there are chaps like Jackson who make deals with private museums. They hand over objects for a finder's fee. It's not properly regulated at all.'

'But why does the government allow it?' I asked.

'It's the system,' he shrugged. 'Been like that for years. France and Germany have made a better fist of it: their governments finance the digs and searches. I suppose our Whitehall Johnnies think they have better things to spend taxpayers' money on.'

'Right.' I nodded, wanting to return to the subject. 'And what does this have to do with Maxwell's murder?'

'Well, if he was murdered, and I'm still not convinced he was...' he swept away his long fringe 'but I've been thinking about it. He was in desperate straits, you know. Beside himself, actually. So perhaps Maxwell did steal the crown, and then Jackson killed him for it. I wouldn't put it past him.'

'Ah ...' About time we got to the grist. 'Do you have any evidence?'

'Not in the least,' Campbell said, sipping his tea. 'Thought that was your and the Inspector's territory. I think you should arrest Jackson, though. He'll stop at nothing, and he probably burned the boat to stop the police arriving. You should arrest him before he murders anyone else.' He stared wide-eyed, as though waiting for me to leap up and dash off with a pair of handcuffs.

'Right.' I let loose a sigh because none of that made sense. 'Well, perhaps later. Campbell, please tell me again what happened between Jackson and Maxwell. And something of Maxwell's background.' I went to fetch my notebook and pen, then settled back into my chair. Tubbs spied my actions and clambered up onto my lap.

'Lovely little kitten you have there,' Campbell remarked. 'Always been fond of cats, you know.'

I handed Tubbs over. It was impossible to write when he sat on the pages anyway.

'Fire away,' I told Campbell, pen poised.

A knock came at the door. I restrained a curse and called, 'Come in.'

Buggins entered. 'Looking for you everywhere, Campers. Lunch! Bully beef and onions. Ready when you are.' He gave a half grin and waited.

'Um, couldn't bring a tin over could you, old chap? Bit involved in a tête-à-tête here,' Campbell replied.

'Wilco.' Buggins turned to me with brows raised in a question. 'You too, Major?'

'I would indeed.' I nodded. I'd given up bully beef at the War's end, but no doubt there were still plenty of left-over rations being sold in the local army and navy surplus stores.

Buggins left and returned shortly with a stack of tins with lids such as the soldiers had used in the trenches. He handed us one each, pulled forward a stool for him-self and sat down. Fogg placed himself dead centre and watched us with pleading spaniel eyes; we all dropped titbits for him as we ate. It was rather good, actually.

'Campers talking to you about Maxwell, is he?' Buggins asked as we placed the empty tins on the stone hearth.

'I was about to,' Campbell replied, and turned toward me. 'Poor old Maxwell had a bit of a disappointment.' He continued as I reached again for my pen and notebook, flattening them out as I did. 'Thought he was going to be rich — and, well, he should have been. Family lived like nabobs: palatial house awash with servants, huge grounds, land, rank, the whole caboodle. Then his father dropped off the twig and Maxwell inherited a stack of debts. Trus-tees forced him to sell the lot, everything down to the last stick of furniture, gone. *Poof.*' He threw his hands in the air. 'Left him homeless, poor chap. Had to rent, and that's not cheap in London.'

'And that was the cause of his financial problems?' I prompted him.

'No, it became worse.' Campbell took his pipe from his pocket again and stuck it in the side of his mouth. 'His mother was still alive at the time, but she wouldn't give up her grand ways, so he tried to maintain her. Then she became ill and the quack's fees drained him entirely.'

He sighed and stared into the fire for a moment. 'Anyway, she died and he was terribly cut-up about it. Started drinking brandy at breakfast. Then some cousin or other stepped in and leaned on the Museum to find him a job and they sent him over to us. He took to it like a duck to water. Never so happy as when he had a spade in his hands; he dug away at anything you'd point him at. Dig, dig, dig.' He shook his head. 'Poor old Maxwell Mole,' he murmured half to himself.

'He hated Jackson.' Buggins took up the tale. 'Profiteer, you see. Spent the war in New York dealing in munitions. Maxwell volunteered for the front and went to France, and Flanders, whereas Jackson just stayed where he was and made a packet. Can't bear the man, he's an unconscionable thief, to my mind.' Buggins's eyes narrowed, then cleared as he glanced at me.

'Yes,' Campbell butted in. 'Maxwell and Jackson have been at each other's throats since we set off from London. And you see, the crown disappearing has made it all worse and if we don't find the treasure, it'll all be for nothing.'

That raised my brows. 'What treasure?'

'You haven't heard about the treasure?' Campbell asked in surprise. 'Erm, actually, I probably shouldn't have mentioned it …' He eyed Buggins, who was trying his best to hide his exasperation. 'Sorry, Buggins, old chap, bit forgetful. That bang on the bonce, you know.' He tapped his head.

'Well, you have mentioned it,' I said, eyeing him narrowly, 'so you may as well continue.'

'Hum.' His brown eyes glazed over for a moment. 'It's the King of the Isles. Somerled. Terrific story.'

'I recall mention of the King of the Isles, but I didn't realise it involved treasure.' I put my pen down with the notebook on the hearth and leaned forward; now here was a story I wanted to hear.

Campbell turned to his friend. 'You'll tell him, won't you, Buggins?'

Buggins's face had turned to stone. Too bad, I thought, because it was too late, the cat was out of the bag.

'Tell me who knows about this treasure,' I insisted.

'Maxwell knew,' Campbell replied in the face of Buggins' silence. 'And Dennis, of course. Carruthers, too, but she is absolutely sound...'

We were interrupted by another knock at the door and Greggs entered.

'May I offer tea, sir?'

He had the most extraordinary knack of turning up just as something interesting was about to happen. Anyone would think he'd been listening.

I gave him a stare of suspicion but he returned my regard with an innocent air.

'Had rather a lot of tea, Greggs,' I told him, 'but coffee would be welcome. I think we'd all like some, actually.'

'I won't be a moment, sir,' he said.

'Good,' I replied. 'And then we can all hear about this treasure.'

CHAPTER 14

'Somerled, wasn't it?' I reminded them.

'Yes!' Campbell replied with great enthusiasm. 'Or Sumarlioi. The monks who wrote the chronicles were better with Latin than Norse …'

A sharp rap on the door was followed by the entry of Swift wearing his trench coat.

'Lennox,' he snapped. 'We waited for you at lunch. You're too late now, we've eaten it.'

'Yes, sorry, Swift, got a bit diverted.' I waved a hand in the direction of the assembled.

He didn't give up. 'And Florence invited Miss Carruthers – thought it would be a nice gesture. You were supposed to be sitting next to her.'

I may have turned a little pink. Everyone looked at me, then looked away with quiet smiles.

I sought to divert attention. 'Just about to have a history lesson, Swift, on the King of the Isles and the treasure.'

'Treasure?' His eyes opened wide in surprise, and then he frowned under hawkish brows at the two archaeologists. 'Right. I'll join you.' He stripped off his trench coat and hung it up.

Greggs came in at that moment and cleared his throat. 'Coffee is served, sir.'

He poured coffee from a pot into a variety of chipped mugs and passed them around, we all clasped them with thanks.

Swift drew a tin out of his pocket. 'Brought some biscuits for you, Greggs.' He handed the goodies over. 'Thought I should replace the ones we ate earlier,' he added.

'Thank you, sir, how very considerate.' Greggs gave a short bow and raised his brows at me.

'I haven't forgotten about your biscuits!' I told him. 'I will find some.' Really, he was so pettifogging sometimes, and I'd only borrowed them for heaven's sake.

Swift pulled up the rickety chair from beside the wash-stand and sat down, spreading his kilt out first. I fetched another oil-lamp, throwing a pool of warm light around us in front of the blazing fire.

Greggs graciously handed the biscuits around, making me feel even more guilty. They were quite tasty, actually — butter and honey with a sprinkling of nuts.

'Florence made them,' Swift told me. 'Now that she's expecting she's developed a passion for baking. Cook's becoming rather fractious about it.'

I nodded in sympathy, although I had no idea why the cook should become upset. She sounded a bit of a Tartar, actually.

'Buggins, old chap.' Campbell turned to his friend. 'You're best at this, could you …?'

Buggins sipped his coffee, deep-brown eyes under black brows watching us quietly, then shrugged and said, 'Very well.' All eyes fixed upon his face. 'Are you ready?'

'Ready,' we all answered.

'Right, then I'll begin. Somerled was born around 1132 Anno Domini somewhere in Argyll on the west coast of Scotland. He was given a Norse name, meaning "Summer Traveller", although "Summer Raider" would be more apt. Despite his name, he was a Gael and he cleaved to the old Gaelic ways.'

Campbell cut in with a solemn nod, 'Somerled is bit of a hero of mine, actually.'

'Thought the Norse were called Vikings?' I asked, feeling as though I should have held my hand up like a schoolboy.

Buggins regarded me steadily. 'Yes, but "Viking" was not contemporary to the times and we historians prefer not to use it,' he paused to see if there were any more questions, but we were silently focused on his rugged features, so he continued. 'You have to understand that the Western Isles had been under the thrall of the Norse for centuries. But in 1156 Somerled finally defeated the Norse King, Godred Olaffson, and wrested the Kingdom of the Isles for himself. It was a magnificent achievement!' His voice warmed in his enthusiasm. 'For the first time in hundreds of years the Gaels had regained control of the Isles. But it wasn't a single battle. King Godred and Somerled fought many times until Somerled and his Gaelic army succeeded.' He paused for a moment. 'Actually, the story of Somerled's life is one long battle, really. He no sooner vanquished one enemy than another appeared.'

'Were they all Vikings, erm, Norse, I mean?' I asked.

'Most of them,' Campbell chimed in. 'They had been marauding about the seas for hundreds of years. Anywhere there was a coastline, there would be longboats full of Norsemen. But Somerled fought everybody: Norse, Scots, English, the whole shebang.' He stopped abruptly, pulled out his unlit pipe, and fiddled with it absent-mindedly as his gaze slipped into the distance.

Buggins glanced at him, and then took up the story again. 'Some years after defeating Godred, Somerled was once again at war, but this time with the mighty forces of Walter FitzAlan, the High Steward. The Scottish King had sent FitzAlan to subdue the growing power of the King of the Western Isles. You know who the High Steward was, don't you?'

'Yes, it was the position of Steward to the Scottish King and was his right hand man, his Ghillie-mor. The family eventually became known as the Stuarts and gained the Scottish crown for themselves.' Swift replied.

I was rather impressed.

'Been doing my homework,' he muttered.

Buggins grinned and continued. 'Somerled took his army of Gaels to Renfrew on the Scottish mainland. He had a fleet of over a hundred ships, which was tremendous for the day. He would need every man he could muster for a battle against FitzAlan's well-armed men.' He paused to look at me and Swift, our faces fixed firmly on his.

'So who won?' I asked.

'Ah.' Buggins frowned and continued. 'The battle never took place. Somerled was murdered in the night.'

Campbell suddenly perked up. 'And that's it, you see. He was murdered and nobody knows who did it. But there were rumours and it's been our pet project for years, because Somerled was such an important chap, and … and he was the father of the Clans, you see. And he won the Islands back for the Gaels. So murdering him was a dreadful deed. It almost put the Gaels back where they started.' He babbled in enthusiasm, his face and eyes shining, then he lapsed into silence once more and chewed on his pipe.

Buggins had relaxed and entered into the spirit of the story. 'Exactly! And it's always been a great mystery who killed him, and we have a theory about it – we believe it was King Godred's base-born son, Ivar.'

'Is that the same King Godred who was defeated by Somerled?' I asked.

'Yes,' Buggins replied. 'Although nobody else agrees with us.' He paused and his eyes darkened, the enthusiasm suddenly dying away. 'It's caused a bit of a rift between us and the scholars, actually. Anyway…' he pulled himself back together 'Somerled was murdered and his army fell to pieces and were slaughtered by the Steward's men. Three of Somerled's sons escaped and fled. His youngest son, Angus, died some time later, but the other two survived him. They were Dougal and Donald.'

'Black Dougal!' I exclaimed.

Campbell leaned forward, pipe clenched between his teeth. 'Got it, old chap!' he grinned.

Buggins raised a smile too. 'And this is where the legend of Black Dougal begins. Dougal's name is Gaelic and it's actually pronounced Dubhgall, and "Dub" means black. And,' he continued, 'he was a fearsome warrior, all of which helped his reputation. He fathered the Clan MacDougal, and Donald founded Clan MacDonald. Mac is Gaelic for "son of", which I expect you already know.' He looked at us.

Swift nodded his awareness and I tried to appear equally knowledgeable.

'Did they continue the fight?' I asked.

Buggins answered. 'Yes, they fought for generations. In fact they never really stopped fighting. Whisky and war, two of Scotland's greatest traditions!'

We laughed. I reached for the coffee pot on the tray by the stone hearth and offered to top up mugs. They held them out as I played Mother. Greggs handed round the biscuit tin once more. Swift tossed a couple of logs onto the fire and set it blazing and we made ourselves comfortable with booted feet stretched out toward the warmth. I couldn't help noticing that Swift had a dirk strapped to the top of his long cream wool socks. He really was taking the old Scottish heritage very seriously.

'How did Black Dougal manage to father the Clan MacDougal if he was walled-up in Swift's library?' I asked, waving a biscuit in Buggins's direction.

'He wasn't,' Buggins replied.

That raised our brows.

'Who is it, then?' Swift and I asked in unison.

'We think it's Ivar, the murderer of Somerled,' Campbell answered with a huge grin. 'And if it is, we may be able to prove our theory.'

I frowned. 'Oh, I see. And that's why you were so keen to come to the castle.'

'Exactly!' Campbell sat forward and took his pipe from his mouth to take up the tale. 'It's really terribly exciting for us. It could be him: Ivar. Well, we hope it's Ivar, but short of finding his name carved on the bones, we can't be sure. We've been discussing it ever since we heard about the skeleton and crown. It would be a huge feather in our caps if we succeeded in proving that it was Ivar who murdered Somerled.'

'And it would repair our reputations,' Buggins added. 'Particularly in the ivory-towered bastions of Oxford.'

He nodded at Campbell, who smiled in return, his fair hair flopping over one eye. He brushed it away absent-mindedly.

'And we might even be given some proper funding from the University.' Campbell continued. 'And it's truly fascinating. It's been a mystery for nearly ten centuries — it would put a bit of fire back into the history of the Isles, too.'

I had a vision of the archaeologists sitting around the fire until late into the evening hotly debating the exploits of the long dead and who killed whom. I must admit I did find it interesting. It's sleuthing of a different sort.

A question occurred to me. 'So you think it's Somerled's crown on Ivar's head? The skeleton, I mean. And that's the evidence that would prove Ivar killed Somerled and stole his crown?'

'Ah, jolly good point,' Campbell spoke up. 'We had great hopes, didn't we, Buggins.' He nodded at his friend.

Buggins took over. 'Yes, but as soon as we saw it, we were sure it couldn't be Somerled's crown.' He turned toward Swift. 'There was a runic inscription on the rim, so...'

Campbell jumped in. 'That means it would have belonged to a Norseman and Somerled was Christian and he wouldn't have worn a pagan crown. It was probably King Godred's. So it's a sort of proof, because it was probably stolen with Somerled's treasure. What we really need is the treasure itself.'

'But you don't know if there is any treasure, and the skull and crown are missing. So you can't prove anything at all,' Swift cut in.

That dropped a damp squib into the conversation and shoulders drooped accordingly.

'I'm sure the crown will be found.' I thought I'd try a bit of encouragement. 'It is a small island, after all, it can't be that difficult.'

Nobody replied.

Swift paused to think about it, then asked, 'When we

showed you the skeleton, did you notice the crucifix that was hanging over the entrance?'

'Yes, I saw it,' Buggins replied. 'You said something about it being with the skeleton, but I didn't examine it. We were concentrating on the crown and remains.'

'It was quite crowded,' Campbell added. 'And Jackson didn't help.'

'Here,' Swift dug out the rubbing from his pocket. 'Do you know what it means?'

Buggins unfolded the paper and turned it around in his hands. He studied it quietly, then said, *"Sun is the light of the lands, I bow to Heaven's doom."* It's a Norse prayer or blessing. It's a fairly common inscription.'

'Did you take it?' Swift snapped the question.

'What?' they replied together, eyebrows raised in surprise.

'Someone stole the crucifix,' I said.

They exchanged glances. 'No,' they both replied.

'Hum.' I looked at Swift, who frowned. I recognised 'Heaven's doom' from the burned paper in Maxwell's room and he would have done too. I decided to keep my mouth shut on that particular subject and turned back to the story.

'Why was Ivar wearing a crucifix if he was pagan?' I asked.

Buggins answered. 'In theory, the Norse had converted to Christianity, but many of them still cleaved to the pagan Gods. I expect he was hedging his bets between both religions.' He smiled. 'It wasn't uncommon.'

'But why would Ivar be here at Braeburn?' I persisted. 'And why was he walled-up wearing Godred's crown?'

'We wish we knew.' Buggins shrugged. 'He may have been hunted down and captured by Dougal and Donald and brought here. Or he may simply have been shipwrecked on this shore. The seas are treacherous, it's quite possible.'

'Bit ironic, though, that he'd be washed-up on the shores of his enemies,' I remarked.

Buggins laughed. 'Every man in the Western Isles was his enemy.'

Swift had been quietly considering the story. 'If King Godred's son, Ivar, was behind the murder of Somerled as you say,' he asked Buggins, 'did Godred regain the Isles and become King again?'

'Dougal held on to Mull, Lorn and much of Argyll. Godred won back the rest.'

'So Dougal must have walled Ivar up,' I proposed.

'No,' Swift cut in. 'The Braeburns would have been here defending the island.'

'So the Braeburns did it?' I said.

Swift frowned.

Buggins answered. 'The curse could really help, you know.' He looked at Swift with a mixture of hope and expectation. 'It may contain some nugget of truth; these old legends often do.'

As Swift concentrated on brushing invisible crumbs from his sporran, a light blush rose on his cheeks. I understood his discomfort: the secret of the curse should have been shared with him. The fact that it hadn't been, made it clear that he wasn't yet accepted by the Laird as true family.

'Clan secret, old chap,' I offered as an explanation. 'Not for public airing.'

Campbell and Buggins's gaze switched to me. I noted their disappointment and changed tack. 'What happened to the Kingdom of the Isles? I haven't heard of it.'

'Donald and Dougal continued the fight, and so did their sons. The clans grew, split, proliferated, inter-married,' Buggins answered. 'The Kingdom of the Isles changed hands many times and eventually devolved to become the Lordship of the Isles, and even that title was eventually taken away by the English king.'

It was all rather complicated and I was beginning to crave some quiet time with my dog, who was currently snoring at my feet. And I'd forgotten to take notes in my notebook, so I'd have to remember it all.

Silence fell for some moments as we digested the violence and duplicity of medieval history.

'And the treasure, sir?' Greggs suddenly asked.

'Ah yes.' Campbell's eyes lit up. 'Quite forgot about that, didn't I, Buggins!' He grinned as all eyes focused very firmly on his face.

CHAPTER 15

Greggs leaned forward looking avid and perky at the same time – no mean feat for the old soldier.

'I've never heard any mention of treasure on this island,' Swift said dubiously.

'Why would you?' Campbell replied with a grin, 'unless somebody knew it was here.'

'Hum,' Swift sat back in his chair and folded his hands over his sporran.

'You carry on telling them, Buggins, would you?' Campbell said. 'You're best at telling the stories.'

Buggins gave an almost imperceptible shrug, and looked at our intent faces. 'Treasure …' His deep voice reverberated around the warm pool of lamplight and into the shadows. 'We must go back to Somerled's offensive against FitzAlan the Steward. Somerled had earned his title of King of the Isles through bitter war and soft diplomacy. He knew that if he failed to win the battle against the stronger forces of the Scottish Steward, he would have to buy peace, and that's why he took his treasure with him.'

His words fell into enthralled silence; we were imagining wooden chests full of gleaming gold and jewels and whatnots of the most costly types. Well, I was, anyway.

'And I assume it vanished when Somerled was murdered?' Swift asked.

'Indeed, and never heard of again,' Buggins replied. 'Just as Ivar was never heard of again.'

'And you believe Ivar may have stolen it and brought it to this island, sir?' Greggs asked, his eyes as round as a schoolboy's.

'Yes!' Campbell exclaimed. 'If he ended up here with the crown, we're pretty certain he would have brought Somerled's treasure with him.' Campbell suddenly sighed. 'And we'd really, truly like to find it, wouldn't we, old chap?' He looked at Buggins, who quietly nodded.

'But…' I was trying to wrap my mind about this 'if you find treasure here, it could be anyone's treasure. This castle has been here for hundreds of years. How could you prove it was Somerled's treasure and that Ivar stole it?'

'Because of Leif Erikson!' Campbell exclaimed – which didn't mean a damn thing to me at all.

'Who?' I asked.

'Lennox, you can be remarkably ignorant sometimes,' Swift cut in. 'He was the Norseman who's reputed to have reached America before Columbus. They've put statues up to him.'

'You're right,' Campbell laughed. 'Marvellous, isn't it! They think he went from the Hebrides to Greenland and then on to somewhere in Newfoundland.'

'Did he come back again?' I asked.

'*Yes,*' they all replied.

Buggins took up the tale again. 'He lived to tell the tale, although the story was considered more a legend than historical fact. It was written in some of the Sagas, although none were contemporary to his lifetime. Leif Erikson called the unknown country "Vinland".'

'Right,' I said. 'And how is this connected with Somerled and his treasure?'

'Because Somerled had Leif Erikson's treasure,' Campbell laughed, holding his pipe up.

'And he'd stolen it?' I asked, very confused now.

'No, Leif Erikson died over a hundred years before Somerled was even born,' Campbell explained. 'Erikson's horde became part of the treasure held by the King of the Isles, and Somerled won it when he vanquished Godred. It was a bit like the crown jewels of the day.' He grinned hugely, thoroughly enjoying regaling us with the tale. 'And that is why it's so fascinating. And it's all part of our theory, you see, and nobody believes us. But if we found the treasure, we could prove everything.'

'How did you arrive at this theory?' Swift asked; he'd drawn out his notebook and was writing as he was listening.

Buggins answered. 'There's an annotation about Leif Erikson's journeys in two different Icelandic Sagas. They're rather garbled, and we only made the connection between those and the Chronicles from the Western Isles fairly recently.'

'How long is "fairly recently"?' Swift cut in, his mind as keen on detail as ever.

'Two years ago,' Buggins replied. 'But until now there has been no clue as to what happened to the treasure.' He paused. 'But it makes sense. It fits. I'm certain that Somerled seized the treasure when he defeated Godred. And it would have included whatever Leif Erikson had brought back from Vinland.'

'Does Jackson know about this?' Swift leaned forward, eyes hawkish as his mind turned to the murder and possible motives.

'No, and he must not find out,' Buggins answered very firmly. 'Jackson would be like a fox in the henhouse if he knew about it.'

Campbell added with a look of something akin to fear on his face. 'And I shouldn't have told you about the treasure. He'd take it away if he found out.'

'I thought you said it was your theory and you learned it through your own research,' I reminded him.

'Yes, exactly, it's ours, not Jackson's,' Campbell replied.

'And you said nobody believed you, so you've made it known,' I reminded them. 'He could have found out from one of your peers.'

Buggins frowned. 'Yes, but those peers only consist of a handful of scholars in the universities. Outside the historians' ivory towers, hardly anybody would know about Somerled having the treasure. And you hadn't even heard of Leif Erikson and Vinland, had you.'

'No, but why would I?' I replied, a bit stung at being

taken for an ignoramus. 'And you said Maxwell knew, so maybe he did tell Jackson.'

'No.' Campbell shook his head, his smile fading. 'He wouldn't say anything. He was our friend.'

'What would the treasure consist of?' Swift continued making rapid notes with a precise hand.

'We don't know,' Campbell replied. 'An Indian head-dress or something would help!' He laughed. 'And there would be real treasure too, gold and silver, even precious gems. But it's not the value of the horde that interests us, it's the fact that it could prove what happened to Somerled, and Leif Erikson. For us, as historians of the Highlands, that's the real treasure.'

Swift wrote this down as I mused on thoughts of gold and rubies, then looked up from his jottings. 'I can't believe it wouldn't have been found by now. It's been centuries.'

'Point taken,' Buggins replied, 'but then you've only recently discovered the skeleton and crown, haven't you.'

'But that was deliberately hidden,' Swift continued.

'And the treasure would be, too,' Buggins reminded him.

Tubbs woke and sat up to look at Campbell, upon whose lap he still rested.

'He needs to stretch his legs,' I said, indicating the little cat, who now turned to stare wide-eyed at the assembled.

Campbell carefully handed him to me and I slipped him into the capacious pocket of my shooting jacket, a place he'd always favoured from his earliest days as a foundling kitten.

'We must be off, too,' Campbell continued. 'Persi will wonder what's become of us.'

'Erm,' I began. 'I was ... I was thinking that perhaps ...'

Buggins gave me an appraising look.

'I'm sure she'd be delighted to take a stroll with you, old chap,' Campbell grinned. 'Ask her. She's quite human, despite her morbid fascination for old bones!'

'Ah, well, yes, I'll do that,' I stuttered in reply as they exited with a cheery wave and a 'toodle pip'.

Greggs gathered the coffee pot and mugs and picked up the battered wooden tray. There was a curious look of intent upon his face; talk of lost treasure seemed to have gripped his imagination. He went off with a light step almost verging on the jaunty.

Swift had stood up too as everyone left, slipped on his trench coat and tightened the belt. He dropped his notebook into his pocket and it occurred to me that perhaps I should carry my journal with me too. All I had in my pocket was a rotund kitten, and he wasn't terribly useful in the art of detecting, or anything else for that matter.

'Treasure?' Swift shook his head with incredulity. 'If the Braeburns thought there was so much as a gold coin to be found, they would have taken this place apart stone by stone centuries ago.'

'But,' I countered, 'Buggins had a point: no one knew about it, just as they didn't know about the skeleton.'

'Somebody here knows something, Lennox,' Swift retorted, and let out a sigh of exasperation.

'If we knew what the curse was ...' I began.

Swift ignored me and cut in: 'Maxwell knew about the treasure and they spent the day at the records office on the mainland. He must have stolen the crucifix, made the rubbing and taken the paper to translate the lettering. Those burned notes you told me about ... "Heaven's doom"? That proves it.'

'Yes,' I agreed, 'and whoever murdered Maxwell stole the crucifix from him.'

'Exactly,' Swift said with eyes alight; then he broke off in thought. 'What if Jackson *has* found out about the treasure?'

'Assuming the murder is connected to the treasure, why kill Maxwell and not Jackson?' I asked.

'I don't know ...' Swift frowned, then shoved his hands in his pockets. 'Why did Campbell and Buggins come to see you, Lennox?'

'Campbell was trying to convince me that we should arrest Jackson,' I told him. 'Then he started talking about Somerled and treasure and it all rather ran on.'

'Did he have any evidence against Jackson?'

'No, nothing.' I shrugged.

'Hum.' Swift paused. 'Jackson and Dennis are the only two with alibis. We need to question Miss Carruthers. Come on.' He jumped up and made for the door.

I wanted to, but hesitated. 'Fogg ...' I said. 'Need to take him out.'

'Lennox, can't you ...' Swift shook his head in exasperation. 'Look, we've invited her to dinner tonight. Make sure you aren't late!' He closed the door with a bang behind him.

Fogg woke up and peered around at me with ears raised in question. 'Come on,' I called. We set off outside into bright sunshine.

I gathered the little dog up and tucked him under my arm to stop him chasing the chickens that were scratching by the byre, then put him down beyond the arched gateway. I made my way around to the path beneath the trees as he ran ahead, ears flapping as he went.

The sharp scent of spruce and fir, bog myrtle and sweet herbs rose from the damp earth. Waves lapped against the shore, seaweed had been thrown onto the beach, gulls wheeled and screamed above my head. The big rock was wet and slippery as I stepped onto it; I stood with hands in trouser pockets and stared out across the water, imagining Viking boats rowed by Nordic warriors cutting across the blue-green waves. They would have been longboats with dragon heads at their prows, a row of painted shields hung along the rails and a single white sail billowing above the bronze and iron helmets of swarthy men.

Fogg chased a squirrel. Tubbs fidgeted in my pocket so I stepped off the rock and onto the beach, extracted him gently and placed him on the ground. He looked around, skipped to a pile of leaf mould between two mossy mounds, dug a delicate hole, peed with eyes closed, then proceeded to paw the leaf mould back in place. I dried him off with my handkerchief and put him back in my pocket, where he purred himself to sleep.

Tales of lost treasure had chased all rational thought entirely from my mind, but I turned resolutely back to the death of Maxwell.

That scrap of paper proved that he was a thief and the burned scrap meant he had found a translation of it. Why burn it? Because it was too important to leave around for prying eyes to discover. Or probably because he'd told somebody, and no longer needed it. In which case, why did he take the rubbing up onto the battlements with him?

I kicked a stone into the loch where it landed in the trough of a wave. Another one rolled over it, white foam forming on the crescent. It was far too rough to fish with the light tackle I'd brought with me. I looked toward the mainland at the line of trees on the rocky shore. It seemed near and yet so distant. I realised I hadn't seen any fishing boats, or indeed any boats at all. I knew the waters between the island and the shore to be dotted with jutting rocks. Nobody navigated them unless they were intimate with the dangers. On the seaward side of the loch, between the Isle of Mull and this island, the sea ran deep, with a treacherous tide. No doubt those who took to these waters were well versed in their ways, and they knew enough to leave their boats at their moorings in this capricious season.

I meandered back toward the castle, hands stuffed in trouser pockets, my mind on Maxwell. My feet led me to the base of the castle wall where the poor chap had landed in a broken heap. Swift had been over it with a fine-tooth comb, as was his wont, but I wondered if there was anything we'd missed.

There were dark stains in small crevices that even the storm had failed to wash away. I drew out my magnifying glass, which I'd remembered to bring, and examined the rocks as best I could. Fogg sat and watched me from a distance; he understood what the spot signified and refused to come near it.

There was nothing to be learned. I accepted defeat and straightened up. I stared again at the towering walls of the castle, imagining Maxwell flailing as he fell, and then the awful bone-shattering crunch of his landing. What had he been doing up there? Had he taken the stairs to the battlements of his own accord, or had he been lured? And the paper he'd been holding? Was it torn from his grasp, but then dropped by the killer, or did Maxwell toss it aside when he realised he was under attack? He had taken drugs and alcohol, so he wouldn't be thinking clearly, but ...

Sun is the light of the lands, I bow to Heaven's doom. The words of the Norse poem slipped back into my mind. Heaven's doom might mean the setting of the sun — had he gone there to watch the sun go down? I turned to stare west toward the horizon, trying to find Maxwell's line of sight, but realised I needed to be higher up. I turned, ran through the gates and raced across the courtyard.

Foggy thought it was tremendous fun and followed, barking as we went. A passing footman, tea-tray in hand, stopped to watch me in bemusement as I took the stone steps two at a time which was pretty foolish as I could barely catch my breath once up there. I found the scratches on the wall where Maxwell had been forced over, and peered along the sightline. I had to admit my mind had been as much on the treasure as the murder. There was nothing of note — trees, rocks, more trees, the sea, and the Isle of Mull on the distant horizon beyond the big flat rock I'd been standing on.

I shook my head at my own idiocy, then drew out my penknife. Idiotic or not, I would mark the spot, and scratched an arrow into the black mould covering the stone wall. I remembered Tubbs, and I stopped to check that he wasn't too shaken. He was still asleep. With a deep breath I turned to walk slowly down the steps.

The footman was making his way back on sturdy boots across the courtyard. He was holding the same tea-tray, now with evidence of depletion.

My mind turned to Greggs and his damn biscuits, so I followed in the chap's footsteps in the direction of the kitchens.

I had to duck to enter the long stone building with its single window cut into the deep whitewashed walls. It looked like a byre that had been roughly converted to a bakehouse and eventually a kitchen.

Warm steamy air met me on the doorstep and I halted to look around and breathe the delightful scent of roasting beef, baking bread, buns and biscuits.

In the centre of the room a large square table stood on a red tiled floor; it was laden with mixing bowls, copper pans, eggs, flour and culinary whatnots. A huge black range was enclosed in a massive fireplace on the far wall, above which knives, ladles, steak hammers, strainers and skewers hung in a row. Next to the ovens was another fire, open and ablaze and fitted with pots and cauldrons hooked onto brackets and chains. A large spit-jack with wooden handle, brass cogs and clockwork wheels turned a side of ribs slowly over the flames, grease dripping onto a tray of sizzling fat.

There was a doorway at the farthest end that opened into another room. By the sounds of clattering crockery and cutlery, I'd say it was the scullery. Murmuring voices reached my ears as I clapped my hands and stepped across the threshold into my idea of heaven.

I didn't get very far. A wooden spoon came spinning out of nowhere to crack against the door behind me with a loud bang.

CHAPTER 16

'Wit ye doin' in 'ere, ye lanky malinky longlegs?' came a screech from somewhere beyond the table. 'Ye've nae right tae be keeking aroond me kitchin.'

'Erm … Greetings,' I called out.

A spatula now flew in my direction. I side-stepped smartly and it bounced off a roof beam and clattered to the floor. I assumed I was in the company of the cook and could just make out the top of a starched white mob cap on the other side of the table, partially obscured by a large pudding bowl.

'I'm from the house. I mean castle. I'm a guest!' I shouted. Good Lord, this was ridiculous. A pastry brush caught me full square on the forehead. 'Ow!'

An undersized termagant in white frock and apron appeared from behind the table brandishing a frying pan. I backed toward the door. 'Madam, will you please desist,' I shouted.

She didn't: she advanced, yelling her incomprehensible battle-cry, and raised the pan above her head. I dug into my pocket and withdrew the only form of defence I had. I held Mr Tubbs to my chest and cried, '*Milk!*'

'Eh?' She halted, peered closely at the little black cat in my hands, and then lowered her weapon a couple of inches.

'I'd like some milk for my kitten. *Please*,' I added.

'Eeee, 'tis a wee kitty ye be havin' there,' she muttered.

'Indeed,' I replied. 'And he's rather hungry.' Which wasn't strictly true as Tubbs was far too well fed to ever be hungry, but I thought it might appeal to her softer emotions.

'Weel, I might be havin' some milk fur 'im.' She put the frying pan on the table and came closer. I handed Mr Tubbs over. Fogg, never one for bravery, peered out from behind my legs.

'Ooh, an' a wee doggie, too,' the pint-sized Tartar almost cooed. She was a very small woman, barely reaching my elbow, but had the spirit of an avenging Valkyrie. Her wizened face suddenly broke into a smile and she gently took Tubbs from my grasp with gnarled hands and held him to her sparse bosom, muttering under her breath.

Turning, she carried him off to a large pantry at the far end of the room and went inside. Fogg followed, so I went too. The walls were white, as was usual, the shelves made of thick stone slabs and ranged up both sides of the narrow room. It was extremely cold in there, remarkably so, given the warmth of the kitchen itself. Rondels of cheese wrapped in cloth were stacked high; other shelves held jugs of cream and milk. I realised that the few ewes kept in the adjoining byre were the source of much of the

166

dairy. There were pots of jams, jellies, pickles and pre-
serves, with lids made from scraps of bright cloth and
tartan fabric. And clutches of fresh brown eggs in baskets
filled with straw.

Still crooning to the little cat, Cook placed a saucer on
a shelf and poured cream onto it. Tubbs lapped it up and
Foggy crept closer to watch, his black nose sniffing the air
in the hope of something falling his way.

'Ee, little doggie, what ye be lookin' after?' Cook
crooned.

'He's quite fond of ham,' I mentioned. 'And beef,
actually.'

That did the trick and she bustled off back into the
kitchen chatting in a tone that sounded almost chummy.
'Ye're master o' the wee beasties, then? Ye'd better be a
canny lad, ye ken?'

'Right, yes, of course.' I nodded, not having a clue
what she meant but wanting to appear keen nonetheless.
'We're, um, we're a bit short of rations. Thought perhaps
you'd be able to help?'

Two beady eyes turned to burrow into mine. 'Ay,
ye're a lanky un with hollow legs now,' she said after a
short pause, and went to forage about underneath the
table. A wicker basket appeared and she placed it on
the scrubbed pine boards, then picked up a knife and
began vigorously slicing beef from the rotating ribs on
the spit. That resulted in a tidy pile, which she dropped
into a deep-sided tin complete with lid. A few scraps were
tossed in Fogg's direction and I had to contain myself

because it smelled scrumptious but it would have been impolite to ask for a piece. There followed thick slices of ham, a small loaf of bread, eggs, more cream in a canister, and a chunk of clootie.

'He's awfully fond of biscuits.' I nodded towards Fogg, who was now sitting drooling onto the red tiles, his eyes like chocolate saucers. A box of biscuits was added to the goodies in the basket.

I gave her my best grin.

'Grannie?' a voice called, and was quickly followed by the maid I'd met when she'd been running from the gin-gang and the supposed ghost.

'Ay, Ellie lass, come in tae me kitchin, now.' Cook called out. 'Do ye ken the wee kitty? An' the doggie? Ach, they're a bonnie pair aw'right.'

Ellie was dressed in the same maid's outfit as yesterday with a fresh white apron, and eyed me warily. 'And what are ye doing in me grannie's kitchen, mister?'

'Just passing by. And … erm, my dog was hungry, you know; kitten, too,' I answered with as much innocence as I could muster. 'He's in the pantry.'

She stepped back and peered into the narrow room, then reached in to lift Tubbs up, and came towards us. 'Ach, a wee kitty, do ye hear his purring?' she said to the cook, and gently handed Tubbs over, his whiskers covered in cream.

'Ay, 'tis a bonnie bairn an' all.' Cook looked back at me. 'An' he needs tae be at the fireside, nae wanderin' aboot the place,' she told me, her eyes now fixing me with a glare.

'Um, yes, yes. I'll return him now, shall I?' I held my hands out, but she ignored me and took a warm tea-towel from beside the oven and wrapped him up like a swaddled babe. Then she placed him carefully in the basket on top of the goodies. He looked at me in wide-eyed surprise. Fogg went to hide behind my legs again.

'Ellie…' Cook turned to her granddaughter 'ye'll see the bairn's put tae bed now. Away ye go.'

And with that, we went. Ellie held the basket on her hip and led the way across the courtyard. The wind was picking up and heavy dark clouds were building above the castle walls.

'Are ye with them archaeologists, then?' Ellie asked.

I shook my head. 'No. I'm a friend of Swift and Lady Florence.' I glanced at her face, freckled and fresh, with pretty green eyes. 'Would you mind telling me exactly what you saw in the gin-gang, Ellie?'

"T'was a ghosty, like I said,' the girl answered guardedly.

'But what did it look like? Could you describe it?' I asked.

'It looked like a *ghost*,' she answered sharply, 'dinnae you hear me say so?'

'Heathcliff? Hello, dear boy,' Miss Fairchild called out, and waved from the shadows of the doorway leading to the Great Hall. She came across to us, her cloak lifting in the wind.

'Greetings, Miss Fairchild.' I came to a halt as I called out to her. 'Please accept my apologies about lunch. I was rather diverted by events.'

'No need, no need,' she replied breathlessly. 'Hello, Ellie, my dear. How are you and your charming grandmother?'

'Ay, we're well.' Ellie's voice adopted a warmer tone. 'And yerself?'

'Marvellous, simply marvellous.' Miss Fairchild smiled sweetly. 'Now, did you speak to Major Lennox about your dreadful experience of yesterday?'

I was beginning to wonder if Miss Fairchild really did have some sort of sixth sense.

'Ach, he'll no be understanding what it was,' Ellie said with a withering glance in my direction.

'Yes, I will!' I replied, rather stung.

They came to a halt to face each other by the well. I was ignored.

'Now, Ellie,' Miss Fairchild began. 'Please tell Major Lennox what you told me this morning at breakfast, if you would?'

Ellie's mouth took on a mulish look, and I thought she was going to refuse. Miss Fairchild leaned forward to place a reassuring hand on Ellie's arm wrapped around the basket, and the maid relented.

'It was on the wall o' the gin-gang. It wasn't very clear at first, there were cobwebs hanging from the beams like tatty curtains. Then it moved. I was feart near to death. *Hovered*, it did, the skull, with black holes for eyes staring at me. Then it went a bit fainter, an' I thought it was going tae disappear, but back 'e came and 'e began to move toward me.' Her voice had dropped to a whisper, then she said loudly. 'An' I screamed me head off, an' *ran*!'

I regarded her and she looked back with angry eyes, daring me to mock her.

'Quite understandable,' I said. 'Frightening, I mean. Did you hear any noise?'

'Ay. Scuffling, like *rats*,' she said, 'but it was from somewhere else, not by the wall.'

'And that's why you went in there? Because of the noise?'

A light blush flushed her cheeks. 'Ay, I told ye that already.'

'Of course, you did, my dear.' Miss Fairchild had been watching. 'Have any of the archaeologists been bothering you, Ellie?'

Ellie looked at her feet, and then at the short figure of Miss Fairchild. 'That older one, Mr Jackson,' she admitted. 'I cannae 'bide him. An' 'e's been botherin' aboot. He's offered a reward, too.'

'A reward for what?' Miss Fairchild asked.

'The head an' crown o' Black Dougal,' Ellie said. 'As if any one of us would be touching such a thing. We'd be *cursed* Dead in our beds before daybreak, my grannie says.'

'Ah.' I nodded. 'Actually, you know, it's not Black ...' They both turned to look at me. 'Never mind,' I added hastily. 'I'll take the basket, if you prefer, and go and tuck Tubbs in.'

Ellie was about to refuse but Miss Fairchild smiled at her. 'Don't worry, my dear. I will accompany the dear boy. Off you go now.' She patted Ellie's arm and the girl nodded as if in a daze and relinquished the basket to my grasp.

'She was meeting her beau, you know,' Miss Fairchild told me as we walked towards my tower.

'The young footman?' I responded.

She smiled and nodded. 'Quite! But he was delayed and I think she disturbed someone.'

I held my tongue, my mind turning over Ellie's account. We approached the tower and I stepped back to let the lady go ahead of me. Greggs appeared on the top step; he simpered at the sight of Miss Fairchild.

'Allow me, sir, and my dear Miss Fairchild.' He bowed and took the basket from my hands, then stared with brows raised when he saw Mr Tubbs looking up at him from the swaddling.

'Greggs, I'm off to see Inspector Swift,' I told him. 'I'll leave Miss Fairchild in your capable hands. Oh, and there are biscuits under the cat.'

I found Swift in his library poring over his notebook.

'Swift,' I said.

He barely looked up. 'This is ridiculous,' he snapped. 'No damn manpower, no resources, not even a damn doctor. How the hell am I supposed to solve this on my own?'

'Well, I'm here, too,' I reminded him, taking a chair on the other side of his desk.

His glance was verging on the withering.

'Swift.' I leaned forward again.

He threw his pen down on the blotter.

'Sorry.' He ran his fingers through his hair. 'It's just … Lennox, it's a murder investigation and I can't run to procedure. I just can't! We should be interviewing everybody properly, and we need the body examined. And someone should go to the mainland, to the records office and ask questions.'

I held up my hand. 'No one's going anywhere. We'll do the best we can and the refined stuff can wait. It's not that desperate, you know.'

'I know,' he admitted, calming down. 'But I don't like wasting time on this history nonsense and all this talk of bones and treasure. We need to *focus*, Lennox – and you're not very good at that, you know.'

I opened my mouth to object but he carried on. 'Miss Carruthers was pleasant enough but didn't add one iota to the facts.'

'We need to interview Jackson,' I interjected before he carried on with his rant.

'I do know that, Lennox.' He slapped an open hand down on the pages of his notebook. 'I was about to go and do exactly that.'

'Jackson's offered a reward to the servants, you know,' I cut in.

That produced a pause and I told him what Ellie had recounted. 'And the story of the ghost must have been someone with a torch,' I concluded.

'A skull painted onto the glass? Yes, easy enough to do, and it would scare off most people.' He stopped to jot a few more lines down. 'Right.' He stood up and tightened the belt on his trench coat. 'We'll interview Jackson first and demand we search his room. We've got good reason now, after Ellie's account.'

We cut across the courtyard at a healthy pace and climbed the steps of the Armoury. I had no idea which room Jackson was in, but Swift did and he marched straight to it and gave a determined rap on the door. Nothing happened. He rapped it again, then cursed under his breath.

'Right.' He turned the handle; it was locked.

We could hear the sound of typing just along the corridor and Swift turned towards it.

'Dennis!' he called as he marched straight into the room.

Dennis let out a squeak. He had been sitting at a small table in front of the fire; now he ceased typing, went red in the face and jumped to his feet. 'You're not allowed in here! This is my room.'

We ignored him.

'Where's Jackson?' Swift demanded.

'Why would I know?' Dennis replied. 'You should go away. I'm very busy with important work.' He returned to his heavy black typewriter and started banging away again.

I took a quick look around. It was just like the dead Maxwell's room: same sort of camp bed, although the blankets were neatly folded, same fireplace with brackets and chains, a spit-jack and hooks; a row of tins of tea, sugar and whatnot alongside a medical kit on the mantelpiece. A kettle on the hearth, a rug on the floor. Nothing out of the ordinary.

'Swift.' I dug in my pocket and withdrew one of the few items I had taken to carrying around with me: a set of lock-picks that I'd contrived to extract from a thief while at Bloxford Hall earlier in the year. 'Here.' I handed them to him.

'Where did you …?' he began with brows raised. 'Right. Come on.'

We returned to Jackson's room and Swift very efficiently picked the lock.

We got as far as the threshold. Jackson was sitting, or to be more accurate, was slumped, on a wooden armchair by a dying fire. He looked rather shocked, which was understandable because he had a crossbow bolt sticking out of his blood-soaked chest.

CHAPTER 17

'Hell!' Swift swore, and stalked across to the extirpated Jackson.

I followed, taking a long slow look about the room, keeping in mind that detecting was about observation — a skill that generally eluded me. There was no sign that Jackson had been entertaining anyone. Nothing seemed out of place, no evidence of a struggle, no extra mugs or tumblers on the low table in the centre of the room, nor on the desk by the window. And it was highly improbable that any guest would have been entertained whilst clutching a loaded crossbow. The killer had probably opened the door, fired the shot, locked it and cleared off. I gave up my perusal and joined Swift by the body. He was feeling Jackson's neck.

'He's still warm,' Swift said.

'Dead?' I asked.

'Of course he's dead. He's got an iron bolt through his heart.'

Swift knelt down to take a closer look at the bolt. Jackson's white shirt was stained with a great deal of bright red blood; he wore the same dark-grey suit under the same black coat as this morning. If he was as wealthy as reputed, you'd think he could afford some proper clothes. I leaned over to better survey the wound.

'You're in the light,' Swift complained.

Really, he was so irritable sometimes.

'I expect it was pretty instant,' I remarked, standing back with my hands stuffed in my pockets.

'Lennox…' he turned to glare up at me 'search the room, will you,' he ordered. 'And make notes.'

'Didn't bring a notepad,' I replied.

'We were going to a damn interview, you knew you'd need to take notes. You really have to learn to think ahead.'

'I am not your sergeant, Swift,' I snapped back.

He scowled at me, then carried on with his examination of the body, digging in Jackson's pockets, pulling out bits of paper, a handkerchief, a bulging wallet, some business cards, and a tangle of fishing line complete with a large, rusted fish hook from his top pocket, which I thought was rather odd. Swift handed them to me and I put them on the window sill, not being sure what I was supposed to do with them. Swift paused and stared closely at Jackson's face, which hadn't been particularly pleasant before he'd been shot and death hadn't improved matters.

'I'm going to take a photograph of him,' Swift said.

'What with?' I asked.

'A camera, of course. Florence has one. I'll borrow it. It will be useful for the police records, considering we can't bring a doctor over here. Or indeed the police,' he added with a note of regret. 'You stay here and guard the place. Don't let anyone in.' He tightened the belt of his trench coat and strode to the door, then turned to add, 'And don't *touch* anything.'

Damn it, who did he think he was! I scowled at the door for a moment, my thoughts rankling, then decided to have a proper look around. I flicked through the wallet, the cards and bits and pieces from Jackson's pockets. None of it contained anything of interest, although he was carrying two twenty-pound notes, one ten, and three fivers. The cards were mostly people with London addresses, a few from New York and one from Paris. I untangled the fishing line, being careful to catch the hook, and wound it into a proper loop, noting that it was the sort used for sea fishing. Then I went to the fire and pushed the logs apart to see if there was anything of interest in the ash. There wasn't.

I went to the bed and knelt to search beneath it, finding dust and a chamber pot, unused, a pair of shoes and mouse droppings. Nothing was revealed by my search of the mattress and covers. I rummaged through Jackson's trunk only to find fancy shirts neatly folded, with all the usual whatnots you'd expect. I dropped the lid down and sat on it.

I turned back to the corpse languishing on his chair. Perhaps I should check his fingernails — maybe he'd been digging and had discovered something and the murderer had shot him? I picked up a flaccid hand and examined the nails; they had tiny grains of soil beneath them and were dirty. I was right! I let the hand drop and searched the room for a trowel or shovel, found nothing and came back to the body. I stood back to take a longer look at him. His hair was greasy and lank; it had slipped over one eye. The other stared glassily at nothing. There were very old, rotted feathers set into the visible end of the bolt. How long are crossbow bolts? Did it go all the way through him? Perhaps it had skewered him to the back of the chair?

I leaned Jackson forward a tad to check. It hadn't gone through him or pinned him to the chair. As I tried to make my observations, he slumped forward, toppled, and fell with a crump to the floor. His knees had buckled and he was lying like an Arab-type chap praying to the Almighty with his forehead touching the floorboards.

I looked at the door, then back at the body. Swift had told me not to touch anything. I grabbed him under the arms and heaved him toward the chair. The chair fell over. Damn it, Jackson was heavier than he looked. I let go of him and he collapsed in an untidy heap, face now flat on the floor. I picked up the chair and tried once more. I manoeuvred him sideways and he was almost in position when he slipped off again and landed on his back. He stared at the ceiling. I ran my fingers through my hair. Right! I rolled him over, got my arms around him from behind and tried to swing him sideways.

'Oh, good God! Lennox, what have you done?'

Persi Carruthers stood in the doorway, her hands held to her face, her eyes filled with horror.

'You're not supposed to come in,' I shouted, then realised things didn't look good. 'I mean … wait. It's not … We found him like this. He fell over. I wasn't supposed to touch him,' I spluttered, then dropped him again and he collapsed like a broken marionette.

Carruthers let a small shriek escape and stepped sharply back out of the room.

'No. Wait!' I called to her. 'Could you help? Swift will be back any minute.'

'What?' she gasped.

'I told you. We found him. He's been killed with a crossbow. Look,' I waved a hand at the crumpled corpse. 'There's a bolt but no bow. I couldn't have killed him.'

She was looking around the room, her eyes wide with shock. She was very pretty when her cheeks were flushed with fear.

'I have to get him back in the damn chair. Would you help? Please?' I implored.

For a moment I thought she would scream and run off yelling blue murder, but she was made of sterner stuff. She took her hands away from her face, straightened up and advanced slowly.

'Who killed him?' she asked.

'We don't know. Swift has gone for his camera and Jackson fell over, slipped off the chair, actually. I was trying to make observations.'

She pushed her glossy blonde hair behind one ear as she came closer, and then peered down at the tangled form of Jackson at my feet.

'I doubt it went through him. Crossbow bolts are usually only about twelve inches long and there's a good six inches sticking out of his chest.' She leaned down. 'It's quite old, you know. They used to be terribly popular.' She straightened up. 'He would have died instantly.'

'Yes, um, that's what we thought.' I forced a reassuring smile. 'Couldn't grab him under that arm, could you? Swift will have my hide if Jackson isn't back where we found him.'

She hooked her arm beneath the corpse and said, 'Ready?'

'Right, I mean, yes.' I stooped to grab the defunct Jackson and said, 'Heave!'

We heaved. Jackson hung like a limp rag for a moment and then landed back in the chair.

'Quick,' I said, and hauled him upright as he slid towards the floorboards again. I straightened him up by yanking on his jacket until he was back in place.

We were both a bit breathless.

'I think that's how he was.' I stood back to survey our efforts, hands on hips. 'He just needs ...' I moved in and placed one of his elbows to lean across the chair arm.

'What do you think?' I asked Persi.

'I can't help, I don't know what he looked like before he fell off,' she replied, then turned her full attention in my direction. 'That wasn't a test, was it?'

'What?'

'To find out if I knew what position he was in when he was killed.' Her eyes suddenly narrowed.

'Good Lord, no! Never even crossed my mind.' I stepped back. She was sharp, and as bad as Swift where it came to being suspicious.

She continued to stare at me, then softened and nodded. 'I'd better go, I doubt Swift would be very pleased to find me here.' She made for the door, then turned on the threshold. 'Oh! Fingerprints. Would you …?'

'Ah, yes. Of course.' I dug out my handkerchief and waved it.

Carruthers raised an elegant hand and left, closing the door behind her. I stared after her, and then at Jackson, who had sagged. His jaw had dropped open in a rather ghastly grin. I sighed and rubbed the arms of the chair with my handkerchief, then thought I should do the door and the handle. I'd just stuffed my hankie back in my pocket when Swift walked back in holding the camera. It was a rather nice little folding Kodak.

'You didn't let anyone in, did you?' He frowned at me. I shook my head.

'And you didn't touch anything?'

'No, no,' I reassured him.

'Good.' He was a bit more subdued than before. 'I, erm, I forgot to note the time we found him. Didn't happen to notice, did you?'

'It was three forty,' I lied, not knowing either, but it must have been around then.

'Procedure, Lennox,' Swift lectured me as he stood back to frame Jackson in the camera lens. 'We have to get a grip on this and we need to follow proper procedure.'

He snapped a couple of shots, then took a few more of the room. I kept out of the way.

'What's this?' He leaned down to scrabble under Jackson's chair and came out holding a squashed feather. 'A white bird's feather.' He stared at it.

He pulled out his magnifying glass.

'Barn owl,' I said, peering at it over his shoulder. 'Probably from the owl we saw in the old militia buildings yesterday.'

He nodded and placed it carefully between two pages of his notebook. 'Strange we didn't find it before,' he muttered.

'Hum,' I replied noncommittally.

He gave me a narrow stare, then stepped back.

'Right…' he withdrew a small jar of fine powder from his sporran, and a soft brush 'I want you to dust for fingerprints.' He dug in his pockets and tugged out a pair of white cotton gloves. 'And wear these. I'm going to gather the archaeologists in their mess and take statements. I'll meet you there when you've finished.'

He walked out as I pulled on the gloves. He really was an annoying nitpicker when it came to dead bodies. I looked at the perished Jackson, sighed and opened the jam jar.

CHAPTER 18

The damn powder went everywhere. How the devil was it supposed to work?

I sloshed the stuff about with the brush, which made me sneeze as small clouds escaped to drift in invisible draughts. I assumed Swift would come and check whose prints belonged to whom because I had no idea. It was rather tedious, actually. I took a last look at Jackson, who was turning greyer by the moment, closed the door and left.

The corridor to the archaeologists' mess took me past their cloakroom and I thought it worth a quick scrutinise. I opened the door and pushed it wide. It was a narrow room, dimly lit by an arrow-slit window, but I could see well enough to spot a crossbow propped up against the farthest wall. I pushed between the heavy waterproofs and stooped to pick it up, but brought myself up short. I pulled the white gloves out of the pocket I'd stuffed them into and donned them, feeling rather pleased with myself. I then examined the bow. It was old, and exquisite in the way only deadly weapons can be.

'Hello, dear boy.' A voice behind made me spin around.

'Ah, greetings, Miss Fairchild,' I said.

She was swathed in her cloak and her short figure filled the doorway. 'It wasn't you who killed Mr Jackson, was it?' she asked, in the sort of way you'd enquire about a sick relative.

'No, but I have found the murder weapon.' I held it up to show her.

'How terribly clever of you, Heathcliff.' She stepped closer to peer at it, then placed her hand on the shaft. 'It holds a presence,' she intoned. 'Evil ... evil ...' She closed her eyes as though in deep concentration.

I opened my mouth to warn her about fingerprints, but it was too late.

'He died in a snap,' she said, opening her eyes. 'His soul — gone in a flash! He's not here at all.' She leaned forward and whispered to me, 'I think he will spend some time...' she pointed solemnly toward the floor '*down there.*'

'Right.' I nodded sagely whilst the phrase 'nutty as a fruitcake' formed in my brain. 'He didn't say who shot him, then?'

'I was drawn here, you know, by his abrupt demise.' Miss Fairchild smiled up at me, the dimple making an appearance. 'I felt the tremor in the spirit world. It was most disturbing and I had just settled myself to take tea with your man Greggs.'

I regarded her quietly for a moment. 'Did you see anything, or anybody, Miss Fairchild?'

'No. I just told you, Heathcliff, I *felt* it, I didn't see it.'

'Not awfully keen on Heathcliff, actually, Miss Fairchild,' I reminded her again.

'Nonsense, dear boy. Now, you must arrest Mr Buggins.'

'What?'

'Are you having problems with your hearing, Heathcliff? Because if you are, I have a solution of oil.'

'No! But why on earth should I arrest Buggins?'

'Because I can feel his hands on this instrument of death.' She indicated the crossbow. 'He has touched it, indeed his fingers may have been the last to touch it.' She smiled sweetly as she made an accusation that could send Buggins to the hangman.

'This is a very grave matter, Miss Fairchild. Arresting people, I mean. Do you have any evidence?'

'No, but I'm sure you'll investigate, dear boy.' She smiled and stepped back out of the scant light and was gone.

I stared at the spot where she'd been, shook my head and then went off to find Swift in the mess.

'Lennox!' Swift exclaimed. 'Where did you find that?'

'Was that the murder weapon?' Campbell asked, eyes widening.

'Someone got Jackson.' Dennis sniggered.

At least they could let me get through the door! I walked over to where they were sitting around the same table in the same places as this morning, with Swift at the head. I placed the crossbow on the table in front of the Inspector and sent a smile in the direction of Persi

Carruthers, who looked absolutely beautiful. In fact every time I saw her I thought …

'Lennox?' Swift was staring at me. 'Are you listening to me?'

'What?'

'I said …' Swift repeated himself.

'Yes, I heard!' I retorted.

They were all staring at the crossbow. It was a work of deadly art and gleamed under the brightness of the oil lamps. It had a sinuous wooden stock, yew by the looks of it, with silver ornamentation chased into the lock mechanism. All the metalwork had been oiled and polished. Someone had recently cleaned it up and put it in working order. They'd made a beautiful job of it, too.

'Right. Did any of you touch this?' Swift indicated the crossbow.

'No,' they replied as one. I eyed Buggins more carefully but he didn't look particularly guilty.

I glanced at Swift, who said, 'You didn't tell them how the murder was done?'

'No, I just got here,' I replied. 'But I think they've guessed.'

Persi was following the conversation closely but kept her lovely mouth shut. She threw a brief glance in my direction and I returned the gaze but she'd already turned her attention back to the men now watching us intently. A log sparked and crackled in the hearth, spitting in the silence.

'He was a bad man.' Dennis, the little archivist jumped up. 'He'll be a ghost now, too.' He giggled with excitement, then sat down again and folded his hands.

Swift picked up the written statements in front of him on the table. I assumed them to be the ones he'd taken today. He flicked through them and withdrew one.

'Buggins, you were in this room "stirring the pot", according to your statement. What did you mean by that?' Swift asked.

'I was cooking tonight's stew. It's in that pot hanging over the fire,' Buggins replied tersely, and indicated the hearth.

'And you say that nobody saw you at any time?' Swift replied.

'Persi came in about fifteen minutes ago, then left again,' Buggins said.

'I'm talking about half an hour ago,' Swift replied.

'Here. Alone.' Buggins leaned back as Swift leaned forward.

'Campbell, where were you?' Swift rounded on him.

'In my room. Idling, really. I didn't feel like going out.' He had retrieved his unlit pipe and started fiddling with it again.

'Dennis?' Swift glowered at him.

'Typing in my room,' Dennis sat with his back straight, very pleased with himself. 'It is my job. I'm very good at it. You saw me.'

'And I was alone too,' Carruthers added with another glance under her lashes at me. 'In my room, except when I stopped by for a drop of milk. Buggins was here.'

'Did any of you see or hear anything?' Swift asked.

'No,' came the reply.

'Did any of you talk to Jackson since this morning?'

'No,' came the predictable reply.

Swift made notes, then lifted his head to glare at them all. 'Lennox, dust fingerprint powder on the murder weapon,' he ordered me. Then added, '*please.*'

There wasn't much powder left but I drew out the brush and did the best I could. Swift took a number of loose sheets from the back of his bulging notebook and spread them out. They each had one set of fingerprints on them with names carefully noted at the top of the page.

He pored over the crossbow with his magnifying glass as the room held its breath. I could see one set of prints quite clearly from where I was standing at his shoulder.

'Miss Fairchild touched it,' I told him.

'What on earth for? And how?' he demanded.

I mentioned that I'd bumped into her and that she'd grabbed it before I could stop her. I didn't repeat the rest of the conversation, I didn't want to point any fingers.

Swift muttered something about procedure again and continued to turn the crossbow over.

'Aha,' Swift called out. 'Buggins. Explain how your thumb print is here on the base of the stock.'

I leaned over his shoulder to take a good long look at the print. It was very clearly defined.

We both raised our eyes to stare at Buggins, who stared back.

'You've touched this,' Swift accused him.

'Yes,' Buggins growled, rigid with anger.

'When?' I asked, beginning to think Miss Fairchild really was on to something.

'It was on the wall of the Great Hall,' Buggins replied through gritted teeth. 'Up on the very top floor. I thought it was rather beautiful and took it down to examine it.'

'What were you doing there?' Swift snapped.

'Going to the muniment room. The Laird had given us the key and his permission,' Buggins said. 'Jackson wasn't interested, but we all went.' He indicated Campbell, Dennis and Carruthers, who were staring in silence. 'Including Maxwell,' he added.

'When?' Swift was writing in his notebook.

'The day before yesterday,' Buggins replied with a shrug.

'Then why rub them off?' Swift turned to accuse him.

'I didn't,' Buggins retorted sharply, a deep furrow between dark brows.

'Barclay Huggins, also known as Buggins, I'm arresting you for the murder of William Jackson, today, October the 30th, 1921, at…' he paused to look at his wristwatch 'ten minutes past four. Stand up with your arms extended,' Swift ordered as he tugged his handcuffs from his trench coat pocket.

That caused chaos: everybody jumped to their feet and started shouting at once, including me.

'Where the hell are you proposing to take me?' Buggins shouted over the racket.

'I'm going to lock you in your room,' Swift informed him. 'You will be supplied with logs and food, but you will not be free to roam.' The noise abated as we stopped to listen. 'There are two dead men on this island; they were unlawfully killed. I will not stand by and see a suspect left at large.'

'There is no need for handcuffs,' Buggins said. 'I'll come.' He stood up.

'But you can't,' Campbell told him. 'Swift. You can't lock old Buggins up. Your evidence is nothing but coincidence. We saw him pick it up. He was just admiring it, he wouldn't harm a fly, he's ...' Campbell's face fell and he stuttered to a halt. I could see his dismay and I wasn't surprised: he depended on his old wartime friend, probably even more than he realised.

'It's true, Swift,' Persi told him. 'We all saw him pick it up.'

Swift's face had set hard. 'He lied about having seen it before, touching it, I mean. That's enough for me.'

'Don't worry, old man,' Buggins told Campbell with a pat on the shoulder. 'He'll let me out when they've caught the right fellow.'

Swift snatched up the crossbow, stalked to the door and held it open for Buggins.

'Lennox, come on,' he ordered me.

'No,' I replied.

He glared at me with hawkish eyes for an instant, then looked a touch downcast. 'Very well.' He tightened the belt of his trench coat and followed Buggins out.

Everyone glared at me as if it were my fault, except Dennis, whose strange little face was staring at the door with eyes magnified behind the lenses of his spectacles. I shrugged and exited.

Foggy was pleased to see me, and I him. I ruffled his long ears and patted his gold-fur head, then found a broken biscuit in my top drawer for a treat. The fire was burning merrily; Greggs must have been in recently. I tossed another log on the flames for good measure and went over to my desk and sat down.

The oil lamp was trimmed and lit, throwing a pool of light across my blotter and notebook at the centre. I picked up my pen as Tubbs came to sit on my book. I gave him a quick back rub to make him purr, then dropped him into my pocket for a nap. I leafed through to an empty page and began jotting down events.

There had been quite a few, actually, and it took several pages just to note down the intriguing history of Somerled and his offspring. I wrote the name 'Ivar', followed by a question mark. Then I inscribed the Norse poem from the back of the crucifix and pondered its import, or probable lack of it. Then I wrote 'Jackson', which caused me to halt and stare into space.

Jackson had tried to bribe the staff, he was a reputed thief and very purposely seeking the crown. And the feather more or less confirmed that it was he who'd been searching the old militia buildings. Shame I hadn't been able to find the spooky torch or his tools. I wondered if he had hidden a trowel or spade or something. Or had he stolen some of the tools belonging to the archaeologists? There was a box of them in their cloakroom; it wouldn't be difficult.

Was there one murderer or two? I could understand the murder of Jackson. But why kill Maxwell? Or had someone killed Jackson because he had murdered Max-well? But Jackson had an alibi? But if he did then Buggins may well be the new killer. Although I really couldn't see Buggins as a cold-blooded murderer. Well, maybe I didn't want to, because I liked the chap, but there were only four archaeologists remaining and Dennis had an alibi for the time of Maxwell's death. And I couldn't contemplate Carruthers – which left Campbell or Buggins, or both. And where was the key to Jackson's room? In the loch, probably.

I ran my fingers through my hair. What was the killer after? The crown? The secret treasure? Or were they trying to stop the search because it risked exposing the curse? In which case MacDonald would remain my prime suspect. And he was the Ghillie-mor: he was in charge of weapons and the like. He was almost certainly the one who had maintained that crossbow, and doubtless knew how to use it. And he hadn't even been questioned or finger-printed, no doubt because Swift didn't dare, for fear of the upset it would cause. And Miss Fairchild remained an utter mystery. Did she really have strange powers? Could she actually commune with the dead?

'Tea, sir?'

Greggs came in with a tray and a plate of biscuits. I greeted him with a distracted smile as my mind had fomented a mass of muddled musings.

'That would be most welcome, old chap.' I stood up to stretch and moved to a chair by the fire while my redoubtable old butler pottered about with cups, saucers, a milk jug, teapot and what have you, and finally served a steaming-hot cuppa to me. The biscuits were oatcakes and very tasty too.

'Another body, Greggs.'

'Pardon, sir?' he replied.

'Jackson, he was shot with a crossbow.' I told him.

'Dead, sir?'

'Yes, yes.' I placed my booted feet up on the hearth.

'How unfortunate, sir.'

'Not really, nobody liked him.' I had just bitten into my biscuit when I noticed that Greggs had adopted a forlorn phiz; in fact the hang-doggedness had returned to etch itself more deeply about his face.

'What's the matter, Greggs?' I enquired. 'You look as though you've swallowed a sixpence.'

'I have not, sir,' he replied.

'I didn't mean literally,' I said. 'Just thought you seemed a bit down in the mouth.'

He didn't reply, just went and fidgeted about, straightening items on my desk, a sure sign that he was agitated about something.

'Miss Fairchild?' I guessed.

I could only see his back, but saw his shoulders sag. He returned slowly.

'She read my palm, sir.'

'Ah,' I had deduced correctly. 'And what was the verdict?'

'That I was a person of solitude, sir. And that my lot was perforce a confirmed bachelor. And I think she may have meant that I held little appeal, sir.'

'Nonsense!' I exclaimed. 'What about that lady in Flanders? And France. Actually, you were very nearly caught out in Burgundy between the redhead and that Spanish signorina. And there was the Belgian nurse, and the strange one you rescued in Amiens. And that dancer, Fifi, I think she was called? And they were only during the War, I've almost lost track of...'

'Sir!' he objected, with eyes wide and brows raised. 'I didn't mean, I ... I wasn't aware that you had known such ... such, personal details, sir.'

'Well, I do, Greggs. And people talk, you know.' I waved a biscuit at him. 'You had quite a reputation as a ladies' man. Still do, actually.'

'Really, sir?'

I nodded solemnly.

'Oh.' He paused. 'Will that be all, sir?'

'Yes, thank you, Greggs.'

He bowed and went off with a gleam in his eye and a considerably lighter step.

CHAPTER 19

A sharp rap at the door was followed by the entry of Swift.

'Lennox.' He marched in.

I waited.

'There's something you have to understand about detecting, Lennox,' he said.

I lowered my brows.

'It's not just about hunting for clues and studying evidence, you know. It's about making hard decisions,' he lectured. 'You have to analyse people dispassionately, not according to whether you like them or not.'

'I'm not a policeman, Swift, and neither are you any more,' I reminded him.

'But I was, and I was trained as a detective. And I know that a policeman cannot shirk responsibility.' He remained by the door, his trench coat tightly belted over his kilt.

'He didn't do it,' I replied with some feeling.

'Can you prove that?' he demanded.

'Can you prove otherwise?' I retorted.

'It's the weight of probability,' he began,' and you have to take into account…'

'Oh, for heaven's sake, Swift!' I ran my fingers through my hair. I hate arguments, particularly when I'm probably in the wrong. 'Sit down and have a cup of tea, will you.'

He hesitated, fidgeted with his belt, then came toward the hearth where the fire burned merrily. 'Fine. Right.' He sat down. 'It's trying to snow outside.'

'Really? It isn't even Halloween yet,' I remarked while pouring him a cup of tea still warm from the pot.

'It is tomorrow.' He wrapped cold hands around the cup. 'Although the weather changes so quickly here …' He didn't finish the sentence, just sipped his tea.

I passed him the plate of biscuits.

'Did you tell Florence?' I asked.

He nodded. 'Yes, and the Laird. They were terribly upset by the murder. And they both think I'm wrong about Buggins.'

'Are you going to let him out?'

'No,' he replied.

I let loose a sigh of exasperation and switched tack.

'How's the Laird?' I asked.

'Bit of a headache but fine now. He doesn't recall anything, I asked him again just to be sure.' He replied.

'Good,' I nodded over my tea. 'When does Fundit come with the supply boat?'

'Day after tomorrow,' he told me between bites of biscuit.

'All Saints' Day?' I confirmed.

'Yes, All Saints' Day is the day after Halloween,' he replied sharply.

'Why was Jackson looking down the well?'

'Lennox, you have a grasshopper mind.' Swift narrowed his eyes, then sighed. 'I have no idea. I imagine he was searching for the skull and crown.'

'He said he was fetching water.'

'Yes, I know he did,' Swift retorted.

'Should we go and have a look?' I put my cup and saucer down on the stone hearth and pulled Tubbs from my pocket. He was sleepy and barely opened his eyes while I placed him next to Fogg in the basket at my feet.

'Do you always keep that cat in your pocket?' Swift finished his biscuit.

'Come on.' I made for the door. 'We've got better things to do than discuss the habits of cats.'

He followed me as I trotted down the steps. He was right about the cold: it was freezing, the wind had picked up and we were jostled about in its swirling blast. It was already turning dusk and heavy black clouds hung above the castle walls, casting dark shadows to smother the roofs of the stone buildings. A few yellow lights shone in high windows; the place suddenly felt stark and forbidding.

'You won't find anything,' Swift said as we strode across the courtyard amid flurries of tiny snowflakes whipping across our path.

'Why?' I asked.

'Because it's very deep and I've already looked,' he replied.

I stopped in my tracks. 'Why didn't you say so?'

'Because I may have missed something,' he said, and carried on, his collar turned up about his lean cheeks, hands buried in his pockets, knees red above long socks and black boots striding across the snow-sprinkled cobbles.

'I already looked, too,' I said. 'But ...' We leaned over the well. I shone my torch down into the dark water several feet below us and saw nothing but the beam reflected back.

'Shine the light toward the pipe, Lennox,' Swift shouted above the wind.

'What?'

'The pipe, look, there.' He pointed at a heavy black hose nosing down into the water.

'What is it?' I called back, trying to make it out. Flakes of white snow swirled about inside the wide mouth of the well to melt in the darkness.

'It's the feed for the water pump,' he called.

I spotted it, snaking over the stone wall and down into the water.

Swift shouted, 'Do you remember that it was malfunctioning yesterday? It was caused by an airlock; I had to bleed the pump in the outhouse.' He pointed a thumb toward the pump house near the kitchens. 'I should have checked the feed.'

Green algae hung from the hose as he hauled it out of the water. The end of the pipe came into view; it was fitted with brass hose rings and a filter had been screwed to the end. And there was something white coiled about it. Someone had attached a long piece of fishing line around the filter. I moved closer to Swift's side and leaned further over the wall to focus the torch beam on the hose's end.

He hauled on the line with wet hands, causing ripples to spread across the black water. I heard a clanking sound as something broke the surface and hit a stone. Swift hauled it up, then grabbed it tightly. We both stared as it glistened wet under the flashlight. It was the iron crucifix.

It was exactly as described and precisely matched the pencil rubbing I'd found. Which was to be expected, really.

'Ha!' Swift exclaimed. 'That's what he was doing, the damn scoundrel. He was making sure we wouldn't find it.'

'You can't be sure it was Jackson,' I said through chattering teeth.

'Lennox, don't complicate things. At least we've managed to find something.' He smiled grimly. 'I'm going to lock this up somewhere safe. I'll see you at dinner.'

He went off toward the yellow lamp hanging below the twin towers of the Keep, snow flurries obscuring him as he reached the shadows around the arch. I took one last look at the wide mouth of the well, its black depths stark and rather frightening, and then strode away across the white-sprinkled courtyard.

The darkness moved as I neared the tower steps. The hairs rose on my neck.

'Who's there?' I called into the blast.

I heard a haunting cry that rose to a howl as the wind rounded the corner of the square tower. I peered into the shadows but could see nothing, then looked up. The sky was starless and black; the buildings loomed above me, indistinct in the darkness. Lamplight shone from the narrow window of my room. I headed up the steps as quickly as my boots would take me.

'Will you be dressing for dinner, sir?' Greggs greeted me as I banged the door shut behind me. He was pootling about with this and that as though it were any ordinary evening.

'Um, yes, I suppose so. It's snowing outside, you know, and blowing a gale.'

'Should I fetch the cloak, sir?' he asked with bright eyes. He had perked up considerably.

'Erm, yes, thank you, old chap. I suppose so. Wouldn't mind a snifter, too,' I suggested.

'Certainly, sir.'

I grabbed the kettle from where it was hanging over the fire, forever simmering in the warmth, and took myself off for a quick wash in the icy confines of the dressing room.

Once suitably spruced up and wrapped in my thick dressing gown, I examined the contents of my trunk. Carruthers had been invited to dinner. What should I wear? What would she wear? Surely not trousers — the Laird would be terribly upset. Did she have formal frocks? Was it an occasion for formal frocks? I wagered she'd looked beautiful in a frock, with those long slim legs outlined in silky fabric …

'I said, "Your brandy, sir".' Greggs was talking to my back. I straightened up and forgot about the lid of the trunk, so it fell down shut with a bang.

'Right, right! Erm, put it by the fire, would you?' I was a tad distracted. 'Greggs?'

'Yes, sir?'

'What should I wear this evening?'

He appeared to be trying to stifle a smile, or possibly a sneeze – hard to tell really.

'I'd suggest country formal, not town, sir.'

'Yes, good idea. Very good, Greggs.' I took a sip of the brandy; it was warming in that reassuring way good brandy always is.

I told Greggs about the most recent strange events as he helped me dress. He made all the right noises in reply.

A blizzard met me as I exited my tower and the gale was blowing even harder than before. Fogg had declined to come with me, so I ran alone to the lofty entrance leading into the Great Hall. Natty Brown was on hand to take my cloak and I straightened my togs as he shook snow from the voluminous garment and deposited it in the room under the staircase. I trotted up the broad steps.

The Laird, MacDonald, Miss Fairchild, Lady Florence and Swift were already seated when I arrived; they were all chatting and didn't get up. This wasn't a country-house formal affair, it was a family and friends gathering and I took my seat among them with a cheerful, 'Greetings.'

'Ah, good evening, Heathcliff,' Miss Fairchild replied, and general words of welcome were warmly offered.

The young footman I'd seen that afternoon was in attendance and he handed me a napkin before pouring me a glass of wine. Swift seemed cheerful and my own mood lifted. Despite the incarceration forced upon Buggins, the discovery of the crucifix was a victory of sorts and it had given our haphazard investigation a bit of a fresh spark.

'Another body in the crypt,' Miss Fairchild said.

'Yes, yes,' I replied. I stared at MacDonald, causing him to stare back from under bristling brows. 'I assume it was you who keeps the weapons in order?' I said.

'Ay, laddie. I'm the Ghillie-mor, who else would be doin' it?' He glowered.

'Where were the shot bolts kept?' I persisted.

'Alongside the crossbow, of course,' he snapped back.

I was now being viewed with a great deal less warmth, so thought I'd better change tack. The Laird looked remarkably well, but I was about to ask how he was anyway, when everybody suddenly stopped talking and swivelled in their seats. The men jumped to their feet, then the ladies did the same. A dazzling vision stood in the doorway. She hesitated, a little shy, then straightened her back, held her head high, and with her blonde hair gleaming under the candlelight she glided toward me on long slim legs outlined in smooth cream silk …

CHAPTER 20

The young footman showed Carruthers to the chair next to mine and I moved to help her sit, but he beat me to it. I frowned at him, but he didn't seem to care. Everyone spoke at once. Florence complimented Carruthers on the silk frock that clung to her lovely form. Miss Fairchild smiled sweetly and leaned across to admire the single row of pearls around her slender neck. The Laird's eyes had fixed Persi with a bright gleam and he was trying to engage her in conversation from the other side of Miss Fairchild. In fact everyone was trying to talk to Carruthers except me.

We were seated at the same round table as the previous evening, the fire was blazing in the hearth, silver candlesticks were gathered in the centre of the table next to porcelain dishes. Sparkling crystal glasses filled with rich red wine stood alongside culinary whatnots, and an elaborate salt cellar added to the clutter on the heavily embroidered tablecloth. It was prettily done. Actually, the whole setting was friendly and convivial, and yet here I was struggling to utter a word.

'Nice … urm,' I managed to stutter before MacDonald suddenly boomed out:

'A fine lady ye are, bonnie lass!' He raised a glass to Carruthers, and downed it.

Persi answered as best she could, then Swift leaned in and told everyone about the crucifix and the conversation grew even more animated. I was pleased when the soup arrived and they all shut up. I hesitated with my spoon, waiting for the piper to arrive and strike up a tune, before I realised the young footman was the same chap who had been blowing on the pipes last evening.

'Is he still there?' Persi asked me over cold soup as I offered her a bun on a plate.

'Who?'

'Jackson. Is he still in the chair?'

I glanced at Swift, who was sitting on the other side of Carruthers and taking an interest in the conversation.

'Shhh,' I whispered.

She frowned at me.

'I … I didn't mean … just need to keep it quiet. You're not supposed to have seen him,' I whispered. 'I think they'll move him later. Probably put him in the Kirk with Maxwell.'

'Maxwell loathed him,' she whispered back as she finished spooning potato soup from her bowl.

'Yes, but they're both *dead*,' I replied – which was probably one of the most stupid things I'd ever said to a pretty girl.

She was very close to me, almost touching elbows, and I caught a faint whiff of her perfume. Her blue eyes were clear rimmed with long dark lashes. She had lovely fresh skin, well scrubbed … I assumed she scrubbed it well, anyway. In the bath, probably … with soap and … something like that, not that I was … I wasn't thinking of her like that … not without clothes … well, perhaps …

'What?'

'Are you all right?' she asked. 'You look rather warm.'

I nodded dumbly and ran a finger under my collar.

Florence leaned over and asked again where Persi had found her frock, the answer being Beirut, and they started talking about the Phoenician Empire. I ate my dinner, which was beef and onions with mash and some excellent gravy.

'What did you think of Ivar?' I asked her later as we ate cheese and sliced apples.

Swift frowned at me and I remembered I wasn't supposed to let on about who the skeleton might be.

'Not Ivar, I meant the skeleton,' I corrected.

'Terribly interesting,' Persi said, turning her lovely eyes in my direction. 'But I hardly had any time to inspect it. I think he had some kind of deformity.'

'Oh.' I couldn't think of much to say about that. 'Could you show me?' I asked. 'Tomorrow, possibly?'

'Yes, I'd be delighted. I've been desperate to have a closer look at him, actually.' A light flush brought a glow to her high cheeks; she sipped wine from her glass and watched me over the rim.

'He's a troubled soul.' Miss Fairchild joined the conversation as we were served crumbled shortcake with baked pears and custard. I assumed she meant the skeleton rather than me.

'Do you think so?' Persi replied. 'I've never been sure about ghosts, although I have had some very strange experiences.'

'Show me your hand, dear girl,' Miss Fairchild demanded, and leaned across me to take Persi's hand and peer at her palm. I had to sit back in my chair and watch my custard go cold.

'An interesting life, Miss Carruthers. But...' Miss Fairchild paused 'there is a shadow awaiting you. *Beware*, dear girl. You will cross the far seas to a place of the greatest antiquity. Things are not what they appear and there is much hidden from you. Love is in your grasp, but do not be diverted from your true path.'

She returned to her pudding as Persi stared at her palm for a moment. I raised my brows, and she smiled back.

We had a jolly meal despite the fresh corpses in the castle – although I suppose questions of mortality must have hovered in the back of our collective mind.

We skipped the gentlemen's brandy and instead escorted the ladies to the upper drawing room, where we all made ourselves comfortable around the hearth with heavy rugs on deep sofas, and tartan cushions to bolster our backs.

Florence sipped fruit juice and looked radiant by the fire. Her condition suited her and I noticed how Swift smiled with loving warmth as he sat down next to her. Miss Fairchild had been seated by the Laird. MacDonald took one of the high-backed chairs, I sat Carruthers on another sofa and offered more cushions and a rug and whatnot until she told me to sit down and stop fussing. The young footman, Angus, I discovered he was called, brought us drinks and left the decanter on a tray when the Laird told him he could go.

The wind had grown stronger and I could hear it raging outside the windows. I noticed they were already white with snow as Angus tugged the curtains across the glass before he left for the night.

'The spirit world is tremulous tonight,' Miss Fairchild began, causing an abrupt cessation of the cozy chatter we'd been indulging in. 'They stir as the night of the dead approaches.'

My eyes slid in Persi's direction, she smiled, then focused her attention upon Miss Fairchild. Florence was entranced, MacDonald looked agog and the Laird eyed the lady with a frown of sceptical curiosity. Swift looked irritated. We were grouped within a pool of flickering candlelight before the fire; it was an evening for tales of ghosts and things that go bump in the night, and I settled back to enjoy the diversion.

'Has anyone here seen a spirit?' Miss Fairchild asked.

None of us spoke; the fire crackled and sparked as the wind blew down the chimney. I sipped my whisky, which was the local brew and apt to take one unawares.

'I saw my mother,' I admitted. 'Last night, when you summoned her.'

'Nonsense, laddie,' MacDonald immediately shouted. 'It was *my* mammie. Naught but a wee slip of a lass.' His voice softened. 'Taken too soon an' sufferin' as she went.' He paused to sniff. 'She went on my account and died in the doin'. An a very shame it was.' He buried his nose in his whisky tumbler.

'*I* saw Mother.' Florence spoke to her father across the expanse of the rug. She leaned forward. 'Daddy, I saw her, she was standing before my eyes. Did you ken?' She slipped into a child's idiom.

The Laird leaned forward toward her, love soft in his eyes for his only daughter. 'I did, Flossie. She'll be watching over you, and your bairn.'

'Miss Fairchild...' I dropped a question into the pause 'how do you explain each of us seeing our own mother?'

She smiled. 'Your mothers heard you and came.'

'But where *are* they?' Florence asked.

'Here, but not here,' Miss Fairchild replied. 'They have their own world within our world. They are *around* us.'

'Hum.' I digested her words but failed to make any sense of them.

'If such things exist outside our own imaginations,' Swift replied tersely, 'why are they still here? And you said Maxwell has gone. Where has he gone and why hasn't Florence's mother gone there too?'

'Dear boy,' Miss Fairchild smiled kindly. 'You cannot inspect this world merely with your physical senses. You know that it is our own minds which impel our limbs to act, not the other way around. But an alien being regarding our movements would find us utterly bewildering;

and yet, once the unseen forces of the mind are comprehended, all is understood.'

I can't honestly say that made much sense to me either.

'But,' Swift returned, 'you could apply that to mean that it is all determined by our own minds and therefore we are merely conjuring our imaginations. And you haven't explained where Maxwell went.'

Miss Fairchild's dimple put in an appearance. 'Take a moment to think upon this physical world of ours. We are a planet, there is an atmosphere. This intangible mass of gas acts as a barrier surrounding our world. It's as though we live in a glass bottle: little comes in, little goes out. So everything within this world simply swirls around. It is born, it grows, it dies. The cycle of life. The difference between life and death is not simply the heartbeat, it is the soul, that ineffable spark of life. Just as the alien being cannot observe the mind, so the uninitiated cannot observe the spirits.'

'Are you saying that the soul, or the spirit if you prefer, moves from the dead to the living, or rather the next living being?' I asked.

'Yes,' she said. 'Usually.'

'So Maxwell has been reincarnated.' Swift patently didn't believe it.

'Perhaps you adhere to the Orphic beliefs, Miss Fairchild; but there are many more people in this modern world than existed in the past.' Carruthers raised this point. 'Where have all the souls come from?'

'Who is to say they weren't already here?' Miss Fairchild answered.

That muddled my mind even further and we all fell silent trying to unravel the concept.

'If the soul recycles, as you say,' Swift contended, 'why would any of them be floating about in the ether or wherever?'

'Because they either cannot move on, or do not choose to move on,' she replied succinctly. 'Heathcliff...' she turned to face me 'your mother has remained; she is waiting for the time you reach contentment. Florence...' she looked in her direction 'your dear mother wants to see you happily settled with your baby and your new husband. Inspector Swift...' she regarded him solemnly 'your mother is fearful that you cannot adapt; and Donald...' she looked over at the gruff MacDonald 'your poor young mother fears your actions. You must apply strength,' she said. 'And do not be deceived.'

As she addressed each one of us, we fell silent in deeper thought.

'What of the spirit of the skeleton? And the curse?' Persi asked.

'Death. Death surrounds the dark soul,' Miss Fairchild muttered. She seemed to be slipping into a trance. 'He watches. He has cast his spell, it catches the greedy, the vainglorious, and it amuses him. His secret is a net for fools; he is in the shadows drawing the avaricious with golden threads of fantasy. He indulges in evil, he revels in it.' She broke off and suddenly laughed. 'Inspector, I'm so pleased you are here. Your prosaic practicality is just the antidote we need. As is your erratic mind, Heathcliff.'

We stared at her. Was that an insult or a compliment?

'Well, I believe I must retire to bed.' She turned towards the mesmerised MacDonald. 'Donald, would you be a dear boy and escort me?'

'Ay.' He blinked under brows like thorny thickets. 'Ay, I will that.'

We all stood and each kissed her pillowy cheeks while MacDonald stood to stiff attention in his Highland dress.

Florence returned to her chair and I picked up the whisky decanter and passed it around. I noted that Carruthers took hers straight but slow.

'Sir,' Swift addressed the Laird, 'I may not agree with Miss Fairchild's beliefs, but on one point I concur wholeheartedly.' He paused. 'The curse. It is a secret that is impeding our investigations, and it is allowing the perpetrator a cloak of secrecy. He's using superstition to divert attention and now there are two people dead. I must ask you most solemnly, sir, to divulge what you know.'

He received a scowl in reply.

'Daddy,' Florence leaned toward her father, 'please tell them. I believe it will help their investigation.'

Swift's head spun towards his wife. 'You *know* the curse?' His face fell on the instant. 'You've always known and you didn't even tell me that you knew?'

'Darling ...' Her voice broke as she spoke. 'Jonathan, I couldn't. Not without permission. I hope you'll understand. Please, darling, don't be angry.' She watched him with pleading eyes, her hand on his arm as his face betrayed his hurt.

'But …' Swift stuttered to a halt, the hawkish look extinguished. 'But, you're my wife. I didn't think we had any secrets …'

Persi instinctively put a hand out in sympathy toward Swift, and I gently reached out to take it, and kept it. She glanced at me and I shook my head. Husbands and wives need to come to their own understanding without outside intervention.

'Sir.' I now took up the baton. 'We need to know the secret of the curse. I can assure you it will not go beyond this room.' I fixed my eyes steadily upon him.

He stared back. The Laird was a decisive man, used to command, unhindered by doubt; he weighed the balance between the ancient fears of the veiled past and the certainty of the present danger. He nodded at last. 'Very well.'

CHAPTER 21

I took the decanter and topped up the Laird's glass, then poured another for Swift. Carruthers declined, so I had an extra-large one.

Swift threw a few logs onto the fire and we sat quietly, waiting.

'I heard you say his name: Ivar. That isn't a name I've heard spoken on this island for many a long year.' The Laird's voice rumbled and I could hear the Scottish burr creep into his speech. 'So you know it's not Black Dougal in the wall. Have you heard the story of Somerled?' He glanced around as we all nodded. 'Then you'll know he was the father of Dougal and Donald and the clans. And you'll know the story of the Norse and the Gaels.' He paused for a sip of whisky. 'Somerled was murdered. Ivar was the base-born son of Godred and a dabbler in black magic; some called him a *draiodoir*, which you English might call a wizard. He was feared because of that, not because he had any fighting skills.' The Laird's lips suddenly curled in contempt. 'Ivar slaughtered Somerled as he slept. The snivelling coward didn't even have the guts to face him, he dirked him in the back.' He sighed slowly, then continued. 'Then he fled in his longboat as fast as his men could row. They were murderers, every one of them. Ravagers of women, drunken thieves, filthy parasites who fed off the carnage of war.' He fell silent in thought for a moment, then continued. 'All was chaos: Somerled's sons escaped with the remnants of the Gaelic army and put to sea. Godred's Norsemen were waiting for them, waiting to destroy them and remove the Gael once and for all from the Western Isles. For days they fought bloody battles until a storm came and scattered the ships on the wind and tide. The storm cast Ivar here upon our shore, and his band of murderers with him. This was the home of Fergus Braeburn, father to our clan. He was also Ghillie-mor to Somerled himself and he was riven with shame that he had failed to protect his master.' The Laird fell silent for a moment, his eyes dark. Then he continued.

'The castle was a simple place, nothing more than the high wall, the Gatehouse-Keep, the Kirk and some wooden shacks for shelter. There were no warriors here when Ivar arrived — the warriors were away battling the Norse and the storm at sea. There were only old men and young boys, and women and children. Ivar and his men slaughtered every one of them.'

The Laird downed his drink and we sat sombre amidst the candlelight listening to the tale, our minds conjuring the hell within these walls. Blood running between the cobbles of the courtyard, the screams of the dying, the anguish of those who watched their loved ones killed. The sobs of those who awaited their fate. The Laird poured himself another dram and took up the story again.

'When the storm's rage abated, Dougal and Donald and the Ghillie-mor, Fergus himself, returned to Braeburn looking for respite. But there was to be no respite because they found Ivar and his cut-throats surrounded by corpses. There were stores of food and drink here and the Norsemen had gorged on it. Dougal, Donald and Fergus put them to the sword. Their rage knew no bounds, they killed every last man of them until only Ivar was left alive. He ran to the Kirk and claimed sanctuary, but Dougal would have none of it: he dragged him out by the hair into the courtyard as Ivar screamed "Sanctuary!", calling him "Black" for abusing the Christian God's succour. Donald helped him and Fergus joined in. It was a mortal sin and they all knew it, but they did it anyway.'

The Laird sighed a long sigh, then continued.

'There were bodies in the well and they threw Ivar in with them. As Ivar was near to death in the bloodied water, he was tossed down a rope. Three times Ivar climbed up to the top of the well and three times they dropped him back down again. Then they dragged him out and he stood before them, and still he was full of arrogance. He had been wearing the crown when they found him in the Kirk, but they had snatched it from his head and now he demanded it back, saying he had won it by right. It was his father, Godred's crown, and now it was his. Fergus Braeburn had claimed the right of execution and he crammed the crown down on Ivar's head and raised his sword to anoint him with death.'

The Laird paused to gaze into the depths of the fire in the hearth. A blast of wind blew down the chimney, causing flames to blaze up, and smoke swirled about the red-hot logs heaped in the black ashes. I gently squeezed Persi's hand; she looked up at me with troubled eyes. The Laird took a drink, and went on.

'As the sword was poised, Ivar shouted out "Treasure!". He told them he had taken Somerled's treasure and hidden it on the island, the crown was proof of it. But it was hidden by magic and could only be raised by magic – *his* magic. He would barter his life for the treasure.' The Laird paused again, his face grim. 'He was wasting his breath. Somerled's sons weren't going to exchange the worthless life of their father's heathen murderer for mere gold and nor was Fergus Braeburn. Fergus once more raised his sword to remove Ivar's head. It was then that Ivar screamed out the curse. *"By the power of the unborn, I curse you Braeburn. Cleave my head from my body, and doom will fall upon this place. Not a soul will survive, not a stone will stand. Hear my curse for you are damned to eternity."*

'Fergus lowered his sword, for he was a superstitious man and Ivar was a reputed *draiodoir*. And he was an *unborn*, and it was well known that the unborn had dark powers that could summon death.' The Laird's voice dropped on the last words, then fell silent.

The clock ticked in the corner and the logs crackled. Swift broke the tension.

'What did he mean by "unborn son"?' Swift asked.

'Ivar was an unborn son.' The Laird answered. 'His mother died in childbirth and they cut her open to save the child. It was not unknown, nor is it uncommon even now. But in those days it was thought to confer special powers on the child.'

'But why did they wall Ivar up?' Carruthers asked.

'Fergus had become fearful, and so they debated the task. It was his castle that was cursed, and his people,' the Laird replied. 'Dougal was the oldest and was now King after his father's death, although in name only. He cut out Ivar's tongue to put an end to his black magic and told Fergus that he should kill Ivar, but Fergus was afraid of the curse and decided to bury him. He built a wall in front of Ivar while he was still breathing.'

The Laird fell quiet, then resumed the story.

'After Ivar was walled up, the men made ready to leave the island. They couldn't stay, the well was poisoned with the dead and there was no fresh water. Fergus pulled as many bodies out as he could and interred them under the Kirk. There's a carving of an angel above the altar in their memory. It's said there were over a dozen children among them.'

Florence pulled a handkerchief from her pocket and wiped her eyes. Swift tried to help, though I could see that he, too, was affected. I took out my own hankie and offered it to Persi. She accepted it with muffled thanks.

The Laird waited as we settled down before continuing. 'The island was abandoned and many years passed before Fergus Braeburn returned. He began rebuilding the castle, but first he poured mortar over Ivar's mortal remains. As long as the head remained on the body there was nothing to fear from the curse. And Ivar was set in stone for all time, and the crown with him.'

'May I ask why the skeleton is assumed to be Black Dougal, even by your own people?' Persi asked tentatively.

The Laird regarded her with a dark expression in his eyes, then gave his answer. 'Dougal berated Fergus for his superstitions and said he should have killed Ivar and damn the curse. He called him a fool and refused to take Fergus as his Ghillie-mor, even though it was his rightful place. It was a grievous insult and a public humiliation. It drove a deep rift between our clans and the name of Black Dougal engrained itself into our history. Over time the legend of the curse became mixed up with the feud and it suited us to leave it so.'

So it was a retort to the humiliation Dougal had inflicted on the Braeburn clan, I thought to myself, but didn't say so.

The Laird downed the rest of his drink. 'That's the tale of the curse. I doubt the story will help you, nor do I want it bandied about. We may not be fearful of old words nowadays, but we are respectful of the Clan secret, even if it is no more than a terrible story. The past is dead; I'll thank you to leave it that way.'

'And the treasure?' I asked.

'They'd have considered the treasure cursed too, although searches have been made at different times by different Lairds. Likely it was no more than a filthy lie. Make no mention of it, laddie, or we'll see more grasping gold-seekers arriving on our shores.'

He stood up and bowed to us, a handsome man in his Highland dress, and then he left, the wind rushing in as he pulled open the door and closed it quietly behind him. Swift put his arm around Florence's shoulders and pulled her to him for a moment, then led her out. They called goodnight as they went. Persi Carruthers and I were left alone.

'A dreadful tale,' I said. 'I'm sorry to have involved you.' We were standing in front of the fire, gazing into each other's eyes.

'I was surprised the Laird allowed me to remain,' she said, 'and yes, it was terrible, but so are many events from history. Mankind is murderous, we all know that.'

There was something about her: serene, beguiling and deeply sensuous. I was entranced and I bent to kiss her parted lips. The door blew open with a bang and a rush of cold air.

'Ye're still here, then?' MacDonald came in with an armful of logs. 'I've come to set the fire for the night.'

Persi and I had jumped apart. I could have hit the man. Persi pushed a strand of gold blonde hair behind her ears as she looked at her feet. 'We were just leaving,' I replied, and went to open the door for the lady. 'Erm, do you have a cloak, Miss Carruthers? Or may I lend you mine?' I offered in an attempt to rescue the mood.

'It's downstairs, I gave it to Natty Brown.' She walked

ahead of me, and I must say she moved sinuously: her dress flowed with her lithe body, causing a ripple of silk right down to the hem at her slim ankles. Her shoes were pretty, like ballet pumps — how on earth was she going to cross the courtyard in *them*? I could offer to carry her, I thought, and smiled.

'It's in here.' She pushed open the door under the stairs and came out holding a dark blue cloak with a hood. I helped drape it around her shoulders.

'Wait!' she turned and came out clutching a dreadful pair of heavy black boots, dropped them to the floor and deftly stepped into them, still wearing the ballet pumps.

'Cinderella *shall* go to the ball,' I remarked.

She laughed, I smiled, then I slipped my arms inside the cloak to catch her gently by the waist and pull her towards me.

'Ye're still here, then?' Natty Brown called out. He too clutched logs. 'Fire needs to be kept burnin'.' He nodded toward the huge hearth in the hall.

'Right,' I said, cursing under my breath. I went into the boot room and yanked out the voluminous black cape Greggs had insisted I wear. I donned it as Persi raised the hood of her own cloak to cover her head. Despite the boots, she looked divine; I looked like a mobile tent. I decided I would await the right moment outside the door to the Armoury, whither I escorted her, clutching her arm tightly, as we were buffeted by wind and stinging particles of ice.

She paused on the snow-covered doorstep of the building and once again gazed up at me.

'Oh, there you are! Persi, come and help.' Campbell walked out of the darkness behind us, also laden with logs. 'Can't have Buggins catching his death of cold, I'm going to pass these under his door. Look, I found some small ones.' He held out some weedy pieces of wood and turned to me. 'Couldn't open the door, could you, old chap?'

I swore under my breath, Persi laughed lightly, I opened the door and the pair of them were gone.

CHAPTER 22

Greggs had retired to bed: I could hear him snoring as I passed his door. Foggy greeted me with an ecstatic yelp as I entered, I gave his ears a good ruffle and he pranced about on hind legs, tail wagging furiously. Tubbs yawned and stared at me with wide eyes. The fire had been banked up, the curtains drawn and my bed turned down; it was warm and cosy and gave a lift to my exasperated spirit.

There was a bottle of Braeburn whisky on my desk; it was down to the last eighth, I noticed. Pouring myself a glass, I opened my notebook, filled my pen from the ceramic ink-pot, blotted the nib and paused above the thick pages still curling at the edges. Now that I was alone and less distracted by the bewitching Carruthers, I could better consider the strange tales told that evening. The whisky helped; I poured another glass.

Miss Fairchild's beliefs were interesting but hardly relevant to the murder hunt. Or were they? I pondered this a while, then shook my head. The curse, on the other hand, was far more serious. Not because I feared being slaughtered at the hand of the 'unborn', but because I'd heard that phrase muttered before. And it was Donald MacDonald who had said it. Why did *he* know the curse? He wasn't family, not blood family, anyway. Then again, the Laird had just told us … so it would be reasonable to assume he'd told MacDonald. And I could understand why such a superstitious man was so fearful of the curse. Jackson had 'cleaved the head from the body' and so let the curse loose. But I wondered if the curse meant more to MacDonald because, from what I understood, he himself was an 'unborn son'? How or why would it make him turn to murder? I couldn't think of an answer to that, but one thing I was absolutely certain of was that it wasn't Buggins. I sighed, because that thought brought me back to the treasure. '*Raised by magic*'? That didn't make any sense, although it confirmed that the treasure could have existed and that it was Ivar's remains in the wall. In fact it seemed to confirm some of the theories Campbell and Buggins had concocted. Rather a shame it was all bound in secrecy by a centuries-old curse. Actually, I didn't really understand why it was still a secret, but then, I wasn't a clansman steeped in clan history, so why would I?

I downed another tot of the smooth Scotch and inscribed the stories as they'd been told, then blotted off my efforts. I decided on one more dram before bed, polished it off, and the bottle, actually, then retired to bed to drop into a deep sleep.

Something jerked me awake. The fire had burned down and I could barely make out shapes in the shadows by the feeble glow of the ashes. Foggy was growling softly. There were footsteps in the distance: faint, as though falling on stone. What the devil was someone doing creeping about at this time of night? It wasn't Greggs: I could hear him snoring below. The footsteps dwindled and fell silent; I strained my ears trying to make them out, then fell back on the pillow. Then I heard them again. It made the hairs rise on the back of my neck. My mind was fuzzy with whisky, but suddenly it clicked into gear — the noise could be the murderer searching for the skull and crown.

I tossed aside the covers and nearly retreated back under them as the cold hit me. But the footsteps were quite clear, they echoed on the wooden floorboards of the room upstairs. I tugged my torch from under my pillow and switched it on. I shone it at the ceiling, which didn't help so I stood up and pulled on my dressing gown. My slippers were nowhere to be found so I shoved my bare feet into my boots. They were cold and wet, my boots, that is, so now my feet were, too. I made for the door still listening to the footsteps above. The torch went out. Damn it! I went back and lit a candle from the remains of the fire. Where were the batteries? Should I call Greggs? No, he was sound asleep and he'd think I was an idiot. The batteries were probably in the trunk. A noise made me whip round, causing the candle to blow out. Foggy's growls became louder from his hideout under the bed. The footsteps stopped. I looked up, which was pointless for many reasons. I waited, nothing happened, and then they started again. Cursing myself for a fool, I fumbled about in the trunk and dug out the damn batteries. The torch lit up and I breathed a sigh of relief. *Right*: whoever was making that noise was going to get a piece of my mind, and then be locked up. I slammed the door open and it hit the wall with a crash, then I bounded upstairs to the next floor, my boots thudding as I went.

It was glacially cold and draughty, with bare stone walls glistening with damp. I tried the door — it was locked. I hesitated. It wasn't that I hadn't rushed into dangerous situations before, but my senses were jangling on full alert. I pulled myself together and felt above the dusty lintel for the key, slotted it into the lock, turned it deftly, and kicked the door open.

Nothing happened.

The room was empty apart from cobwebs blowing in the breeze from a broken window. I ran the flashlight across wooden floorboards smothered in a thick layer of dust. Not a solitary footstep had disturbed it. That was unexpected. I took an involuntary step backwards, then ran the torch-beam around the walls. They were standard castle walls, solid and thick. There was no other doorway than the one in which I stood. I flicked the beam upwards to see bare rafters holding up dark roof slates. There was no one here, nor had there been for a very long time.

The hairs rose once again on my neck as I shone the torch around one last time. Somewhere in the distance I thought I heard a strange screech; it was far away, but it ended as a distinct cackle of laughter. I looked around again, then gave up and returned to my dog. I coaxed him out from under the bed, gave him a cuddle, pulled the eiderdown over Tubbs, him and me, and tried to sleep.

The smell of frying bacon woke me next morning. Bright sunshine shone through the window, lightly glazed with frosty crystals of ice. Snow was piled white outside against the bottom of the pane. It hurt my eyes, and my head, which ached. Greggs came in with a tray of fried everything, including bread soaked in dripping. He must have opened the curtains earlier in an effort to wake me up. I noticed that he'd placed the empty whisky bottle in the middle of the window sill, where it sent refracted rays of pale gold about the room.

'Will you be rising, sir? Or remaining in bed?' Greggs asked, making it sound as though I were some idle loafer.

'I'll eat by the fire,' I told him as I donned my dressing gown and found my slippers in the dust beneath the bed. The place was rather a mess actually: my boots lay in a heap in the middle of the floor, the trunk was open with the contents strewn about, and an expired candle lay on the rug. Greggs must already have seen the disarray, as he now stepped deliberately around it to put the tray on the table by the hearth, and then ostentatiously proceeded to tidy up.

'It wasn't intentional, Greggs,' I said as he began folding my shirts.

I sat down to tuck into my favourite meal of the day. Fogg came to sit and stare at me with pleading eyes, so I gave him a slice of sausage. Tubbs had decided to remain curled up in bed.

'Didn't happen to hear anything last night, did you?'

'I did not, sir. I sleep very soundly, as you know.'

'Hum,' I mumbled through a mouthful of fried egg. Greggs slept soundly on account of being deaf. I eyed my little dog: he had wet feet and was dripping onto the rug; Greggs must have let him out while I slept — which put me firmly in the doghouse. 'Well, there were strange noises in the night, so I got up to investigate, that's why I was tired and the place is rather a shambles.'

'And these noises were in the trunk, sir?' He was straightening out my tweed jackets now.

'No, of course not, Greggs. Ghosts don't lurk about in people's trunks.'

'Ghosts?' he turned to stare at me with raised brows.

I paused with a forkful of bacon halfway to my lips. 'Well, probably not *ghosts*. It was footsteps, and screaming.'

Greggs's brows shot further toward his receded hairline.

'But far away,' I added hastily. 'Very far away. Nothing to worry about, Greggs. One of the staff playing games, probably.'

He turned a lighter shade of pale. 'When did you say the boat is arriving, sir?'

'Erm…' I tossed a scrap of black pudding in Fogg's direction and swallowed the last of my tasty breakfast 'tomorrow, I think. Probably. Depends on the weather, really. Anyway, must get on, Greggs. You can take the tray while I scrub up.' I put it in his hands and he hovered for a moment and then went off, bemused.

I had the skeleton in my sights – well, it was Persi, actually. I was seriously miffed that my attempts to kiss her last night had been constantly interrupted, and was very keen to see her again. Not that I would kiss her in broad daylight, of course, but we might at least be able to come to an understanding. If she was amenable, that was. But what if she *wasn't*? What if …? I tied my mind in knots while I donned a fresh shirt, clean trousers, socks and the usual whatnots. I carefully brushed my wayward hair, pulled on my shooting jacket, instructed the little duo to remain by the fire in the warmth, and set off.

It was cold, it was freezing, actually; my breath formed white clouds as I stood on the snow-covered doorstep and clapped my hands. I set off to crunch through the icy crust covering the courtyard. Icicles hung from roof-tops, frost sparkled over dark grey slates under a crisp blue sky, the sun shone and all felt well with the world. Admittedly, there were a couple of corpses in the Kirk, and I was now apparently being haunted, not to mention the missing skull and the creepy curse; but apart from all that, it felt marvellous to be out in the fresh air.

I trotted up the Armoury steps and rapped on the door of Persephone, my Goddess of all things sensational.

'Hello!' She answered fully dressed in the usual archae-ologists garb and holding a hairbrush in her hand.

She looked stunning … her eyes, and hair and … My mouth opened, but nothing came out. I stuttered a bit and finally forced a strangled, 'Greetings, old stick.'

'I have my tools,' she said.

'What?'

'For the skeleton,' she smiled. 'Won't be a moment.' She closed the door again.

Hum. I stared at the scarred oak boards, but that didn't achieve much so I wandered along the corridor. Maybe I should have brought some flowers? Actually, there weren't any. Perhaps some logs, everybody seemed to be wandering about with armfuls of logs.

There was a window at the end of the corridor, glazed with ice. I went back to Persi's door, lifted a hand to knock, thought about it, then wandered off again. Buggins was in the other room; I could hear voices; he was talking to Campbell, who must have delivered his breakfast. There was a faint clacking noise coming from above; that would be Dennis, tapping away on his typewriter. He was very fast; must have taken a course in it. I'd had a bash at typing once; it was more complicated than it looked. He would be alone up there now – the occupants of the other two rooms were dead. If it were me, I'd have been demanding a different billet. I went back to the window, but spun around as a door opened. It was Campbell with an empty dish of what looked like porridge.

'Breakfast for Buggins.' He raised a half-grin as he locked the door with a large iron key and placed it on top of the lintel.

'Thought he was supposed to be incarcerated?' I asked.

'He is.' Campbell pushed his fair hair away from his forehead. 'Swift came by, he's relented on the terms. Said he's putting him on Scouts' honour to stay behind the door. Not sure why we bother locking it, really, Buggins won't break his promise.'

'Hum,' I murmured.

'Well, toodle pip, old chap,' Campbell called as he returned to his own billet in the next room.

'Ready,' came the call. I turned around: Persi awaited.

I offered my arm and we trotted off together. I'm not sure that many first dates include a skeleton, but I can't say I minded – at least he was dead.

Neither Swift nor Florence were at home when we called in through the doorway of the Keep. Ellie, the cook's granddaughter, was there and told us 'Do as ye whist'. Apparently, Swift and Florence were at breakfast with the Laird.

It was sunny and bright in Swift's library, the window placed at exactly the right angle to gain the morning sun. I tugged the tartan rug from across the opening in the wall and stood back to let Persi enter first.

'It's rather strange to see him again, isn't it.' She hadn't moved, just stood and regarded the white bones of the headless skeleton.

'Knowing the history? Yes, it is. And that he was alive when they walled him up,' I replied.

'He deserved it,' she said, and stepped across the jagged stones forming the threshold. She pulled out a slim chisel and hammer as she approached the mortal remains of Ivar. 'I think we'll need a lamp,' she suggested.

I went and fetched a storm lantern from Swift's desk,

lit it and joined her. It was quite a tight fit with two of us in such a small, cavern-like space. I regarded her from a very short distance; she didn't seem conscious of the proximity; her concentration was entirely focused on the skeleton.

'Would you hold it a little higher, please?'

'What?' I said.

'The lamp.'

'Oh, erm, yes, of course.'

She chipped mortar away from around the bones at the skeleton's wrist. It crumbled away easily under the chisel.

'I had assumed he was already dead when they put him in here because I couldn't find any evidence of constraints, but there's so much lime in this mortar it must have dissolved whatever he'd been tied up with,' Persi said whilst stooping to chisel the mortar with small but expertly placed hammer blows. It fell away in powdery chunks. 'Oh, look,' she bent down further and pointed. 'See that hollow? That's where the rope had been before it disintegrated. It's left a mould in the mortar.'

I looked. It wasn't very interesting.

She chipped away some more and kept on chipping. She uncovered a rusted iron ring on a skewer that had been driven into the wall behind the skeleton. She found that terribly exciting.

'They drove this into the back wall and tied him to it,' she told me. She stood back to survey the bones; the light of the lamp caught golden strands in her hair and made them gleam. 'Oh, Lennox, can you see this!' She moved closer to the skeleton's right shoulder and indicated the bone with the tip of her chisel.

'Um …' I replied.

'Well, if you follow the line of his shoulder to the neck…' she ran her fingers over the collarbone 'you can see that it's deformed. I thought there was something odd about him. He would have had a twisted neck.'

I peered at it. Part of the spine was still hidden within the mortar but I could see where it emerged and would have joined the skull.

'He'd have held his head at an angle, a bit like Quasimodo,' Persi said. 'Perhaps he lay crooked in the womb and that's why his poor mother died trying to give birth to him.' She chipped a bit more at the top of the spine. 'And look, another mould. He was tied by the neck, too.'

'Hum.' I was more interested in the hollow caused by the missing skull: it formed a concave void, and I reached up and felt the smooth surface of the mortar. A shiver ran down my back as I thought about how it had been formed. 'What did you make of the crown?' I asked.

'Difficult to say, without being able to examine it properly. I only had a brief glimpse before Jackson grabbed it. The Laird was very angry and made him hand it back.'

I watched her as she examined the mortar where the crown had been.

'Did you know Jackson before he joined the expedition here?'

She took a brush from her top pocket and began gently

brushing the mortar. 'No, although I knew his reputation. I was in the Lebanon last year with a team from Oxford.' She turned to smile at me, then went back to the brushing. 'We were uncovering a Phoenician necropolis, it was utterly fascinating, simply tons of bodies and plenty of grave goods. Anyway, Jackson turned up and started offering money to anyone who wanted to sell artefacts. The team banned him from setting foot on the site, but I heard later that he had three or four crate-loads of goods shipped out from the local port, so he must have purchased the antiquities somehow.' She stopped brushing and turned to look at me. 'He was nothing but a well-connected thief. We despised him.'

I gazed into her eyes, then pulled myself together. 'What happened the day you all went to the records office? The day Maxwell was murdered?'

She lowered her eyes and sighed. 'I do wish you hadn't locked Buggins up, you know. It has made it more difficult for me to help you.'

'What do you mean?'

'Well, Lennox.' She looked away, then back again. 'We didn't tell the whole truth. When we arrived in the town, we split up. Dennis, Maxwell, Campbell and I went to the library and records office, but Buggins and Jackson went to the procurator fiscal's office. I promised not to say anything, but ...' She hesitated. 'But I think in the circumstances, you should know.'

'Why did they go to the procurator's office?' I asked sharply.

She took a deep breath. 'To legally register the crown. It's important enough to be designated as treasure trove, and Jackson wanted to make sure it was recorded. I don't know the law terribly well, but he called it *bona vacantia*. Jackson knew all the legal loop holes, he was very clever like that.'

'Why would Buggins agree to such a thing?' I asked, trying not to snap. 'He's denying the Laird his legal rights over his own property and he knew Jackson would find a way to filch it, he told me so himself. I thought Buggins was a decent man,' I replied with rising anger.

Persi hesitated. 'He's trying to save the team. He and Campbell are at their wits end. Nobody will give them funds because of their reputation. They've gone out on a limb about the murder of Somerled and not a soul agrees with them. They are laughed at, actually. If they can't prove what they say, they'll lose everything and they love their work, it's their life. I don't know what they'd do without it.'

I stifled a curse. I hadn't thought Buggins or Campbell were deceitful types and it came as a nasty surprise. 'What did Jackson know about the treasure?' I asked.

'Nothing. And it was imperative he didn't find out,' she replied. 'Buggins thought that as soon as Jackson got his hands on the crown he would leave. Go back to New York, probably.' Her eyes were troubled as she looked up at me.

'Leaving the coast clear for Buggins and Campbell to search for the treasure themselves,' I mooted.

'Yes, assuming it could be found,' she said slowly. 'I thought it was a bit of a dream, really. Campbell believed it implicitly, but then he's like that. Whereas Buggins is far more pragmatic – but I suppose he thought it was worth one last desperate try.' She shrugged. 'Although … well, it's just such a remote possibility. And then the crown was stolen and …'

'And the boat was burned,' I added.

'Exactly. And it all turned rather horrible. Especially for poor Maxwell.'

'If there's only a remote chance of finding the treasure, is it really worth killing for?' I asked.

She turned her eyes to gaze steadily up at me. 'It would have great monetary value, but it's the context rather than the treasure. It's Leif Erikson and Vinland. It may not seem much to you, but for some archaeologists and American museums it's like the Holy Grail. It would cause a sensation if someone could actually prove America was discovered hundreds of years before Columbus. It would be headline news. It's far more important than finding Somerled's killer, that's just a footnote in Highland history; but Vinland? That would shine the spotlight of the world upon anyone who found the evidence.'

'And of course vindicate Buggins and Campbell's theory,' I said, 'not to mention cover them in glory.'

She turned back to the spot she'd been carefully brushing, dug her fingers into the crumbling mortar and extracted something. She dropped it into my palm. I peered down at it, then turned it over in my fingers. When I raised it to the light, it shone in sparkling facets of deep blue. It was a sapphire the size of a sparrow's egg.

CHAPTER 23

'It must have been part of the crown and got dislodged by the mortar,' she told me, staring at the jewel in the lamplight.

I rubbed it between thumb and forefinger, knocking off the grains of mortar still sticking to it. 'Were there any others?' I asked.

'There was a ruby on the front, a large one. You should have seen Jackson's face when he saw it. He was mesmerised.'

'And no doubt weighing up its value,' I replied. 'Here,' I held it out to her.

She shook her head. 'No, it's not mine. I don't keep the items I discover, that's not what archaeology is about.'

'Fine. The Laird should have it – until the actual crown turns up, and then it will all have to be taken away.'

'Lennox.' Persi placed a hand on my chest. She was very close and gazed up at me with blue eyes shining in the lamplight. 'Don't be angry. Campbell and Buggins have their backs against the wall. Whatever they did or said, they would not have been able to stop Jackson taking the crown. And the Braeburns will be properly compensated. Anyone who discovers artefacts is always rewarded.'

'And if Campbell and Buggins should discover the treasure, how will they be rewarded?' I retorted.

'Only by enhancing their reputation and proving their theory,' Persi replied calmly. 'There is a world of difference between archaeologists and treasure hunters. We seek knowledge and we sign pledges to promise we will neither receive nor take any reward, other than the honour of discovery.'

My anger still simmered but I was listening to her, she was too entrancing not to. 'How well do you know them, Persi? You said you were in the Lebanon last year, so you haven't been a member of their team for very long.'

She suddenly laughed. 'I'm not a member of the team. They called me in because of my specialisation in old bones. But I've known them for years, they were both students of my father's before the War and we'd already virtually adopted Campbell. He was orphaned very young and left at boarding school most of the time. My parents took him on digs during the holidays. He became fascinated by the Highlands and the Somerled story; it's an obsession with him now.'

'What about Buggins? Is he obsessed too?' I asked, staring, quite fascinated, at her eyes.

'Not really; not to the same degree, anyway. Lennox, they're like my big brothers, I love them and I know that neither of them would murder anybody for anything.'

'But they went through the War, Persi, just as I did. It changed people. We were all killers, we had no choice,' I argued.

'Killing during war and cold-blooded murder are two entirely different things. They were in Intelligence – Campbell was captured and tortured, you know. They nearly killed him. He pretends he was injured by a bomb, but he's never been the same since.' She took a deep breath. 'Would *you* murder? Truly, Lennox, would you?'

'No, Persi. No, I wouldn't.' I sighed and looked into her face. Something was troubling her. 'Something else happened, didn't it?'

She looked down again, her breath coming a little too fast. 'Maxwell told Jackson.' She held up her hand as I opened my mouth to question her. 'We don't know when he told him, not exactly, but I'd say it was on the way back from the records office.' She reached out and took one of my hands. 'He didn't confront us straightaway. I suppose with Maxwell being killed there wasn't much chance. But there was a terrific row yesterday afternoon after Buggins and Campbell returned from lunch with you and Swift. I heard it: Jackson was waiting for them in Buggins's room and he almost exploded in fury. He said they'd never work again and he would destroy their reputations once and for all. It was terrible.'

'So that was why he was so angry yesterday morning when Swift and I interviewed you all? He was waiting to take his rage out on them,' I said and sighed in exasperation. 'But this changes everything, Persi. And you're saying this happened just before Jackson was killed?' I questioned.

She nodded, then looked into my eyes. 'About an hour before you found him. Once they'd finished shouting, the boys went back to their rooms. They were cut up about the whole situation. But they didn't do it. I swear to you, Lennox.'

'So why are you telling me about it now?' I demanded.

'I've been awake most of the night trying to decide what to do. But I think you have to know.' I could smell her scent, see the smooth outline of her lips. 'You can't find the real murderer unless you know the truth,' her voice dropping as she stared up at me.

I put my arms around her slim waist and pulled her toward me. I was just about to …

'Lennox! What on earth are you doing?' Swift shouted from the opening.

I swore under my breath and let my hands drop.

'Investigating, Swift … What do you think we're doing?' I retorted.

'Hum.' He sounded dubious. 'Well, we're supposed to be going into the ruins today, I hope you haven't forgotten.'

I let Persi step out of the cavity first. She pushed her hair back from her face, then pocketed her tools as she joined Swift and gave him a dazzling smile, which softened him up.

'Good morning, Miss Carruthers.' He remembered

his manners and made a slight bow, then frowned at me. 'Did you find anything?'

I held out my hand, he extended his palm and I dropped the sapphire into it. 'Persi found this in the wall, it must have been dislodged from the back of the crown,' I told him. He stared at the stone, turning it over in his fingers.

'Sapphires were believed to have magical powers to protect against poison,' Persi told him. 'They were very rare; it would have probably come from ancient Persia and been traded along the coastal routes.'

'She said there was a ruby in the crown, too,' I mentioned.

'Yes, I know, Lennox, I found it,' Swift retorted as he tucked the gem into the slit pocket of his black Highland jacket. 'Thank you, Miss Carruthers, I'll ensure it is kept safe. Actually, my wife was hoping to see you, she was talking about a knitting pattern or some such thing. For the baby, you know.' His voice softened as he turned the subject.

'Oh, yes,' Persi laughed. 'I'm afraid I don't know much about babies, but my mother insisted I learn to knit — she said it taught patience and dexterity. I'll go and find her. Bye-bye.' She went off with a brief wave of her hand. My eyes followed her out of the room.

Swift was wearing his trench coat over his kilt and Scots garb. 'Ready?' he asked.

'Shortly,' I replied. 'Need to walk my dog.' I turned and left, no doubt to his irritation, but he'd have to wait. I wanted some quiet time to think.

Despite the cold and snow, Foggy was delighted to gambol about in the fresh air. The chickens were absent and we ambled out of the gateway and toward the trees. I halted at the old shack on the shore where the snow spread in a soft layer on the roof, glistening in the bright sunshine. The door was open, with a pile of sea-washed slush beside it.

'Ay, 'tis yourself and the wee doggie.' Natty Brown emerged with a length of rope and greeted Fogg and me.

'Indeed, it is. Greetings, old chap.' I regarded the rope. 'I thought this shed belonged to MacDonald.'

'It belongs to the Laird, laddie, as does everythin' else on this isle,' Brown replied as he expertly coiled the line. 'Fundit will be comin' with the boat on the noon tide tomorrow, an' we're needin' to be ready for him.'

'Right-o,' I nodded, 'jolly good.' I left him to it, my mind distracted by the morning's revelations.

Swift would have to know about registering the crown as treasure trove, and about the row with Jackson. He'd probably want to lock Campbell up now, too.

Maxwell must have sold Jackson the information on the treasure and that gave both Buggins and Campbell the motive to kill Maxwell and Jackson. Although they didn't know what Maxwell had done until after he was killed … Or perhaps they did? My shoulders drooped as I walked.

Foggy spotted a squirrel, its chestnut fur gleaming against the pristine snow, and he set off at a gallop. The squirrel clambered to the top of the gnarled pine before the dog reached the trunk and he ran in circles barking, long ears flapping. I couldn't help but smile; gloomy thoughts were hard to sustain in such soul-stirring surroundings. My weaving passage knocked ice crystals from fragrant pine needles, sending tiny particles to sparkle in the sun. I breathed in air sharp with spruce and snow and tangy sea salt.

I stepped onto the large rock at the island's end to gaze out to sea. It was almost flat calm, with a single sailing boat on the far horizon where the mountains of Mull lay pale blue with white caps. On the opposite shore the mainland was lined with spiky pines decorated with a frosting of snow. Winter wasn't far away.

I turned back to the castle with its high walls and deep secrets. Dark clouds had formed above the Keep — another storm was brewing and it wouldn't be long before the sun was swallowed by shadows. I lengthened my stride, only just gaining the arched gateway as the first hailstones began to fall.

'Tea, sir?' Greggs asked as I blew in.

'That would be very welcome, old chap,' I replied. Foggy had acquired a sprinkling of ice, so I dried him off with his blanket. He settled into the basket by the fire with Tubbs as Greggs returned with a tray of tea and whatnots, plus Swift hard on his heels.

'I brought a lamp for you.' Swift held two lighted storm lamps and gave one to me. I placed it on the hearth. 'Come on,' the Inspector said.

'Not yet,' I replied. 'Sit down, Swift.'

He didn't. He fidgeted on the other side of the blazing fire. He was dressed as before in trench coat, kilt and sporran. No doubt he had a torch, magnifying glass and various detecting paraphernalia about his person.

'Have some tea, Swift,' I told him as Greggs poured each of us a cup.

'No, Lennox, we must get on. Stop prevaricating,' he snapped.

'Need to tell you something,' I replied, 'sit down and learn some damn patience, will you.'

He finally sat down, perching on the edge of a chair. I told him what Persi had said about Jackson and Buggins registering the crown at the procurator's office and the row just before Jackson's murder.

As predicted Swift was furious and jumped up determined to go and interrogate the remaining archaeologists.

'Stop being so damn hasty,' I argued with him. 'And sit down, will you.'

'They *lied*. First of all they colluded with Jackson to let him claim the crown and they kept the treasure a secret from him, and then when he finds out about it, he's murdered a short time later,' he shouted. 'It's unconscionable. Damn it, how could they lie to us like that? There are two corpses in the Kirk,' he continued. 'Who's next? Miss Carruthers? Florence? One of us? The Laird? Are you willing to take the risk?'

That made me stop and think, but then I shook my head. 'Evidence, Swift. Or lack of it, it's all circumstantial. There's nothing concrete to implicate Campbell.'

He opened his mouth to quarrel but I cut him short and said, 'Look, let's stick to facts. And tell me what this *bona vacantia* law is about?'

Swift sat back down on the edge of his seat, obviously rattled and snapped. 'It means "unclaimed goods". Or "abandoned chattels". It applies to items that don't have any known owner so they devolve to the British Crown.'

'Is that it? The authorities just requisition them?' I remarked. 'Seems a bit precipitous.'

'There's an inquest or an assessment made. Jackson wouldn't have been able to just walk off with the crown, he'd have had to go through the legal procedures. But as registered finder of treasure trove he would have right of first refusal to *buy* the crown.'

'So that's how he gets his hand on treasures?' I replied, understanding the tactic now.

'In Britain, yes,' Swift said. 'I don't know about other countries.' He stood up again and yanked the belt of his trench coat tighter. 'Come on. And bring the lantern.'

He really was quite irritating and there was so much to think about. For instance did the *bona vacantia* principle apply if the Laird knew who had put the crown there? On the other hand, that was a secret …

'Lennox!' Swift snapped.

'Yes, I'm coming.'

I left Greggs in charge and we set off in the direction of the ruins. The weather had taken a dramatic turn for the worse: a mass of roiling clouds hung heavy above the island, pouring a mix of hail and snow on top of the layer already smothering the courtyard. We loped across the frozen cobbles, our shoulders hunched, barely able to see for the blizzard. We entered the dark doorway of the gin-gang and paused to shake snow from our hair.

It was deathly quiet inside but at least I wasn't being blinded by hail. The place was dark; shadows gathered in every corner and the cold numbed my face. It felt a world away from the warmth of the room we had just left.

'Where was the owl?' I asked Swift, thinking of the feather we'd found under Jackson.

'Beyond the old Smithy and stores,' he replied, lantern held above his head. 'Be careful, the older buildings have earth floors, it will be slippery with mud.' He led the way, placing his boots carefully among the debris.

I held my lamp up as we made our way slowly through the labyrinth of rooms. I shone the bright yellow light up along rotted roof joists and down crumbling stone walls, some of them tumbled into the mud. Snow had fallen through holes in roofs, adding to the bone-chilling cold. Roots, broken branches, dead leaves, stones, slates and rat droppings lay in mounds and we wove our way around them and sometimes clambered over them. We squelched and slipped and now and then fell and cursed. If anyone was lurking, they would have plenty of warning of our approach.

Swift halted in the middle of a building.

'The owl flew out from here,' he said, swinging the lantern around for a better view.

I flashed my lamp upwards too and saw the remains of

a nest on top of a ragged wall where the roof beams jutted into the stonework.

'Doesn't seem to be much here,' I remarked, and turned my attention to the floor. 'Swift,' I called. 'Look: footprints.' I moved towards another doorway on the far side and shone light onto the glistening black mud. 'See.'

Heavy boots had stamped a trail leading deeper into the ruins. There was only one set, and we knew it hadn't been made by our earlier incursion because we hadn't come this far.

'Come on,' Swift said, and set off, head and lantern held low.

'Ow! Damn it.' I had walked into a half fallen rafter.

'Can't you go quietly?' Swift hissed at me.

'What for?' I retorted, rubbing my brow.

'Just in case someone's down here.'

'Don't be ridiculous, Swift, who would be stupid enough to be down here in this weather?'

'Us,' came the tart riposte.

There wasn't much I could say to that, but I muttered under my breath anyway.

'*What was that?*' Swift stopped suddenly and I almost walked into him.

'What was what?'

'Thought I saw a light. Be quiet a minute.' He stood stiffly still.

We didn't move; our breath blew white in the lamplit dark.

And then I saw it: a faint glow that flared briefly, then

was gone. There was a noise, nothing more than the spilling of small stones, but I heard it.

Swift stepped forward, waving me to follow.

We saw the flicker of light again through a narrow gap between broken stones; it was pale and indistinct, and resembled neither candle nor lantern.

We quickened our pace. I caught another glimpse when it paused to hover briefly on a skein of grey cobwebs — the light was in the shape of a skull! My heart skipped a beat, but I told myself to get a grip. It was just a painted skull on a torch, it must be, we'd already deduced that. Swift had halted too when he saw it, and then he started to run toward it.

'Stop where you are,' he yelled. 'Police!'

That didn't seem to impress them. The light moved rapidly in the other direction, deeper into the maze. We followed at speed, our breath coming quickly, cold damp air filling our lungs, our lamps flailing in our hands, boots pounding as we raced forward.

Suddenly the beam stopped still, and then it went out. We skidded to a halt.

'Damn it, he's turned it off,' I swore through sharp breaths. We stood stock-still, chests heaving for air, listening for our prey, eyes straining into the darkness around us, trying to detect movement.

Suddenly another light appeared. It was further away but we could see the glow reflecting off stones glittering with damp. The light flickered and we ran through a maze of small rooms, then careered into a larger space.

There it was, in an alcove on the other side of the chamber: it was the skull itself, the skull of Ivar! And it wore the golden crown. It was placed on a flat stone like an altar, and it had a single candle burning at its side. We darted forward. There was a mound of rubble ahead and we both leaped across the heap. We landed in the alcove on the rubble-strewn floor, and fell into a chasm of blackness that opened beneath our feet.

CHAPTER 24

Blood ran into my eye. I raised a hand to wipe it off, but that was bloodied too. I was lying on my back, head angled on a pile of debris, my wits knocked out of me along with my breath. What the hell had happened?

'Swift?' I called out, my voice croaking.

No reply. I threw a hand out to reach for him, but he was neither to my right nor to my left. Then I lay still, too sore to move. I couldn't see anything, it was pitch dark, our lamps had smashed in the fall and there was not a glimmer of light. I moved to peer upwards and it sent my head spinning. There should at least be a gleam from the opening we had fallen through, but there was nothing. The darkness was so black it was almost physical, and it felt suffocating.

'Swift?' I tried again. I thought I could hear him breathing. I listened – maybe it was, or maybe it was the distant sea, waves beating against the shore. Or perhaps it was my addled brain.

'Swift?'

'Lennox?' A hoarse whisper echoed back.

'Where are you?'

'Here.'

'Where the devil is here?'

I leaned in the direction of his voice and reached further out. My hand was cut and becoming numb with the cold. My fingers touched a slim stick and I picked it up on a reflex, before dropping it again. I turned over, and groaned. Damn it, I was sore, and bruised, and bleeding. I swore again, then crawled over to where I thought Swift must be.

'Ow!'

'Sorry.' I must have hit his head. He was bleeding too. I wiped my hand on my sleeve, and then some of the fog cleared from my brain and I fumbled in my pocket for my torch. It lit up with a brilliant beam of blessed light. I could have laughed, or cried, but I groaned and rubbed my eyes.

Swift was lying in a tangle of coat, kilt and boots on a pile of rubble. It must have fallen as we did because there was scattered debris around us on a thick floor of oozing black mud.

'Are you in one piece?' I asked.

'I think so.' He turned over and dragged himself up to a sitting position. 'It was a trap.'

'Yes.' And we'd fallen into it like a couple of idiots.

I ran the beam around me and saw the lamps. Red blood had been splashed on the smashed glass. I peered at my hand, which was filthy, but the blood had stopped dripping from the gash in my palm. The mud we were lying in was deep and foul but it had probably cushioned our fall and saved our lives.

'Lennox.'

'What?'

'I think we're in an oubliette.'

'A what?'

'Dungeon,' he snapped, sounding more like his old self. 'Except unlike a dungeon, there's no way out. It's French for "forgotten". Prisoners get tossed down into an underground cavern and the trap door is shut above them. Then they die, eventually.'

I picked up the stick again and shone the torch on it. It was an arm bone, a human one. I threw it as far as I could. He was right about the cavern bit: I shone the beam at the walls, which were rough-hewn stone. We were in a cave. I aimed the beam upwards into the blackness; the top was a long way above our heads, fifteen feet or more. Right above us was a wooden door. I could barely make it out, but it must be the trap door. The killer had opened it, disguised it with branches and rubble, and had closed it after we'd jumped into it. I swore I would kill him when I got my hands on him. If I ever did …

'Lennox.' Swift shuffled closer. 'Good God, this mud stinks.'

'Hum,' I muttered. My throat felt harsh, 'you're plastered in the stuff.'

'We have to get out.'

'Yes…How?'

He groaned. 'Wait a minute, I have a torch, too.'

'No, save it,' I warned. 'We don't know how long we'll need the light.' My heart suddenly felt cold; I couldn't contemplate being trapped down here in the blackness: it would feel like being buried alive.

'They'll find us,' Swift said. He crawled over to me and rested his back against mine. 'Might take a while, though.'

'Do they know where this place is?' I asked.

I felt him shrug.

'I've no idea. I didn't know it existed, I've only read about them in history books.'

'There are bones.' I shone the torch on the tibia I'd thrown against a wall. There were others gleaming white in the mud and a heap of them on a pile of stones to our right. I didn't want to dwell on the nature of their deaths.

'It wasn't the crown,' I said.

'What do you mean, Lennox?'

'No ruby. I realised, just as we started to fall: there was no ruby in it.'

'Damn it,' he swore. 'Damn it. Probably just foil and card on an old skull. There are plenty of them in the crypt.'

We lapsed into silence and contemplated our stupidity.

'He must have a plan of the castle,' I said.

'The killer? Yes, or seen one, anyway. But there's no complete plan held at Braeburn,' Swift replied. 'I've studied them, from the oldest to the new. This area is shaded and marked as the old militia buildings. There are no details.'

'The records office? Do you think the killer found it there?'

'Possibly, I don't know, I've never been. It may even have come from a museum somewhere.'

'Or it could be someone who lives in the castle and knows it like the backs of their hand,' I suggested.

Swift shut up.

'We need to find a way out or we'll freeze to death in here. Can you move?' He tried to climb to his feet and slipped in the mud. 'Damn it!' He tried again, his hand on my shoulder. Then he helped me haul myself to my feet. We leaned against each other, bloodied and bruised and with nasty bangs on our heads.

I nearly sat down again.

'They'll follow our footsteps.' I brightened up.

'If the murderer doesn't cover them up, along with his own,' Swift replied dryly.

My shoulders sagged again, then I straightened up.

'Right, come on.' I shone the torch into the blackest corner and advanced. We didn't get very far, but we found another skeleton, or the tangled bones of one, anyway. He grinned at us from a fleshless skull on top of his ribcage.

'We should follow the wall,' Swift said.

It wasn't a round cave, more the shape of a wonky bee-hive with cracks and crevices splitting off. We explored one such dark passage, which dripped with water and green slime. The mud was even deeper and caught our boots up to our ankles. It petered out in a dead end. We retreated slowly, the cold numbing our muscles, bones and minds.

'Got to keep going, Lennox.' Swift put a hand on my shoulder and caught his breath. 'Think I might have cracked a rib.' He bent over, then straightened up.

'We can rest,' I said.

'No. No. I'll be fine.'

'Let's try down here,' I shone the beam into another ragged route in the rocks; water streamed down its grey and black surface, running over the hard contours in rivulets and dripping from outcrops into the mire under our feet. The opening was high, starting from a 'v'-shaped cleft, then dropping rapidly to half a man's height as we stepped inside. I squatted down and shone the flashlight into the space beyond.

'Looks like another cave,' I said, and crawled in.

We couldn't stand up so we kept crawling for what seemed like a long way. Then it opened up and I climbed to my feet.

'It's a tunnel, made by water by the looks of it.' Swift ran a hand down smooth rock, very different from the jagged stones of the larger cave.

A scrabbling noise made us spin around and then look up; a slick brown tail disappeared into a slit in the cave wall above us.

'Rat,' Swift snapped. 'I hate rats.'

'But it's alive,' I said. 'It must have a way of getting in and out or it would be dead by now.'

That buoyed us up and I tried not to think of the fact that rats could use holes far too small for humans to wriggle through.

255

Blackness lay further ahead and we extended our steps to follow the tunnel, and then stopped. A wall of stone met us, and the wall was man-made.

We frowned at it as I ran the beam over the roughly formed stones. Water seeped out of every joint, the old mortar was sodden; the rivulets ran into the mud beneath and formed pools of slime and water.

'It's the well,' Swift stated. 'They must have plugged it up to make the well. My God, it's centuries old.'

'That explains the smooth rock in the tunnel,' I said.

I was examining the wall higher up by standing on a pile formed of surplus stones left over from the building work.

'It's over ten feet high before it joins the natural rock,' I called.

Swift stared upwards where my torchlight was concentrated. 'They made the well by plugging it.' He sounded excited. 'It's the old burn. *Brae burn.* Brae means hill and burn means stream. The rainwater must have collected on the hilltop and run down into this hollow, and they blocked it off to collect the water. The island would only be habitable with fresh water, you see.' He turned to look at me, eyes bright with enthusiasm in a muddied, bloodied face. 'They probably did it in the dead of summer when it ran dry.'

'Yes, fascinating, Swift,' I didn't want to dampen his ardour but we had slightly more pressing matters to attend to. 'And how does that help?'

'Hum.' His mouth turned down. 'Well, if someone worked down here, there may be another way out, or in.'

'Right, yes. Look, there's something up there.' I moved the torch beam. 'It's just a shadow, but it might be something.' I started to climb the pile of loose stones. 'Give me a push up, will you?'

'No, I'll go,' Swift insisted.

'You're wearing a kilt.' I gave him a wry eye, 'I'm not pushing *you* up over my head.'

'Ah,' he replied. 'Right, well you can stand on my shoulders, but don't dislodge the stone wall whatever you do. There are tons of water on the other side of it.'

'That had already occurred to me, thank you.'

The stones were loosely piled and a few tumbled down as I clambered higher. The opening narrowed the further up I went and I was able to force my back onto one side of the crevice and my feet on the other to leave the stone pile behind. With my torch between my teeth I edged upwards, then fumbled above my head for the cause of the shadow. It was a space; I couldn't feel the size of it from where I was standing below, but I grabbed an outcrop and swung up letting my feet scramble in thin air. For a moment I dangled in great discomfort, then hauled myself up, feet kicking out for a toehold. I heaved, knocked against a piece of rock, and dropped the damn torch.

'Are you all right?' Swift had picked it up as it clattered by his feet.

I scrambled into the hollow and lay panting for a moment on the rough floor. A rat ran over my outstretched hand. I swore.

'Are you sure you're all right, Lennox?'

'Yes,' I shouted out. 'But I can't see a damn thing.' I sat up, feeling my way around. Then I stood up, the ceiling of the cave just above my head. I heard scrabbling ahead of me. More than one rat, then. 'Wait there.'

It was the same awful inky blackness as in the oubliette and I almost felt nauseous for a moment with claustrophobia. I stumbled, my arms flailing ahead of me, then banged my head again. Crawling seemed the better option. I could hear Swift calling out, but not his words; the tunnel went on ahead but it was going downhill, not up. Now there was scrambling behind me.

I returned to the opening.

'Help me up,' Swift called. He was standing on the pile of stones.

I lay flat out and dropped my arm as far over the edge as possible. He grasped my hand and I pulled — nearly yanked my blasted arm from its socket, but we made it.

'Didn't see any point being down there and you up here without a light,' he gasped.

I didn't say a word, I couldn't. I could hardly breathe.

'It's going downhill,' I finally managed. 'And there are more rats.'

We manoeuvred slowly into a sitting position and rested for a few minutes. The cold wasn't quite as intense in here but it was still taking its toll. The exertion had helped to get the blood moving but it had also drained our reserves.

'Come on,' I said at last, and crawled forward, the torch once more in my hand.

The passage narrowed. It, too, was smoothed by water and must have been another outflow from the hollow where the well was formed. We crawled along on hands and knees praying it wouldn't close up into a mere slit in the rocks. A turn in the tunnel took us further down still, but I suddenly heard a muffled crashing sound … it was the sea. Somewhere ahead of us lay the shore. More minutes passed and my knees began to bleed, but they were so frozen I could barely feel it. Then a light, faint but clear; and I could taste a mixture of snow and salt. I managed to get my feet beneath me and stumbled forward, then stood up. It was a grotto. The walls were layered with bright white frost clinging to the cave walls in spiky crystals, and there was a frozen pool at my feet. It was like the opening to the realm of an ice queen. Except that it wasn't – I knew where we were: we were in the jumble of gorse-covered rocks near the far end of the island.

CHAPTER 25

It was bright in the grotto, or bright in comparison to the Stygian depths we'd just emerged from. Swift struggled into the cavern and let out a long deep sigh of relief.

I looked at him and laughed, my voice echoing back down the tunnel. He was as filthy as a mudlark, with pale flesh showing in streaks where he'd rubbed his hands across his face.

He raised his brows, which I found even funnier, so he frowned, and then a grin spread across his face. 'Lennox, you look like you've just bathed in the peat bogs.'

I slapped him on the shoulder.

'Come on, old chap,' I said. 'Let's get out of this hole, there's someone out there I want to beat the living daylights out of.'

'Not if I get to him first,' Swift replied. He looked up and around. 'We're in the gorse bushes, aren't we?'

'And under a mound of snow by the looks of it,' I replied. 'Where's your dirk?'

'I'll do it.' He drew his knife from the sheath bound to his calf in the Scottish tradition and reached toward the only gap in the rocks that appeared large enough for us to squeeze through. He couldn't quite reach. 'Here.' He handed the knife to me.

I thrust it upwards with my hand and shoved it all the way through the frozen snow. It left a fist-sized hole that let the wind blast in, then a heap of snow fell on top of me and I fell on my backside under it.

Swift burst out laughing.

'Very amusing.' I wiped my face and rubbed my hair, I'm not sure if it improved the mud plastering me or not.

Climbing back to my feet, we both surveyed the opening I'd made. A face suddenly appeared and stared down at us, then barked.

'Fogg!' I yelled. 'Foggy.'

He yelped and would have fallen down on top of us had someone not grabbed hold of him.

'What are ye doin' in there, ye daft beggars?' MacDonald peered down at us.

'You're a sight for sore eyes, MacDonald.' I called up.

'We're trying to get out,' Swift shouted up. 'Can you help?'

'Ay, I can that,' MacDonald replied.

We could hear sounds of furious digging and chopping and more voices, one of them belonging to the Laird.

'Jonathan,' the Laird called as MacDonald hacked away with an axe to clear the thorny branches of gorse. 'Florence has been frantic, and so has Miss Carruthers – we all were. Where on earth have you been?'

MacDonald slid a rope down the gap, with a noose tied at the end. 'Put yer foot in there and we'll haul ye up.'

'Go ahead,' I told Swift.

He placed a boot in the loop and was quickly pulled upwards; he had to squirm and twist to escape the narrow opening but there were hands to help and he disappeared quickly. The rope was dropped again immediately and I went up the same way. I sat on the snow-covered rocks in the fresh air and picked up my ecstatic little hound and gave him the biggest fuss he'd ever had.

We tramped back to the castle through fresh snow. The storm had abated but had left deep drifts under the trees and piled up against the castle walls. They plied us with anxious questions about what happened and I let Swift relate the details as we trudged through the snow.

'There were footsteps, Jonathan,' the Laird told us when we'd run out of answers. I was behind them, moving slowly with Foggy in my arms.

'Where?' Swift asked.

'From the castle. We followed them, didn't we Donald?'

'Ay, that we did.' MacDonald agreed. 'And yon wee doggie did, too, but he was actin' strange. Had his tail down.'

'The footsteps went to the grotto?' I asked, not really following what they were saying.

'Ay,' MacDonald answered, 'there an' back again.'

We were approaching the Keep and I stopped in my tracks. The men turned toward me.

'I think you need to put a guard on the grotto, sir,' I told him. 'Until dark at least.'

'Why?' Swift demanded.

'You believe it to be the killer?' the Laird asked.

I lifted a filthy hand and ran it through my matted hair. 'Yes, I do think it was the killer, and if he was down by the grotto he would have had a damn good reason for it.'

'I'll see to it, Major,' the Laird replied. 'And it's not a grotto, incidentally, it's the old well.'

Swift and I were too weary to take in the import of that remark, and we parted at that point. I told them I'd join them later.

I staggered into my room with Fogg under my arm and placed him gently in his basket, whence Tubbs stared up at us both.

Greggs appeared.

'Sir! You have caused an alarm. There have been search parties and activity, sir. I must ask, where have you been?' His old face was lined with worry. 'And you are *very dirty*, sir.'

'Long story, old chap.' I sighed. 'Don't happen to have any hot water to hand, do you?'

The kettle over the fire was steaming as usual and he brought the washbasin from the icy dressing room and filled it. I kicked off my boots and plunged my feet, socks and all, into the warm water.

'I am aware of the whereabouts of a *bath*, sir.'

'What?'

'Downstairs; a tin bath. I will have it fetched.' He left

as he spoke. I was about to tell him not to bother but suddenly the idea of a bath sounded like heaven.

He returned a short while later with young Angus the footman, who wrestled in an old-fashioned hip-bath. Half an hour later I was sitting in it before the fire, steam rising from my body with my legs extended over the edge because they were far too long to fit in it. I had a tumbler of whisky in one hand, a pork pie in the other and the undivided attention of my cat and dog.

There was a brief rap on the door.

'Come in,' I called.

Carruthers stepped into the room and nearly dropped the box of biscuits she was carrying. I grabbed a towel.

'Sorry, sorry,' we both gabbled at once.

She blushed, a delightful flush that spread across her high cheekbones.

'I just wanted to drop this in and to see if you were recovering. I'll... erm, I'll see you at dinner. Or drinks,' she stammered. Then she laughed. 'I'm so pleased to see you again. Florence and I were dreadfully worried.'

'I survived intact, thank you.' I replied. 'I can show you if you like,' I teased.

'No, no.' She put a hand over her eyes in mock horror, laughing as she did.

'Sir!' Greggs exclaimed. He halted in the doorway, his brows up in his hairline.

'I'm going, I'm going!' Carruthers spun around, thrust the box into Greggs's hands and dashed off.

'*Sir* ...' he said again in his most admonishing tone.

'Oh give it up, Greggs, I didn't mean it. I wouldn't dream of doing such a thing,' I lied. 'Couldn't pour me another drink, could you, old chap?'

He did, and then he sat down and I told him all about Swift's and my adventures in the ruins.

'If you managed to escape, sir,' he asked, 'why didn't the deceased?'

'Those skeletons, you mean?' I replied. 'I suppose they wouldn't have had any light. Without the torch light we'd never have spotted the opening.'

'Ah, yes, sir.' He nodded.

'Who raised the alarm?' I asked. 'And put Foggy on the trail?'

'Miss Fairchild requested the search an hour after you set out, sir. She said you and the Inspector were in the doom where the lost dead lay, but that you'd return again with our help.'

'Really? She is a most mystifying woman,' I remarked.

'But most insightful, sir. It is the greatest of good fortune that you brought the lady, although I thought it peculiar at the time.'

'Greggs, I did not *bring* her.'

'As you say, sir.'

I shook my head in defeat. 'Then what happened?'

'The Laird and Mr MacDonald and Mr Brown the factotum began a search of the ruins, sir. I attended in my outdoor wear. We took lanterns and spread throughout the buildings, calling as we went. There was no sign that you had even been there, but Mr Fogg ran about with his nose to the ground and we knew you must have passed through.'

'There were no footprints in the mud?'

'None, sir.'

'Hum.' I wasn't surprised, but I was filled with fury at the ease with which we had been tricked and left for dead. 'And I assume Fogg led you outside the castle eventually?'

'He did, sir, he must have heard you below ground. I was sent to inform the ladies that you had been discovered while you were helped to safety. Mr Fogg has very sharp ears, sir.' The old chap bent to ruffle the little dog's fur, then drew a treat from his pocket and gave it to Fogg. I had no idea Greggs kept treats about his person – but then he was a constant surprise.

'Do you know the culprit responsible, sir?'

'I do not, Greggs; not yet, anyway.' I finished my food and drained my glass. 'I'd better be getting some togs on, old chap.'

'Very well. I will leave you to dress, sir.' With that he went off to do whatever he did when I wasn't around.

I didn't get out of the bath, it was too comfortable and I was a mass of bruises. Any movement was going to hurt, so I decided to stay where I was. I leaned forward and grabbed the kettle on its iron hook to swing it toward me, and upended it in the water. The act of leaning back in the enveloping warmth, my feet extending toward the blazing fire, almost banished the horrors of the adventurous afternoon. I glanced idly at the mechanics of the roasting-spit above the kettle. There was a long black chain hanging from its end and it swung gently like a pendulum. I watched it, mesmerised. There was something niggling in my mind, and my thoughts drifted to the loop on the rope. And suddenly I realised how it had been done. It was so damn easy, as easy as laying the trap; as easy as shooting Jackson and killing Maxwell.

'Eureka!' I thought, although I wasn't going to jump out of my bath and run off naked to proclaim my enlightenment. Instead I remained soaking for some time longer, unravelling the murderer's machinations in my mind.

I dressed in fresh clean clothes. Everything hurt but I was keen to see Swift and tell him my conclusions. We had to prepare for the evening; it was Halloween and I was going to present one particular person with a very nasty surprise indeed.

I called Foggy to join me. He was the hero of the hour and deserved to be feted as such. It had stopped snowing and the wind had died away with the storm. It was rather beautiful actually: dusk was falling and the windows were ablaze, throwing yellow rectangles across the soft white drifts piled against panes. I put Fogg under my arm and set off across the blanketed courtyard, crunching unblemished snow beneath my boots, and called into the doorway of the Keep. 'Up the stairs,' I was told to go by Ellie, the cook's granddaughter.

Swift and Florence were in their drawing room. It was a cosy delight of candles in sconces, a merry blaze in the fireplace, curtains drawn against the cold, chintzy cushions, deep wing chairs, soft sofas, and signs of a woman's touch in every direction. I settled with a contented sigh on a chair in front of the hearth while Florence made a huge fuss of Foggy.

'How are you, Lennox?' she asked.

'Fine,' I replied. I watched Swift go to the sideboard to pour a dram for me. I nodded in his direction. 'How's Swift?'

'Bruised, with a few gashes,' Florence told me while ruffling Fogg's ears. 'He was dreadfully angry about the subterfuge that was played on you both.' She wore a tartan dress today the colour of heather and juniper, her pale-blonde hair caught in a headband; she looked divinely lovely. 'Are you any nearer catching this killer? It really is quite frightening, Heathcliff.'

'Um, *Lennox*, old thing; and yes, I have an idea I'd like to discuss with your husband.'

'What?' Swift thrust a tumbler of amber liquid into my hand and sat next to his wife and Foggy on the sofa. 'It was Campbell, had to be. Or he let Buggins out and I put him on his honour, you know.'

I sighed. This was going to be a long night.

He argued, I argued. Florence listened and tried to calm us both down.

'We need to examine them, Lennox,' Swift said.

I nodded glumly. I really hadn't wanted to go there.

I told Fogg to stay with Florence; he was quite comfortable on the sofa and didn't demur.

Swift and I strode to the little Kirk together to visit the dead.

It was a small building and as cold as the tombs it pro-
tected. I switched on my torch as Swift raised his lantern,
he seemed to have an endless supply of lamps, which I
suppose was understandable given the nature of island
life. We advanced into the unlit interior, and I admit I'd
had quite enough of cold, dark places, but this one held
a stark charm. It was very narrow and not terribly lofty,
only a storey and a half high. It had been adorned with
carvings, a rare occurrence in this island's military bas-
tion, and there were oak pews with tapestry kneelers and
cushions. On the stone walls plaques had been mounted
bearing the names of the dead. I aimed my beam at one,
which bore the date 1538 to the memory of Lady Mary,
the beloved wife of the one of the old Lairds.

Swift lit candles ranged on the altar; adding the scent
of melted beeswax to the smell of cloistered dampness
and something indefinable and rather earthy. I paused in
front of the altar to say a quiet word to the man upstairs
and take a glance at the angel carved in memory of Ivar's
victims, all those centuries ago. They had long memories
in this corner of the world.

I followed Swift to where he was quietly waiting beside
a door in the far corner.

The smell of sodden stone and something far worst
rose to meet us as we wound down the stone steps. Swift
was in his Highland best and I'd donned tidy togs with
the intention of impressing the lovely Carruthers. I hoped
we weren't about to mire ourselves in muck again.

The corpses lay on neighbouring tombs in the centre

of the crypt. There were alcoves built into the walls and shrouded in cobwebs and shadows that slid darkly aside as we passed by in the light of Swift's lantern. I caught a glimpse of rotting casks and coffins, a few white bones visible through gaps in the wood.

'He's been down here,' Swift said as he stopped to raise his lamp and gaze around.

'Yes,' I agreed. 'He came to fetch a skull for his trick with the fake crown.'

Our words fell loud into the darkness, echoing beyond the edge of our lamplight.

'How big is this place?' I asked.

'I'm not sure,' Swift replied with a tone of doubt. 'I haven't explored it. It may just be the size of the Kirk's floor space, or it might be bigger. I don't know.'

We arrived at the body of Maxwell and I shone my torch over his length. I would have preferred not to look him in the face, but aimed my beam there nonetheless. He'd turned a rather dreadful shade of grey with over-tones of green. He had been laid out neatly with his arms crossed over his chest and his wrists tied together to keep them in place. His broken legs were lined up to give a semblance of decent order.

Swift came and held his lamp high.

'Go ahead,' Swift said.

'Could *you* …?' I asked.

'Lennox, you're not turning squeamish, are you?' He looked at me from below dark brows, his face in the pool of lamplight. 'Oh, very well.'

He deftly unbuckled Maxwell's leather belt and slipped it from under the body, barely disturbing it. I was quietly impressed, actually.

'Where's Jackson's wallet?' I asked.

'In his pocket,' Swift replied. 'Just a minute.'

A noise in the dark sounded behind us. We both swung around and I shone my torch among the tombs built into the walls, but saw nothing other than mouldering decay.

Swift returned his attention to Jackson. The hairs were standing on end along the length of my spine. Death had shrunk Jackson's lean cheeks into cadaverous hollows; he too had been arranged in tidy order, although someone had tied his hands either side of the bloody crossbow bolt protruding from his chest.

It took only a matter of moments for Swift to slip a hand beneath the corpse's coat and extract the wallet.

'Why did you leave it on the body?' I asked.

'Because it belonged to him,' he replied, which didn't make any sense at all.

Something moved behind us. I pivoted on my heels, flashing my torch every which way.

'Lennox, will you stop jumping at every damn shadow,' Swift snapped.

'Fine. It's probably just rats.'

That made him stop and turn around. 'Right, come on,' he said, and made for the stairs. I followed with a backward look and a warm desire to leave the place to the dead.

CHAPTER 26

'Right, we need to assemble the evidence.' Swift stated as we once more settled into the Keep's drawing room with Florence and Fogg.

'Do you have everything now?' I asked.

He had laid the belt and wallet on the low table before the fire; we had examined it and confirmed our suspicions. Which I was rather pleased about because I'd had enough adventures in the dark.

Swift opened his notebook and flicked through to a list he'd made. 'Feather,' he began, and found the owl's feather pressed between two pages. He gave it to Florence to place on the table. 'Just a minute, I'll fetch the rest.'

He went out and returned with a wooden box while I poured another dram.

'Here's the fishing line.' He handed it to me and I placed it on the table. 'The crucifix, the pencil rubbing, Maxwell's hip flask, batch of statements, and the crossbow,' he recounted, lifting each item from the box and passing it over. 'Oh, and there's this.' He pulled the sapphire from his jacket pocket and added it to the collection. 'I forgot about it in all the excitement.'

We regarded the pieces of evidence on the plain oak table.

'There doesn't seem to be very much there, darling,' Florence remarked.

'Enough to send a man to the gallows,' he said coolly. 'Come along, dear wife.'

I put the items back in the box. The hook dangled from the fishing line and caught the crucifix, clinging to it. It hadn't hooked it: it had been attracted to it by magnetism. I tugged it off. It struck me as rather strange.

We had sent instructions to MacDonald to arrange the evening. We would assemble in the drawing room before dinner, drinks would be served and all the archaeologists were to attend, including Buggins, who was to be escorted by MacDonald himself. I had told Greggs to come, too. (He demurred of course, but I insisted.) Naturally, Miss Fairchild and the Laird would be present. Dennis was asked if he would bring his typewriter and record the proceedings; it would keep the little fellow busy.

Natty Brown was standing by the open door of the Great Hall; light streamed out and fell across the white snow blanketing the courtyard.

There were two carved turnips with small flickering candles placed inside them on the doorstep, and a saucer of milk each side.

I stopped, box in hand, and stared down at them.

'We keep the old Halloween traditions here, Lennox,'

Florence smiled. 'The milk is for the Cat Sith and the fiery faces are to ward off the Sluagh.'

'Ay, ma Lady,' Natty Brown said. 'An' the Saints will get a burnin' in the yard and a prayin',' he told us all.

I had no idea what they were talking about. Fogg took an interest in the milk, so I called him away. He was in enough trouble over the chickens.

'Thank you, Brown,' Swift said as he helped Florence to remove her cape and handed it to the factotum.

By the sound of chatter reaching us from upstairs, most of the guests had arrived. We waited for Brown until he was ready to escort us up and open the door for us.

'Oh, there you are,' Carruthers smiled as we arrived. She was clad in the same silky frock as last evening; my heart skipped a beat.

I handed the box to MacDonald and strode to her side, raised her hand and made a formal salutation with a bow. She laughed with delight.

'Lennox, Swift.' The Laird made himself heard above the noise. 'Get on with it.'

I excused myself and joined Swift by the fire.

'Sit yerselfs down now,' MacDonald instructed the assembled, 'and take yer drink. Ye'll be needin' it.' He looked at me and Swift. 'Away ye go, laddies, and ye'd better be canny about it.'

I took up a position with my back to the hearth, a whisky in my hand and Swift at my side. A small table had been set up and MacDonald had placed our eclectic collection of evidence upon it.

Ranged on the assorted chairs and sofas were Persi Carruthers next to Campbell and a silent Buggins, who looked to be brooding but otherwise none the worst for his incarceration. Then came Miss Fairchild dressed in lavender and pink, her face framed, as usual, by wispy curls. She was seated on a deep-sprung Victorian chair with Greggs standing sentinel behind her. He had spruced up and looked rather dapper. Florence sat alone on a small sofa in the centre. The Laird, attired in High-land dress, was in his customary high-backed seat; Mac-Donald, sporting the same, settled himself in a similar chair at his side.

Dennis had been placed between him and the huge fireplace, where he could most easily watch proceedings and record them with his heavy black typewriter on a fold-up desk. His fingers were poised over the keys and he held the hunched position of one ready for the off. His spectacle lenses reflected the flames of the fire and his cheeks glowed red because he was probably quite warm, despite his shorts and khaki attire.

Fogg sat at my feet staring at the throng.

'It's all yours, Lennox,' Swift said, and went to join Florence on the sofa.

That made me frown, but he smiled grimly and explained. 'You made the analysis. You can deliver the evidence.'

'Fine.' I took a deep breath as all eyes fixed upon me. I picked up the silver hip flask from the table and turned it over in my hands. 'Maxwell ...' I began.

I raised the flask so it glowed in the light of the overhead candelabra. 'Maxwell was murdered. He was killed within an hour of arriving back from the mainland two days ago.'

Dennis had started typing noisily and it was already annoying. At least he was fast.

I took a breath. 'The cause of his murder lay in the past; indeed it could be said that it lay many hundreds of years in the past. It lay with another murder, that of the Gaelic King of the Isles, Somerled. He was supposedly slaughtered by Ivar, the son of Godred, the defeated King.' I noticed Campbell lean forward eagerly in his seat and I hastened to muddy the water, aware that I couldn't expose the clan secrets.

'We cannot be sure whose bones were uncovered by Chief Inspector Swift. The myths surrounding Black Dougal have echoed through this castle for centuries. No physical evidence exists to prove the story of Somerled's murder, nor of Ivar's hand in it. The legend remains simply that. But the crown is a very real entity; it once belonged to a king, and its ancient history, its gold and jewel content and its dramatic discovery make it very valuable indeed. It is an extraordinary piece of the history of the Highlands, the ousting of the Norse and the regaining of their own lands by the Gaelic people.' I paused for a drink. Fogg had already become bored and fallen asleep.

'Its discovery had attracted the attention of archaeologists and treasure hunters alike. William Jackson pulled strings to come here and he brought a team of historians with him. His intention was to remove the crown from this island one way or another. Jackson had money, he was experienced in dealing in antiquities and he was totally unscrupulous. And he was arrogant, and this arrogance infuriated the Laird of Braeburn Castle.' I looked at him. 'You were not going to stand by and allow this money-grubbing scoundrel to steal the crown or anything else, were you, sir?' I turned to the Laird, who was watching me intently from under white brows.

'I didn't kill him, Lennox, if that's what you're suggesting,' he retorted. 'I stopped him by my command.'

I nodded. 'And you had to consider the curse that had been hanging over all your heads for centuries. You knew what the discovery of the skeleton would mean for the people living on this small island. It would raise fears, fears that could lead to hasty actions, actions that could be deadly.' I turned to stare at MacDonald, hair and beard pristine white, straight-backed and unmoving in his chair, a tartan sash flung over his shoulder, his kilt spread about his knees, long cream socks, a dirk strapped to his calf above shining black boots.

He bristled and growled. 'Are ye accusin' me, laddie?'

I didn't reply, just returned his stare for a few moments, then turned in the direction of Buggins and Campbell on the sofa next to Persi.

'Buggins, your team were offered the chance to come here and investigate. But you must have had misgivings when you heard the financing was to be provided by

William Jackson, because his reputation and methods were well known.' All eyes now moved toward Buggins.

'Jackson used the principle of *bona vacantia* to acquire legal rights over antiquities. Miss Carruthers told me this, and the whole team knew how it worked.' I turned my regard toward her lovely face. '*Bona vacantia* is Latin for "abandoned chattels", or "unclaimed goods". It means nobody knows who they had belonged to.'

'To *whom*, Heathcliff – you really must be correct in your grammar,' Miss Fairchild reprimanded me with a bright smile. I had the impression she was thoroughly enjoying herself.

'Yes … Thank you, dear lady,' I replied briskly, and returned to Buggins. 'Jackson went to register the crown as treasure trove at the procurator fiscal's office and you went with him, Buggins, knowing full well that Jackson would gain legal claim to the crown.'

'That's nonsense, man,' MacDonald snarled. 'How could he claim something that doesn't belong to him?'

'Let me explain. Once an item is declared as treasure trove, two things happen. First, it must be handed over to the British authorities for assessment, and secondly, the person who has registered the item can claim the right of first refusal to buy it. And it didn't actually matter that it was missing because once it did turn up it would have to be handed over to the British authorities on pain of prosecution. That is how Jackson manipulated the law to gain whatever antiquity he was pursuing.'

A general rumble of anger rippled about the room as they understood the duplicity at play.

'You knew this, didn't you, Buggins?' I now fixed him in my sights. 'You knew how Jackson operated, and yet you agreed to help him claim the crown. You helped him in his chicanery.'

Open anger was now squarely aimed at the stony-faced Buggins, who was sitting with his arms folded across his broad chest and a deep furrow between his brows.

'Why did you do it, Buggins?' I asked. He didn't reply so I answered the question myself.

'I think you agreed to it because you had your own plan. A plan that would not only thwart Jackson's nasty legal tactics but would finally vindicate your theory about the murder of Somerled.' Apart from Dennis's annoying clatter on the typewriter, everyone in the room was silent.

'The law of *bona vacantia* only applies to ownerless goods. In order to stop Jackson using it for his own gain, all that needed to happen was for the crown to be claimed by the true owner, the Laird.'

'Ay, so what are ye bletherin' about, laddie, when everyone knows it is the Laird's?' MacDonald said.

'The only way the Laird can prove his ownership is by revealing the history of the crown and how his long-ago predecessor put it there. In other words, he would be forced to reveal the secret of the curse in open court.' I paused to let them digest this. 'And that was your plan, wasn't it Buggins? Because you were convinced the history of the curse would prove your theory and save your and Campbell's reputations and careers.'

'I say.' Campbell jumped up, pointing his unlit pipe at me. 'That's jolly unfair. Buggins never thought such a thing in his life. Did you, old chap?' He turned to his friend for confirmation. 'Buggins? It isn't true, is it. We thought we'd find the treasure, didn't we?'

Buggins closed his lips firmly and looked away.

I sighed, suddenly rather depressed. I understood the pragmatic reasoning Buggins had followed, and even sympathised with his plight, but I didn't like the duplicity. And I didn't like being responsible for stripping away the veil of deceit either. I gave myself a mental shake, stiffened my shoulders and continued.

'In your defence, Buggins, I expect you thought the Laird would have had an extremely good chance of overturning *bona vacantia* and legally retaining the crown.' He regarded me with a steady gaze as I watched him.

'But although the disappearance of the crown didn't affect Jackson's legal claim, it did affect your plans, didn't it? It was a disaster wasn't it?'

I saw Carruthers raise her hand to her cheek, her face pale and troubled. 'Jackson should have taken the crown, delivered it to the British authorities and cleared off back to America to await the legal process. But the crown went missing and so here he still was, breathing down your necks and demanding that you find it.'

I now regarded each of the archaeologists in turn. 'The disappearance of the crown was disaster enough. Only

THE CURSE OF BRAEBURN CASTLE

one event could make it worse and that would be if Jackson discovered the story about the treasure. And he did, didn't he? Because Maxwell told him.' I watched for their reactions but their faces were uniformly frozen.

'Maxwell stole this and hid it in the well.' I picked up the crucifix and waved it about so they could have a good look, and then returned it to the table. 'Somebody saw him do it. I believe it was a man, and a very determined man. He was convinced there was treasure on this island and he was determined to find it. He knew the story of Leif Erikson and Vinland and the glory it would bring.'

The tension suddenly heightened as talk turned to murder and treasure. 'While this man had been searching the ruins, he spotted what Maxwell was doing at the well. It raised his suspicions and I'm certain he began spying on Maxwell, including at the records office.'

I was very aware of Carruthers's gaze upon me.

'Maxwell went to the library to translate the runic writing scratched into the back of the crucifix.' I picked up the pencil rubbing and quoted: '"*Sun is the light of the land, I bow to Heaven's doom ...*"' It was a vital clue to the whereabouts of the treasure. Perhaps Maxwell considered hunting for the treasure himself, but he must have thought how much easier it would be to sell the story to Jackson, because that's exactly what he did.'

'Can you prove this?' Buggins rather growled the question at me.

I didn't reply, but instead picked up Maxwell's belt, still cold and damp from the body in the crypt. I turned it over to reveal the discreet lining within which money could be slipped. I slid out the carefully folded notes that had been hidden there, and unfolded them to reveal ten five-pound notes. I said nothing at all as I took Jackson's wallet and spread out the crisp white fivers he'd kept there. Then I looked up.

'The serial numbers are sequential. This is proof that Jackson paid Maxwell for the information.' I stopped and took another sip of whisky.

'Betrayal.' I continued. 'A nasty, selfish act which raised fury in the heart of a man whose mind now turned to murder.' I paused because there was one piece of information I didn't have.

'Did anyone see Jackson and Maxwell in close conversation during the trip to the mainland?' I asked.

Dennis stopped typing and stood up. 'Jackson and Buggins didn't tell me they were going to the procurator's office. I should have been told, I make all the reports.'

'Dennis, I asked if anyone saw Maxwell and Jackson together,' I retorted rather sharply.

'I did see them,' Dennis said with the air of the school snot. 'After Jackson came back, I saw him and Maxwell behind some shelves and they were talking. They didn't tell me what they said.'

'Did you see or hear anyone else?' I pursued.

'No. And now I must continue.' He sat down abruptly and began thumping away on his typewriter again.

I shook my head, then went on. 'Whatever was said was enough to sign their death warrants. Personally, I'd have killed Jackson first, but Maxwell was undoubtedly the easier target and he had been drinking heavily that day.' I picked up the flask again and turned it over in my hands. 'It may have been because he felt remorse, or maybe relief that his problems were over. Whatever his thoughts, he was drunk and under the influence of morphine. I doubt it was difficult for the murderer to persuade him to lean over the wall and simply upend him over the top.' I placed the flask down yet again with a sigh.

'The killer had one more task that night. He went to the boat, threw lamp oil into it, tossed in a match and pushed it out to sea.' I heard the sudden rumble of anger emitted by MacDonald and the Laird as I spoke. 'Why did he burn the boat? I imagine it was to prevent the arrival of the police; and he wanted time to complete his search. He now had a clue to the whereabouts of the treasure in the form of the Norse blessing. All he had to do was deduce its meaning and prevent anyone else finding it first. The hunt was on.'

CHAPTER 27

'Jackson had learned the secret of the treasure and his reaction was predictable: he was enraged, and he wanted to get his hands on a prize far greater than the value of the crown. As soon as he had the opportunity to confront Buggins and Campbell alone, he exploded in wrath. He would force them to search for the treasure, and if they didn't agree to his demand he would see to it that they were ruined.'

The room was once again quiet. The killer was sitting amongst us, and we all knew it.

'Campbell.' I turned my attention toward him and he sat up. 'You and Buggins were with Intelligence during the war. You were captured and tortured, weren't you. It affected you; it damaged your nerves and your memory. Did you deliberately inform Maxwell about the treasure, or did you drop it absent-mindedly into a conversation? Did you fear what Maxwell would say in his drunken state? Or, once you knew that your friend Maxwell had betrayed you, did you react in a murderous fury and kill him, and then mete out the same to Jackson?'

'N-n-now, you-you look here ...' Campbell began to stutter.

'You're digging in the wrong spot, Lennox,' Buggins warned me.

'Am I?' I faced him in reply. 'We shall see.' I turned away. 'There was certainly no shortage of people who wanted to see Jackson dead.'

The oiled stock of the crossbow gleamed in the light of the fire. I picked it up, waved it about, then put it down again. 'The first murder had been rather risky and complicated, so why not devise a simpler act next time? Everyone knew where the crossbow was, they'd seen it in the Great Hall. It even had bolts with it. It would be so much easier to merely open Jackson's door and shoot him. And so it was. Simple, quick and easy. The killer even remembered to wear gloves, which was a good precaution given the presence on the island of a former Chief Inspector of Scotland Yard.'

I took a few paces about, being stiff with cuts and bruises from my earlier adventures.

'Swift and I were becoming a nuisance. We'd found the crucifix, we had the translation and we knew about the treasure. And we were on the murderer's trail. So the killer planted a feather from the ruins on Jackson's body for us to find and set a trap.'

I picked up the owl feather and showed it around. The end broke off and fluttered to the floor; all eyes watched it fall, then returned to watch me. 'The murderer was aware we had seen the owl and knew the layout of the ruins. I don't how, perhaps he'd found an old map somewhere, or he was familiar with the layout already, or he had a chum within the walls. Or he may have simply discovered the oubliette during the search for the treasure.'

I threw away the remnants of the feather and took a couple of paces to stand in front of the fire. 'Miss Fairchild, could you please tell me what on earth you are doing here?' I asked her outright.

She laughed delightedly. 'Oh, you dear boy, do you think I may have done some terrible deed? I do assure you, I have not.' She dimpled and smiled and the Laird and MacDonald and even Greggs started to bristle, so I gave up because nothing she'd said had ever made any sense to me anyway.

'Heathcliff,' Florence called out. 'Did this awful person mean to kill Daddy?'

Swift answered for me. 'No, darling, it was just to enable a search of his desk.' He gently squeezed her hand as she smiled up at him.

'Exactly,' I replied, and returned to my tale. 'So we were lured into a trap and fell straight into it. I imagine we would have been rescued before long, or at least I hope so because it was one of the most unpleasant experiences of my life.'

'And mine,' Swift added.

'We escaped the oubliette and ended up in a grotto, or rather, as we were told later, the old well. Now, this must have come as an enormous shock to the person who lured us into the trap because one of the reasons he had dropped us into the oubliette was to focus the search party within the castle walls.'

'And why?' I raised the rhetorical question and answered it myself. 'Because the killer had finally worked out where he thought the treasure was. But no sooner had he arrived at the site of the old well than he heard my little dog on his heels. Fogg, of course, was looking for me, not the murderer.' I bent down to wake the little dog up with a ruffle of his head; he sighed and rolled over, snoring gently. 'The murderer had no choice but to retrace his footsteps and wait until the coast was once again clear.' I paused for a drink as my throat was dry, before beginning the drama's final act.

'*Treasure* ...' I said to an audience now hanging on my words. 'The glittering prize, hidden for centuries with an enthralling story to add a gleam of gilt-edged glamour to it. This wasn't only the treasure of a long dead king, it held a legend, one of deep significance not just to the ivory-towered citadels of history, but to the whole of the western world. The treasure would prove the discovery of America – or Vinland, as Leif Erikson named it – hundreds of years before Christopher Columbus. What glory would be showered upon the shoulders of the man who proved that journey really had taken place! His name would be written forever into the annals of discovery.'

I turned to Miss Fairchild. '"Vainglorious" was the word you used, wasn't it?' As I regarded the lady, she smiled merrily.

'Indeed, Heathcliff,' she replied lightly. 'And they shall reap their reward by your hand.'

'A vainglorious enterprise,' I stated, then continued. '"*Sun is the light of the lands, I bow to heaven's doom ...*" That was the clue they needed and it came from the crucifix that had been found about Ivar's neck.'

'Ivar!' Campbell jumped to his feet. 'So it *is* him. Buggins, it's *him*, they know it is, and now we can prove it. Good Lord, old chap, we'll be vindicated. Ha!'

I stepped back. Damn it! I'd let the blasted cat out of the bag. I put my hands to my head, and then looked at Persi, who offered a wry smile.

Everyone started talking at once and Dennis was typing like fury, his fingers whizzing over the keys.

'Silence,' the Laird shouted. 'Lennox, you blithering idiot.'

I downed my dram. Swift was grinning. I wish they'd all thought it was so amusing.

'Right. Well, I must apologise for that inadvertent admission, sir.'

'For heaven's sake, man, just get to the blasted point will you,' the Laird snapped.

'Please sit down everyone, would you.' I looked up, paused, and waited until they were all seated and watching me with keen expectation.

'And so, our killer must have realised the same error I myself had made. Somerled, a Norse name meaning "Summer Raider". The Norse went raiding in the summer when the seas were less dangerous. "*Sun is the light of the lands, I bow to heaven's doom"*; think about those words. The rising and falling of the sun forms a trajectory, and that trajectory is determined by the time of the year. Today is October the thirty-first and summer is long gone. When Maxwell and his murderer went to the battlements to watch the sun go down, they were looking in the wrong place. They should have been looking further north.'

I glanced over to the door, which had been quietly opened by the young piper, Angus. He talked to Natty Brown and then withdrew.

'Did he find it?' I asked the factotum.

'Nay, he dinnae,' Natty Brown replied.

'Find what?' the Laird asked.

'The torch,' Swift answered. 'We sent Angus to search for the torch. The killer had painted a skull on his torch and was using the beam to frighten people.'

'Does that mean you don't have evidence to convict your man?' the Laird asked.

'No,' I replied. 'But it would have made it easier.'

'Well, put a name to this murderer,' he commanded. 'And put an end to your blethering.'

'On one condition, sir,' I replied. 'That you reveal your secret now.' I fixed a steely eye on him. He leaned his head slightly to one side and stared back; then the ghost of a smile crossed his lips.

'Ghillie-mor,' he ordered.

MacDonald rose to his feet and went over to the suit of armour in the corner. He pulled the breastplate to one side, placed both hands in the cavity and withdrew the white skull and the golden crown from within. There was a concerted gasp of '*ahhh*' while he carried it across the room and placed it carefully on the table with the other exhibits. It grinned at me with white teeth in smooth bones, the heavy gold of the crown glittering in the firelight, the ruby glinting a deep, dark red.

The clock ticked on the far wall; even Dennis's bashing on the typewriter had ceased as we all stared at the skull. It was rather disconcerting actually, and Swift was right, he had very good teeth.

The Laird broke the collective trance. 'Lennox!'

'Right!'

I turned towards Dennis, who started furiously typing again and reached the end of a sentence. He pushed the return lever and the carriage whizzed back to start the next line. I stood on the other side of the fireplace watching him silently. He was looking intently at the paper, fingers hovering above the keys, but as the silence grew, he hesitated, then glanced up at me.

'Dennis, would you please type the name of the person who murdered Maxwell and Jackson, and left me and Swift for dead in the oubliette.' I walked at a leisurely pace around him and leaned over his shoulder to examine his work.

'What name should I type?' he asked in his high voice. Sweat had broken on his forehead and his cheeks were very red because the fire was blazing and he was far too close to it.

'I'll spell it out for you, shall I?' I offered.

The atmosphere in the room was tense and breathless. 'D.E.N.N. ...'

He stopped typing, his fingers froze and he stared at the black letters imprinted on the white page.

'Is there a problem, Dennis?' I growled, my rage barely suppressed.

His face turned puce. 'I-I-I don't ...'

I grabbed him by his bloody neckerchief with both hands and hauled him to his feet until he was suspended almost a foot from the ground.

'You snivelling little runt, I'm going to...'

'Lennox! Stop!' Swift raced over and grabbed my arm along with MacDonald and the Laird.

'Stop, put him down!' they yelled, and pulled me off. Natty Brown yanked Dennis away and had him gripped by the arms. The little squirt was yelling at me. 'You're not allowed. I haven't done anything. You're not allowed to touch me. I'm ... I'm ...' He was struggling and kicking as they hauled him off his feet and Swift snapped handcuffs on his wrists. I moved toward the struggling prisoner with violent intent and he started screeching. 'Don't touch me, you can't, you can't!'

Carruthers appeared suddenly at my side. 'Heathcliff, stop.' She put her hand on my arm. 'Look at me.'

I looked. I gazed into her eyes. Then I headed straight for Dennis. He was still shouting but had changed his tune. 'I know where it is, I know where it is, let me go or I won't tell you!' Natty Brown and Angus held him between them and he suddenly stopped struggling and stared at me, almost goggle-eyed with fear and fury. 'You can't touch me. I know the secret and you will never find it without me.'

I glared down at him and said. 'I know where the treasure is. Nobody needs you.'

'No, you don't, you can't,' he squealed.

'It's in the old well.' I replied.

The shrieks became incoherent, then Dennis ranted, 'It's magic. You don't understand it, you have to know the magic.'

Buggins and Campbell had come over and stood at my shoulders.

'The old well? We'll go there now,' Campbell said excitedly. 'We can dive down, can't we, Buggins? I can swim.'

'It's too narrow, young man.' The Laird had joined us in the circle of men facing the cowering Dennis. 'It's a few feet of a pool and then it narrows to a cleft between rocks. When I was a boy, we used to swim in the shallows in summer, but I assure you, you can't dive down it. Nobody can.'

Dennis stared up at me, eyes magnified by the thick round lenses, hatred and malignancy glittering in those orbs. He almost laughed. 'See! You can't raise it, you need to know the magic. I know how it's done. It's raised by magic, no one else can do it.' His voice rose to fever pitch.

'Really?' I almost smiled. 'Tomorrow will prove the truth of that. Swift.' I turned to him. 'Could you take him away?'

'Yes. Follow me,' Swift ordered Natty Brown and Angus, 'and keep a tight hold of him.'

'You can't lock me away. You'll have to let me go or I won't tell you,' Dennis kept bawling, but nobody listened.

Natty Brown and Angus exited, Dennis between them. I could still hear him as they crossed the courtyard.

I sank into a chair by the fire as Buggins and everyone else in the room shot questions at me. I was tired, but Greggs came to the rescue; he poured a whisky and handed it to me. Fogg looked up with liquid eyes and cocked ears, enquiring whether it was dinnertime yet.

I found a treat in my pocket and gave it to him, ignoring the chatter in the room until Swift came back.

'Would you like me to finish?' he asked.

'No, I'll do it.' I stood up. 'Quiet,' I called. They didn't quieten. 'Silence!' That did it.

'Where's your evidence, Lennox?' the Laird said.

I picked up the length of fishing line that we'd found stuffed in Jackson's pocket. No doubt Dennis had planted it there; he probably thought it would be clever to throw such a confusing clue into the mix. The rusted hook swung gently at one end and caught on the small noose that had been tied at its other. I unhooked it and went to Dennis's heavy black typewriter, abandoned on the fold-up desk. I upended it and placed the hook on the metal arm of the letter 'Y', then unravelled it. I ran it over to the spit-jack in the huge fireplace and looped the small noose onto its handle. I pulled down the lead weight to set the clockwork mechanism off and let it go. As the handle circled around with the rotation of the mechanism, the taut fishing line pulled the typewriter key, then released it, pulled, and released it. It went bang, bang, bang, quite slowly.

I went and unhooked it because it was annoying, then returned to the typewriter and pulled out the two wheels holding each end of the ribbon. I unwound the inky black fabric until I found what I was looking for and held it up to the light. 'Here,' I said. 'On this section of ribbon there is a single letter stamped over and over again. The one Dennis chose to hook was actually the letter "T". And that was his alibi for the time Maxwell was murdered.'

I rather expected a 'bravo' or something, but no one said a word. Then Campbell piped up.

'I say, Lennox. That's jolly clever! Did you think of it all on your own?' he asked, coming over to stare at the typewriter.

'He did,' Swift answered for me.

Buggins came over and gave me a slap on the back with a quiet grin and shook my hand. 'Well done, old man,' he said.

I thanked them both, then turned to Swift. 'Dennis knows the curse, Swift. He said "raised by magic".'

'I know, I heard,' he said, and looked discomfited. 'The Laird's desk?' He suggested.

I was about to reply when we were interrupted.

'I think we should have dinner, now,' Miss Fairchild said, eyeing me.

There was a general murmur of agreement as they all stood up and milled about preparing to leave. Swift offered Florence his arm, and there was some hasty manoeuvring to claim the arm of Miss Fairchild, which Greggs, to his credit, won. Carruthers appeared at my side.

'That was awfully clever, Heathcliff.' She smiled up at me.

'*Lennox*, old stick – unless you want to be called *Persephone*.' I grinned. 'Or Nefertiti.'

She laughed.

Dinner was rather subdued, or rather, I was; everybody else was laughing and chatting away. The Laird invited Buggins and Campbell to eat with us and that added to the festive air. They all plagued me with questions, but after I'd repeated 'tomorrow' three times in answer, they let me eat in peace.

It was late by the time we all walked into the courtyard. Frost had formed over the snow and it sparkled in the lamplight. A myriad stars were visible overhead in a midnight-blue heaven far above us. On every doorstep a carved turnip had been set, grinning faces flickered in the darkness, illuminated from the candles within.

Natty Brown had lit a bonfire and it roared with yellow flames filling the air with the smell of woodsmoke. Sparks drifted upwards to hiss on snow-covered roofs and icicles hung from eaves. I drew in a sharp breath; there was a touch of magic about it.

The staff had all gathered around the fire and trays of whisky were served. We gathered together in a circle about the heat of the fire, glasses in hand. I looked at the faces glowing in the blaze, bright-eyed and rosy.

The Laird lowered his head and began a quiet prayer. It was in Gaelic, but I listened carefully to the tone and the lilt. It was moving and solemn. I understood the sentiment. It was a blessing to the dead, a remembrance of their lives and a wish for peace for their souls.

He stopped and raised his glass of whisky, and we all followed suit.

'Samhain,' he shouted.

'Samhain,' we shouted back, and as our words echoed around the old castle walls we tossed our whisky into the fire.

It flared and spat, blue and green flames rising up into the dark night sky swirling in smoke and fiery splinters.

Angus the piper appeared and breathed life into his pipes and played a haunting tune. Three times he trod behind our circle about the fire, the notes melting one into another, rising and falling until they died away into silence and he had completed his lament.

Natty Brown refilled our glasses and we again held them to the sky.

'Samhain,' the Laird shouted again, and we downed the liquid in one.

CHAPTER 28

The night ended with each of us being handed a flaming length of burning wood from the bonfire to take to our own hearth. I escorted the lovely Carruthers to the door of the Armoury. There were too many people milling about for any romance, so I placed a solemn peck upon her hand, a chaste kiss upon her cheek, and wished her a very good night.

Fogg trailed in my footsteps toward our tower and Greggs opened the door. He had evidently beaten us to it.

'Sir...' he began.

I cut him off with a firm hand held in the air. 'No, sorry, old chap, but I'm weary to the bone.'

'But...'

'Greggs, please, let me go to bed,' I entreated him. 'I'm sore and tired.'

'Yes, indeed, sir. I wanted merely to say, bravo!' He almost smiled. 'I was most impressed.'

I stopped in the doorway to my room and faced him with brows raised in pleasant surprise. 'Thank you, Greggs.'

He left with a dignified bow and I made my way bedward and slept soundly through the night.

Tubbs was purring loudly in my ear the next morning. The curtains had been drawn to reveal sunshine sparkling through a glaze of frost on the window. The smell of bacon, eggs and various fried delights wafted from below and I stretched, yawned and greeted my little duo on this bright new morning. It felt good to be alive.

'Lennox.' Swift marched in without so much as a tap on the door.

I groaned.

'Come on.' He was dressed in his now customary trench coat and kilt.

'No. Not until I've had my breakfast.'

Greggs arrived with said repast on a tray.

'Good morning, sir,' he greeted me. 'Will you be dining in bed or at the fireside?'

'Fire,' I confirmed, and reached for my dressing gown. 'Have a cup of tea, Swift,' I told him.

He grumbled a bit, but agreed. 'They're all ready to go,' he said as he sat on the edge of his chair clutching a steaming mug.

'Need a few things first, old chap.' I was sharing a sausage between Fogg and Tubbs. 'A ladder, an anchor and a couple of long ropes.'

He frowned at me from under dark brows. 'An anchor?'

'Yes.' I said through a fried egg. 'I saw one in the boat shed. That should do it.'

'Right …' He drank his tea. 'I assume you know what you're doing.'

'We'll soon find out, won't we.' I looked at him and

laughed, and he frowned with hawkish eyes. 'By the by, that talk of magic. Did you ask the Laird if there were any documents in his desk that Dennis may have read?'

Swift's frown deepened and he nodded brusquely. 'There were a few cryptic notes left by one of his predecessors. They were in Latin and he didn't think anyone would be able to translate them, but...'

'But an archaeological archivist would.' I finished the sentence.

'Exactly.' He stood up, 'I'm going to the well, I'll meet you there.'

'Good.' I waved a fork at him. 'And bring Dennis, will you, in handcuffs if necessary.'

He grinned suddenly. 'Don't worry, I'll have him trussed up like a Christmas turkey.'

Breakfast complete, I hurried my ablutions in the icebox masquerading as a dressing room and emerged ready for action. Greggs was waiting for me in muffler, gloves and overcoat.

'Come along, old chap. Bring Foggy,' I told him as we made for the door.

It was crisp and clear outside and we strode past the heaped ashes of last night's bonfire. The snow encircling the remains was trampled and pitted with soot. It smelled of winter with the scent of woodsmoke still hanging in the air.

We made a small procession out under the Keep, our breath steaming as we went. Foggy, too, had been picking his way through the snow, but he suddenly raced ahead as we neared the trees.

There was a small crowd assembled around the newly cleared opening to the old well. They called out greetings as we arrived, or most of them did, anyway. I noticed that Dennis in the centre was bundled up in a heavy duffle coat with his wrists pinned together by Swift's handcuffs. His nose was red and his eyes swivelled furiously about.

'One more word from you, laddie, an' I'll be tossing you in yon loch and it'll be the last anyone ever hears from ye,' MacDonald warned him.

'Greetings,' I called, my breath white, my boots breaking across snow already well trodden by assorted feet.

'Lennox,' Campbell called, 'you're going to perform some sort of magic, are you?'

I didn't respond.

Carruthers was standing beside Campbell and Buggins; she too grinned a welcome.

'Hello, old stick.' I smiled at her.

I could see that she was cold. She wore a dark-blue woollen coat belted at her slim waist, with her gloved hands thrust into its pockets. 'Hello, you,' she returned the smile.

'Where's Swift?' I asked.

'Down there.' Buggins indicated the opening in the rocks. 'He has already lowered a ladder and we're about to go down with our pick and shovel.' He hefted the large pickaxe that he had been leaning on. I noticed Campbell had a spade.

'The Laird?' I looked about.

'Behind you.' I pivoted to see the Laird and Florence making their way under the trees towards us. Greggs was bringing up the rear with Miss Fairchild on his arm.

'Come on,' came the muffled order from Swift below us in the grotto.

'Right.' Buggins moved forward and deftly manoeuvred himself into the opening in the rocks. He lowered himself down the ladder, waiting half way for Campbell to pass down the pick. I waited for him, then peered over the edge.

Swift had cleared away all the snow that had fallen into the grotto, shovelling it to one side. He and the other two were looking up at me, grouped around a long ladder. I put my hand out to let Carruthers go ahead, then twisted about and climbed in after her.

'We'll need to break the ice covering the pool,' I said, going over to peer at the thick layer showing pale green water beneath its depths.

'We'll do that, stand aside.' Buggins moved into position. He hefted the pick, raised it and let it fall onto the ice. Icy splinters flew. He stopped to grin at us, evidently in his element. Then he continued hammering the steel point of the pick deeper into the cracked surface.

Natty Brown came down and was followed by a complaining Dennis, who was hampered by the handcuffs. MacDonald came close behind. The Laird was next and we formed a tight huddle to watch Buggins and Campbell at work.

Miss Fairchild, Florence, Greggs – with Fogg in his

arms – remained in the snow at the surface. They peered down as best they could.

Buggins was making short work of the ice and had cleared a hole in it. Campbell shovelled it away as quickly as it piled up.

'Is that wide enough?' Buggins asked.

I knelt at the edge and looked into the green depths. I had no idea. 'Erm, possibly, I suppose …' I turned towards Swift. 'Where's the anchor and rope?'

'What are you *doing*?' Dennis suddenly shouted out. 'That's stupid, you can't do that. If you promise to let me go, I'll tell you how to do it.'

'One more word from you, laddie,' MacDonald growled, 'and you'll be down there head first.' He shook Dennis by the shoulder. 'Ye hear me now?'

Swift had tied the coiled rope to the end of the rusted iron anchor from the boat shed.

'I doubt you'll be able to hook anything with this, Lennox,' he said.

'I'm not going to hook it,' I replied. 'Pass it to me.'

He handed it over and I dropped the anchor with a splash into the ice-framed pool. I could see some way down through the clear water and realised the Laird was right about the narrowness of the cleft: a man could not possibly dive down there between the rocks. The anchor disappeared from view as I let the line out after it. I reached the end of the rope but could feel that the anchor wasn't on the bottom yet. 'Give me the other line, would you,' I asked.

MacDonald stepped forward and took it from Swift. 'I'll tie it fer ye,' he said, and expertly knotted the two ropes together.

I continued to feed the line into the water until it suddenly stopped falling. I tugged at it and decided that it must be bouncing on the bottom but nothing else was happening. Oh hell, I thought to myself, perhaps I was entirely wrong about the whole thing.

I jerked the rope again, trying to swing the anchor around on its line. Everyone was watching me intently, expecting something to happen. I paused and pushed my hair out of my eyes to better peer into the depths. I suddenly felt the slightest tug on the rope. I pulled it very gently, and encountered resistance. Something was connected to it. I tugged again. 'Got it,' I murmured. A buzz of excitement rose around me.

I pulled the rope up inch by inch. Swift coiled the length behind me as we lifted it with its extra weight very, very slowly to the surface. Hands reached out about me, wanting to help.

The anchor broke the surface first and we all saw a chunk of metallic-looking rock stuck to it as if by magic. A hole had been made through the strange rock, and through the hole was fixed a bronze chain.

'What the devil is it?' The Laird asked in amazement.

'A lump of magnetite,' I answered. It's a huge magnet and is attracted to the iron in the anchor.'

'Of course,' Persi laughed. 'The Norse used magnets to navigate with. They called them lodestones.'

'"Raised by magic",' I quoted. 'That was what Ivar said, wasn't it, sir?'

The Laird nodded silently, a look of wonder on his face.

'Did you hear that, Buggins?' Campbell said, almost beside himself with excitement. 'It's magnetite. It was Ivar's; they said so.'

'Pull up the chain, will you, Lennox,' Swift instructed me.

I did, and he helped. There was a heavy weight on the end of it, and whatever it was, it got jammed between the narrow rocks a number of times and we had to drop and twist the chain to free the load.

Everybody had formed a circle leaning over the edge of the ice-fringed pool, watching intently.

Swift and I continued to pull until something black and bronze came into view. Buggins and Campbell reached down into the water to grab it as we tugged up the final few feet of chain.

'Got it,' Campbell shouted. They yanked it clear and dragged it onto the snowy floor of the grotto, everyone shuffling backwards to make room for it.

It was a small chest, black and slimy and made from ancient wood that had shrunk and warped and filled with grains of sand that ran away in rivulets. Thick bronze bands bound the body; a large hoop was on its top, to which the chain was attached.

Dennis started yelling. 'It's mine, you stole my idea.'

'One more word from you, laddie ...' MacDonald threatened again, and he shut up, glowering as he did.

We looked at the dripping chest and then at each other. 'Open it,' the Laird ordered.

Buggins raised his pick and hammered it down on the clasp that had held it shut for almost nine centuries. The wood and bronze forming the chest groaned and buckled, and then the lock broke.

They sat back on their haunches and waited for me.

'Go on, man. Open it,' the Laird ordered.

I raised the lid slowly; it creaked on verdigris-encrusted hinges.

The chest was full of water.

I let it drain away.

It looked as though something revolting had crawled in there a very long time ago and died. A bundle of shrivelled skin was all that was visible. It wasn't my idea of treasure, and I sat back, having no desire to touch it.

Carruthers was made of sterner stuff. She removed her gloves and put a hand out to touch it. 'Leather,' she half whispered. Then she lifted an edge very slowly and carefully. It had been rolled up and she began to unwind it.

'What is it, old girl?' Campbell asked, almost breathing down my neck as he leaned over me.

'*Wheesht*, man,' MacDonald told him to keep quiet.

Persi pulled the roll open and revealed a necklace made of fine white shells that looked like long, hollow needles of bone, threaded together with a fine gold wire to form a loop.

'Dentalium!' Dennis yelled, and lurched forward. He grabbed the necklace in his cuffed hands, and as he did

305

so it disintegrated between his fingers. 'No!' he screamed. '*No* ...' his anguished screech echoed around the place.

Carruthers, Campbell and Buggins all shouted at once, 'No ... no ...', and lurched forward, hands out to stop him, but they were too late.

'Come away, ye mad dafty,' MacDonald shouted, and he and Natty Brown dragged him off by his shoulders. The little man was shaking, his hands covered in white mush, which was all that was left of the shells. He started to sob. Brown and MacDonald sat him down at the back of the grotto and left him there.

'What on earth was that about?' I asked, brows raised at Persi, who had turned very pale and shocked.

'Dentalium,' Buggins answered for her. 'It's from North America; it was highly valued by the native tribes.'

'Ah.' I understood. 'It would have been given to Leif Erikson after he made contact with them when he reached Vinland?'

'Yes,' Campbell replied, his voice cracking. 'And it's gone. It's just disintegrated. There's nothing left. Buggins, it was, it was ...'

'What else is in there?' the Laird interrupted sharply having no more interest in a bunch of crumbled shells than I did.

I dragged out another layer of rotting leather and pulled it apart, half expecting to find more shells, but it was empty. But there was something below it and it glittered under the light of the lantern in Swift's hand.

It was gold.

And there was *lots* of it. It lay in a tangled mass: bangles, belt buckles, elaborate brooches chased with intricate patterns, bracelets formed into coiled snakes and strange dragons. Below the gold lay silver: two goblets engraved with sinuous shapes and each filled with delicate jewellery; earrings and necklaces made from beaten bronze wound with gold and silver thread and hung with precious gems. And at the very bottom lay dozens of thick golden coins punched with savage faces and strange lettering. It was all rather exciting.

Despite their disappointment at losing the old shells, the archaeologists had perked up at the sight of proper treasure. Swift and I lifted items out of the chest and handed them round. Everyone was now holding bits and pieces in their hands before passing them on. Amongst the coins I found a strange little figure.

'Heart of oak,' Carruthers said. 'Isn't it beautiful.' She looked at the carving in my hand as I turned it over: a knight on horseback. He wore armour and a helmet and an expression that looked rather startled.

'What is it?' I asked, staring at the little chap's face.

'A chess piece,' she replied. 'Quite a few have been found in the Hebrides, although they were usually made of ivory. I expect most of this horde came from there.'

'What have you found, darling?' Florence called down.

Swift rose to his feet, his knees red from kneeling on the ice. '*Treasure*,' he called back up, his voice reverberating with delight.

'You found it?' she called back down. 'Truly, Jonathan, you *found* it?'

'Yes,' he shouted back. 'We'll bring it up and show you.'

There was suddenly loud chatter all around as everyone started to talk at once. We were dazed and exalted and terribly excited. Buggins and Campbell shook each other's hands then slapped us on the back; everyone hugged Carruthers and she was quite pink by the time they started the climb back up the ladder.

I waited until last, and put a hand out to stop Persi from stepping up. At long last we were alone and I reached out, took her in my arms, looked long into her gorgeous eyes, and kissed her.

CHAPTER 29

'An' 'e's really nine hundred years old, sir?'

Tommy Jenkins was sitting on a chair in front of the fire staring at the carved knight in his hands. Tubbs was asleep in his lap, so the boy wasn't fidgeting quite as much as usual.

'Yes, I told you he was,' I said again.

We were both in my library, sitting by the hearth with Fogg snoring at our feet, as an autumnal breeze blew against the window.

'An' what did they do with the crown? Is it still on the skull? Did it scream when you found the treasure, sir?'

'Of course it didn't scream,' I replied. 'It's *dead* – how could it. And we put the skull and crown back on the body, there was no point in leaving it about the place.'

'So it weren't taken away, then?' he asked, swinging his legs.

'No.' I sighed because it was complicated and small boys weren't interested in tedious legalities. 'The Laird and Swift and Donald MacDonald went to the procurator fiscal's office. They showed them some of the treasure and after a lot of argument the Laird persuaded them to tear up the papers registering the crown, and then they registered the treasure instead.'

'What 'appened to the skeleton, the evil Ivar?' Tommy asked, more fascinated by bones than I considered healthy for a youngster.

'We left him in Swift's library. He's going to put a glass window in front of him so he can keep an eye on him,' I said.

'An' 'e still has his crown on?' the boy asked.

'Yes, I told you he did.'

'What did the words say on the rim? You said there was Viking words.'

'Norse, not Viking,' I reminded him. 'I asked Miss Carruthers and she said it meant "Fear not death, your doom is set." I think it means "be brave". They seemed to be rather obsessed with doom.'

'So it wasn't a curse, then?' Tommy asked, then rattled on, his freckled face shining with enthusiasm. 'Can we have a skeleton, sir? Please sir, it would be terrific, we could sit him in a chair an' talk to him.'

'No,' was my short and emphatic reply.

Greggs arrived with a tray. 'Tea, sir,' He announced.

Cook had been baking and ginger cake was arranged in slices next to the cups and whatnots.

'Thank you, Greggs,' I replied. 'Has the post boy been yet?'

'He has, sir. There are two letters for you in the hall; I was in the kitchens but will fetch them shortly, sir.' He poured tea as Jenkins helped himself to cake.

'Have you heard from Miss Fairchild?' I asked Greggs.

'She is remarkably well, I believe. She is in John O'Groats attending to a particularly bad case of poltergeists, sir.'

'Oh, she does get about, doesn't she,' I remarked through a slice of ginger cake.

'Only north of the border, sir. She prefers the cooler climes of the Scottish Highlands.'

'Will you be seeing her again?' I asked.

'Indeed, sir,' he responded, 'although, possibly not for some time.'

'Hum.' I eyed him, looking for signs of disappointment at this news, but he seemed perky enough. And I'd heard him humming arias recently, and suspected he'd taken up with the Operetta company again.

'I will fetch your mail now, sir,' he replied, and turned to Tommy and said, 'Jenkins.'

The lad slid off his chair, carefully handing the carved knight and Tubbs to me first, then went off munching cake in Greggs' footsteps.

There were two letters and I opened the blue envelope first. It was from Swift.

Lennox,

Dennis will go to the hangman. He is without remorse, and apparently boasting to all and sundry of his accomplishments. He believes that he alone has proved America was discovered by Leif Erikson, although no evidence remains.

He confessed to the murder of Maxwell and Jackson. It was as we deduced. He saw Maxwell hide the crucifix when he was in the ruins searching for the treasure. He spied on him in the library and eavesdropped on the conversation between Maxwell and Jackson. He decided to kill them both because he believed they had found a vital clue to the whereabouts of the treasure and might discover it before he did. He wanted all the glory himself. On returning to the island, he called on Maxwell, told him that he'd witnessed his actions in the library and offered to help. He laced the hip flask with morphine and stole the fishing line from Maxwell's room, which he subsequently used to set off his typewriter. He instructed Maxwell to tell Jackson to retrieve the crucifix at dusk while he and Maxwell went to watch the sunset and identify where the treasure may have been hidden. Then he followed Maxwell up to the battlements and pushed him over the wall.

He shot Jackson with the crossbow. He said it was more efficient than his first murder. He left the owl feather for us as a deliberate ruse to lure us back into the ruins because we had disturbed him and he thought we were getting too close. He left the fishing line in Jackson's pocket to confuse us. He tossed the torch into the loch.

Apparently Dennis is one of the leading experts on Norse Mythology. He knew all about lodestones, and Vinland, he can read runic script as well as Latin. The Norse used magnetite extensively; it is commonly found in Scandinavia. Attaching lodestones to hidden items is mentioned in some saga or other, so he understood the meaning of their 'magic'. Some credit should go to you for deducing the same.

We are all very well here at Braeburn and preparing for winter. Florence is blossoming. The treasure will eventually go to one of the larger museums after it has been assessed, but the Laird will be rewarded a portion of its value. This will help greatly in rebuilding the castle. Florence has asked me to refrain from any more projects until we have more funds and I have agreed.

Yours etc., Swift

Damn good thing, I thought, because according to Mac-Donald, Swift was very good at demolition but his efforts at building were less than successful. He hadn't understood how to underpin the stone steps, causing poor Florence to tumble down them, and MacDonald himself had surreptitiously rebuilt Swift's library whilst Florence took him off elsewhere. Swift was better suited to detecting than do-it-yourself.

I sighed and turned to the pale-pink envelope. It was from Persi Carruthers. We had spoken on the telephone since Greggs and I had left Braeburn just a few days ago. It had been a leisurely train journey but we'd been very pleased to arrive back in our cosy home. The archaeologists had stayed on, poring over the treasure and the crown, making elaborate lists of their origins, taking measurements and making drawings. They had found it terribly exciting whereas I'd begun to feel the need for the quiet of the Manor. The Braeburns had waved Greggs and I, Fogg and Tubbs off from the mainland train station. I was very pleased for them all.

Dear Heathcliff,

I wish you had stayed on, we have made so many intriguing discoveries and we will all be writing articles for many years to come on the subject of the 'Braeburn Treasure' as we are beginning to call it.

I ran some tests on the water in the old well and discovered that it had a carbon dioxide seep from the volcanic rock upon which the island is built. This slowly dissolved the dentalium, which is why it disintegrated. It was a dreadful blow to our hopes.

But despite losing the link with Vinland, we are terrifically pleased with the proof that Somerled was indeed murdered by Ivar. Campbell and Buggins are already being mentioned in Oxford and news is circulating amongst the scholars. They are vindicated at last!

I'm afraid I have some rather sorry news. I had hoped to come and visit you once we had completed our work at Braeburn but I have received information that will take me away for a while. I must go to the Lebanon. I will contact you as soon as I am able.

I miss you, you have a special place in my heart and I hope I am dear to you, too.

With deep affection,
Persi Carruthers

Well, that rather put a dampener on my day. My heart sank lower as I gave the remains of my cake to Fogg and stared into the fire. I had put the oaken knight in my pocket and now withdrew it; he had dried out after his long internment and was a nice glossy black colour now. I ran my fingers over the carved features, then placed it up on the mantelpiece. It had been a parting gift from the Laird. Fogg looked at me and wagged his tail, Tubbs yawned. I picked the little cat up, dropped him gently into my jacket pocket, called my dog and headed off for a long walk in the peaceful countryside.

Author's Notes

Please don't read this unless you have first read the whole book!

I do hope you enjoyed the story. The setting is an ancient castle at Halloween and so ghosts, ancient sins, and enigmatic mystics are pretty much *de rigueur* for the time and place. Well, I thought so and rather hoped you would too.

Miss Fairchild is indeed an enigma, and she was intended to be. She is a medium in tune with the spirit world, or so she thinks. Her arrival is a mystery to Lennox and the assorted inhabitants within the castle walls. She may be smoke and mirrors, or perhaps she was the real thing, but this is a story of Halloween, so, like the existence ghosts, we'll never really know.

Which brings us on to the footsteps in the night. They could be someone playing tricks, which is perfectly understandable given the season, or perhaps they really were a lost soul wandering the empty halls in the dark of the night.

Somerled, on the other hand really did exist, as did his sons, Donald and Dougal. And they really were the fathers of many clans which exist today. It is not known if Somerled was defeated in the battle at Renfrew or murdered before it took place. There is great debate amongst historians about his death. I thought murder quite likely, but then, I suppose I would.

Godred was the Norse King of the Isles, he was beaten by Somerled and he did regain part of his Kingdom after Somerled was killed. Dougal retained the southern half for the Gaels . And although his Gaelic name did mean black, I am not aware he was ever actually known by that nickname. 'Black Dougal' was a fiction on my part.

Ivar also existed, but apart from his name and his being a baseborn son of Godred, nothing more is known of him.

Magnetite is common in many parts of the world, including Scandinavia. The Norse did use Lodestones as compasses, although I have never heard of them using chunks of magnetite to hide their treasure. But, I thought it perfectly reasonable to invent such a method.

Leif Erikson is thought to have travelled to Newfoundland and much has been written about his exploits.

And the typewriter alibi. I'm sure fans of the great lady herself, Agatha Christie, will recall in 'Evil under the Sun', that one suspect was heard typing and was exonerated. But I always wondered if such an alibi could be fabricated. So I bought a 1920 typewriter, rather a pretty thing actually, and tried it out. It can be made to tap away if pulled intermittently by a rotating device, such as an ancient spit jack. So this clue was made in deference to one of my greatest heroines, Dame Agatha Christie and I hope you don't think I was taking liberties.

I do hope you enjoyed this book. If you would like to keep up to date with this series, you can do so on the Karen Menuhin readers page here…

https://karenmenuhin.com/

By signing up you will be updated about latest releases, stories, pics and news, including Mr Fogg, Tubbs and more. It would be great to see you there!

***

Murder at Melrose Court is the first book
in the Heathcliff Lennox series.

The Black Cat Murders is the second book.

The Curse of Braeburn Castle is the third book.

Death in Damascus is the fourth book.

The Monks Hood Murders is the fifth book.

If you like this book, please leave a nice review!!
It really helps.

If you feel there is something amiss, please do get in touch with me at karen@littledogpublishing.com and I'll do all I can to help.

A little about Karen Baugh Menuhin

1920s, Cozy crime, Traditional Detectives, Downton Abbey – I love them!

Along with my family, my dog and my cat.

At 60 I decided to write, I don't know why but suddenly the stories came pouring out, along with the characters. Eccentric Uncles, stalwart butlers, idiosyncratic servants, machinating Countesses, and the hapless Major Heathcliff Lennox.

A whole world built itself upon the page and I just followed along...

An itinerate traveller all my life. I grew up in the military, often on RAF bases but preferring to be in the countryside when we could. I adore whodunnits.

I have two amazing sons – Jonathan and Sam Baugh and their wives, Laura and Wendy, and five grandchildren, Charlie, Joshua, Isabella-Rose, Scarlett and Hugo.

I am married to Krov, my wonderful husband, who is a retired film maker and eldest son of the violinist, Yehudi Menuhin. We live in the Cotswolds.

For more information my address is:
karen@littledogpublishing.com

Made in the USA
Monee, IL
04 May 2021

67670522R00184